THE REVENGE PLOT

A Love Story

Sienna Waters

Find out more at www.siennawaters.com. And stay up to date with the latest news from Sienna Waters by signing up for my newsletter!

TO N.–

Who thinks there's a story in every moment
xxx

CHAPTER ONE

The hair was blonde, which wouldn't have been a problem except Elizabeth was a brunette.

She held it up to examine it better and then, for lack of a better place to put it, replaced it on Eli's jacket. It shone slightly in the light streaming in through the hallway.

Elizabeth's heart beat a tad faster, her mouth was a little dry, but all in all, she thought she was handling herself admirably. In fact, this was probably more of a comment on her house-keeping skills than anything else, she told herself. She really should have taken the jacket to the cleaners last week.

She stood and stared at it for a moment longer, toes itching in her new shoes, until the taxi outside beeped its horn and she remembered that she had places to be and people to see. It was a Tuesday, after all.

It was drizzling and cold enough that she should be wearing a winter coat. The cab, on the other hand, was warm and stuffy enough that she had to roll down a window as soon as she got in.

"Where to, love?"

She huffed. "Portman Square," she said sharply. She disapproved of being called 'love.' Not just by the balding, overly cheerful taxi driver, but by anyone at all. Even Eli never called her that.

She settled into her seat and let herself be driven. And the hair preyed on her mind.

In another world, she wouldn't have noticed it. In another world, she'd have taken the damn jacket to the cleaners when she was supposed to. In another world, she'd have been less observant and more in a hurry to get into town for lunch.

Unfortunately, she lived in this world, with its drizzle and rude cabbies and long, blonde hairs. Why blonde? She just knew it was dyed, could tell by the shine of it. So common. She flicked back a long curl of her own dark brown hair as she thought about it.

Eli and a blonde. She found it hard to picture them together, not just because she didn't have a face for the blonde, but because Eli had always chosen brunettes before. Maybe just so that he didn't get caught out as often.

She'd heard that clever men brought their mistresses the same perfumes as they gifted their wives, so that they'd always smell like home. Eli was definitely clever. He was a financial analyst, after all. Not that Elizabeth had any idea what that was, other than that it provided for an enormous deposit in their joint bank account every month.

So it wasn't beyond the imagination that Eli might restrict himself to indulging in extra-curricular activities with brunettes just so that there'd be less evidence.

Until now, of course.

"You alright, love?" asked the taxi driver, glancing into the rear-view mirror.

"Perfectly, thank you," said Elizabeth crisply.

Of course, the most sensible approach would be to clone one's wife and then have the affair. That way, there'd be no clues at all. Though she supposed that probably defeated the purpose of cheating. 'Eating away from home,' her mother had once called it. Which implied that it was normal, desirable even, because who didn't enjoy lunch in a restaurant every now and again?

The cab was approaching Hyde Park and had started to rumble along more slowly now that the traffic was worse.

"Gonna be a few minutes, love," said the driver. "Traffic's always a nightmare around lunch."

"I'll get out here," Elizabeth said. Apart from anything else, she didn't want to be called 'love' again.

"Please yourself."

She handed over the fare, considered deducting the tip and then didn't because it would be rude, and got out. She extended a plain, black umbrella over her head against the incessant drizzle and began to walk.

It wasn't far. A block or two at most.

As she walked, she composed a mental list of anyone she and Eli knew that had long, blonde hair.

"DRINKIES ARE ALREADY in," boomed Amanda as Elizabeth was shown to the table.

"Lovely to see you, dear," said Arabella, standing up and dropping a kiss in the vague region of Elizabeth's cheek.

"Horrid weather we're having," Alexandra said, not bothering to stand up. "Do sit down, you must be gasping, you poor thing."

The three As. Elizabeth wasn't exactly sure how she fit into an equation that by definition really shouldn't include her, though Arabella had once tipsily suggested that they change her name to Augusta.

She *was* sure that the three As were her normal Tuesday lunch date, and that throughout the rest of the year there'd be a sprinkling of invitations to garden parties, dinner parties, and the occasional special event.

Which she supposed made them her friends. No, she was being uncharitable. They were her friends. They shared recipes, complained about their husbands, and in the case of the three As had an awful lot to say on the topic of school fees.

"So Angus and Amy did get in," Amanda was saying, as if to prove Elizabeth's thoughts. "And now George is making the most God-awful fuss about the fees. Honestly, you'd think that we were sending them to Eton or something."

Arabella and Alexandra both grimaced in sympathy.

"Don't get me started," Alexandra said. "I hate talking finances with Alessandro, but he just will not accept that in England we don't talk about money the same way as the Italians do."

Alexandra was far too fond of dropping the fact that her husband was Italian into the conversation. As far as Elizabeth knew, no one had ever mentioned how distinctly odd it was that the couple had practically the same name.

"Hugh says that the Italians have no idea how to make money," said Arabella. And she should know, Elizabeth thought, since her husband was high up in some bank or another.

Which meant it was time for her to inject something into the conversation. She blinked, remembering how the sunlight through the front door reflected off the blonde hair on the dark jacket.

"Oh poor old sausage," said Amanda. "We're wittering on about our husbands and here you are miserable as sin. Eli off on another business trip, is he? Leaving you all on your own again."

Elizabeth could spot a life-raft when she saw one. "Yes," she said simply.

"He'll be back soon, don't you worry," Alexandra said, just as large glasses of wine were placed in front of each of them.

He'd be back tonight, Elizabeth thought. She made a mental note to take his jacket to the dry cleaners this afternoon. That way neither of them would have to look at it.

Elizabeth wondered if Alessandro ever played away from home. He was Italian, after all, and didn't they have some sort of cultural pass for infidelity? She wanted to ask, but took a large sip of wine instead.

At least she could imagine Alessandro cheating, with his wild dark curls and his lean figure and his eyes like pools of chocolate. Elizabeth resisted the temptation to fan herself. She was sure that she wasn't the only one around the table that occasionally fantasized about Alessandro.

Apparently, Queen Victoria had advised her daughter to 'close her eyes and think of England' on her wedding night. In north London the saying might as well be 'close your eyes and think of Alessandro.'

She gave a little shudder and moved on. Arabella was talking about the new wine merchant she'd found. Which was probably just as well, because Hugh did like a drink. Not women though, as far as Elizabeth knew. In fact, Hugh had that red-faced look of someone that would deny an affair with his male secretary until the cows came home. And Arabella would stand by him too, prim and proper as the papers snapped pictures of Hugh hanging his head.

George, on the other hand, was devoted to Amanda and as cynical as Elizabeth was, even she wouldn't deny that. Every now and again she'd catch George glancing at his wife during a dinner party, or at a barbecue, or during a Christening, and he looked as though he couldn't believe his luck.

Which was more or less surprising because in her most private and least kind thoughts she did think that Amanda looked rather like a prize bull dressed in a Liberty print dress.

She downed the rest of her glass of wine and ordered another one.

"What is it, old stick?" Amanda asked as the waiter walked away. "You're all out of sorts, care to share?"

She thought about it. The words were on the tip of her tongue and the shining golden hair was at the forefront of her mind. But then she saw Arabella's frown of pity and heard Amanda giving out advice and knew Alexandra would roll her eyes at the indiscretions of English men, and so she didn't.

"The damn Aga," she said.

And that was enough to get all three of them talking about the temperamental stoves and how best to deal with them, leaving Elizabeth time to sit back and sink another two glasses of wine and nibble at a salad before the bill came.

"No, no," she said. "It's absolutely my turn." She pulled out her purse and slid a credit card out, slipping it discretely to the waiter.

When he brought it back, she settled it back in with the others and spared all the cards a small smile before she zipped her purse closed again. Because being married to Eli did have its advantages. She really did need to remember that.

CHAPTER TWO

When Poppy Robbins opened her curtains to reveal the gray, drizzly morning she grinned so hard her face started to hurt.

There was nothing like a rainy day to make her feel like she really was living in England. Plus, there was the chance to wear the bright yellow rain boots that she'd picked up at the charity shop just yesterday.

"Pops?"

"Yep?" She sat down and started pulling on her socks.

"Did you use the last of the coffee?" Mel, best friend, roommate, and current psych student- though this was her third attempt at a degree and her sixth new career- stuck her head around the door.

"I get enough caffeine at work," Poppy said, sitting up straight to see a look of gloom spread over Mel's round face. "What?"

"You haven't packed anything," said Mel, sliding into the room fully.

"I will, don't worry."

"Two weeks and we've got to be out of here. Roger was pretty definite about that. I don't think he's going to let you squat or anything. His sister needs the place."

"I know, I know, don't worry about it."

Mel sat on the edge of the bed. "You know how you are, Pops. You can't just wait for something to change the circumstances.

These circumstances aren't going to change. You need to box up your stuff. You need to find a new place to live."

Poppy grinned at her. "You worry too much. Probably a symptom of not enough caffeine. I'm guessing you'll find the coffee in the fridge."

"Is that a Canadian thing?" Mel asked suspiciously.

"It's a… coffee thing."

"There is a coffee jar," pointed out Mel.

"There was a coffee jar," Poppy said. "You packed it already."

Mel sighed and patted Poppy's leg. "I am sorry, you know."

"About what?"

"About all this blowing up."

"It's not your fault that Roger's sister needs the flat, it's fine." She still felt a little thrill using the word flat rather than apartment, though after five years it really was second-nature.

Mel wrinkled up her nose. "Stupid sisters." She patted Poppy's leg again. "And I'm sorry that my sister can't put you up as well. What with the baby and everything, there's just no room right now."

"It's fine, I completely understand. Rather you than me, changing all those diapers."

"Nappies," Mel said, laughing. "But yeah, I'm pretty sure there's going to be a price to pay for a couch to sleep on."

Mel had been her best friend since she'd moved to England and they'd met on a tube platform. Poppy had been marveling at the fact she was actually in the real London tube, and Mel had been hurrying from university, a stack of books in her hands that she dropped all over the platform when she'd bumped into Poppy.

The rest was history. They'd been friends ever since and room-mates since the year before. A situation that was now changing.

"You gotta find a place, Pops," Mel said, getting up.

"It'll all work out," said Poppy, absolutely certain that it would. After all, most things did. She was here, wasn't she? She hadn't given up hope, even after everything had gone wrong.

Even after Evelyn had dumped her and her whole reason for being in the country in the first place had disappeared.

Mel had stepped up, given her a place to live, and then there was always work. Shit. She checked her phone. Work that she was definitely going to be late for if she didn't get a move on.

"You don't want a cup?" called Mel on her way to the kitchen already.

"No time," squeaked Poppy, looking under her bed for the yellow boots.

When she finally emerged, three minutes later, her blonde hair tussled and a boot in either hand, Mel was standing in the doorway again, a cup of coffee in either hand.

"I put extra milk in so it's cool enough to drink," she said, passing one over. "And you've got dust in your hair." She plucked two dust bunnies out of Poppy's curls.

"Thanks, you're an angel," said Poppy, slurping down the coffee. "God, I know I shouldn't say it, but this instant stuff is so much better than the fancy stuff at work."

"That's probably because Canadian coffee isn't really a thing," Mel said, leaning against the door frame and sipping at her own cup.

"Yeah, well, you try explaining that to Jeremy," said Poppy, draining the rest of her mug and handing it back to Mel.

"Your boss is an idiot," Mel said.

"My boss is anxiously awaiting my presence," Poppy said in the poshest accent she could muster.

"Not bad, not bad at all. We'll have you working at the palace yet," Mel grinned. "Go on then, off with you. I'll grab you some boxes from the supermarket on my way home from class. At least that way you'll have somewhere to put your stuff when you're living under that bridge."

"There won't be a bridge," Poppy said, pulling on first one boot then the other. "I told you, something will turn up."

"Not if you don't start looking," said Mel, but Poppy was already halfway down the hall.

"Bye, don't wait up," she shouted as she stepped out into the cool morning.

RIDING THE TUBE was one of Poppy's favorite things to do. It was the most foreign thing that she did daily, and every time she got into a silent carriage it made her smile. There was something about the smell, the people buried in their phones, the quiet, that made it distinctly English.

The train shuddered to a stop somewhere between stations and a garbled announcement was completely incomprehensible. There was a murmur of grumbling and a rustling of newspapers, but no one complained. Poppy hung on to the arm strap and waited until a short while later the train rumbled and took off again.

Three stations later, half the commuters got off and Poppy snagged a rare seat. She jumped straight back up again as an older woman got on.

"Thank you, dear," said the woman, as she settled into Poppy's seat.

Poppy grinned and went back to swinging from the arm strap.

Five years she'd been here and she had no thoughts of going back home. No thoughts of anything other than just gently living every day with a smile.

The tube rolled to a stop again, and this time Poppy got out.

"Morning, Paul," she said as she reached the top of the stairs to the street. She dropped twenty pence into the homeless man's cup.

"Cheers, Poppy."

"You doing alright in this weather?"

"Warm as toast, don't you worry," he said. "And you're running late, Jeremy will have your guts for garters."

"Don't say that," she said, pulling a face. "I'll just make it. Pop by after the lunch rush and I'll see what we've got in the kitchen. Might be nothing, but I can at least promise you a warm drink."

"Ta very much."

She rushed out onto the sidewalk, turning right and

practically running down the street to the corner. Only when she'd turned the corner and seen that the lights were on and there was no queue of people out front, did she slow down.

The Canadian Coffee sign glowed, a red maple leaf on either side of the name, the light a beacon on such a gray morning.

It had been no use explaining to Jeremy that Canadian coffee wasn't really a thing. He wasn't stupid, he knew that. "But it'll be a thing," he'd said, and Poppy hadn't had the heart to try and dissuade him. Besides, she'd needed the job, and Jeremy had been cutely over-excited about having a real, actual Canadian working for him.

At the beginning he'd wanted them all to wear uniforms. Poppy had said that Canadians really didn't do uniforms and Jeremy had said that the Mounties certainly did and Poppy had pointed out that Mountie uniforms were probably terribly expensive. Jeremy had given up on the idea after that, though he did still make the baristas wear aprons.

She looked down at her rain boots, bright yellow against the dark, wet sidewalk, and deliberately walked into a puddle. Immediately, her left foot felt cold wetness seeping in. Huh. Well, she supposed there had to be a reason that someone had donated them to the charity shop. At least her right foot was alright. She made a note to herself to remember only to puddle hop with her right foot, then she squelched on down the sidewalk until she reached the steamy windows of the coffee shop.

CHAPTER THREE

T he salmon was in the pan resting and the couscous was steaming and the wine was in the fridge cooling. Everything was very much in hand.

Elizabeth untied her apron, patted at her immaculate hair, and went into the living room to make sure that the coffee table was arranged and the cushions were straight.

He'd be here any minute and it was important to her that her husband entered a clean house. Twelve years they'd been married and not once could Elizabeth remember a time when Eli had seen the house a mess.

It would have been different, of course, if they'd had children. But they hadn't. First because Eli hadn't thought they were ready and then after because Elizabeth couldn't. It was unfortunate, sad even, but not something that she dwelled on.

It didn't do to dwell on things.

Instead she'd thrown herself into her charity work, into making their house into a home, into being the perfect wife. And if part of that meant over-looking the occasional dalliance with a co-worker or assistant or whoever else, well, then that was just what needed to be done.

Her mobile rang in the kitchen and she hurried to get it, wondering if it was Amanda about the museum fundraiser or Arabella about collecting for the children's hospital.

As it turned out, it was neither.

"Darling," Eli said, as soon as she picked up the phone. "How are you?"

"Absolutely fine. Where are you? Please don't tell me that your flight was delayed again. I mean, honestly, what are the airports coming to?"

There was only the slightest of pauses. "No, it's not that, darling. Actually, I, uh, I'm still in Frankfurt."

Elizabeth looked over at the pan of salmon. Frankfurt seemed like an awfully long way away. For an instant she felt bad about the fish, bad that it died for this, just to be cooked and thrown away uneaten due to some… some what?

"Oh." It seemed an appropriate response.

"I'm afraid something's come up, darling and I really couldn't get away."

Something? Or someone? That long blonde hair like spun gold glinted in her memory. She'd taken the jacket to the cleaners. And just to be sure, she'd taken Eli's winter coat and his good blue suit as well.

"Oh."

"I'm so sorry, I know that I said I'd be home tonight, but it really was unavoidable."

"And when will you be home?"

In the background of the call she heard a siren screaming and then fading as it passed wherever Eli was standing.

"Tomorrow for certain," Eli said as the siren passed by. "I'll definitely be home tomorrow."

"Okay, darling," Elizabeth said, stomach cold and mouth dry again. "I'll see you tomorrow."

"I miss you," said Eli, his voice dropping a little in a way that used to make her pulse race.

"Me too," she lied, and then hung the phone up before she could lie any further.

She looked at the phone in her hand for a long time. The siren had been a police siren, she'd recognize it anywhere. A distinctly British police siren, the swirling sound of it very different from the two-note German sirens she knew from sailing weekends in

Hamburg.

Hands as steady as they could get, she put the phone down and went to the stove. Quickly, she scraped the salmon into the rubbish bin under the sink. There was no point in keeping it, it wouldn't be edible tomorrow.

The couscous and vegetables she carefully packaged in Tupperware and stowed in the fridge. Maybe she could use them for lunch the next day.

Then she pulled out the bottle of wine, uncorked it, and poured herself a glass. Halfway back to the living room she turned around, picked up the bottle, and filled her glass to the very brim, before putting the bottle down.

Eli had been smart and handsome. But it was his smile that had attracted her across the university bar. The smile that had made her feel like she was the only girl there, that he was paying special attention to just her.

Which was why when she walked in on him and Rebecca Marshall, her best friend and maid of honor, a week before the wedding, she'd been more shocked than she'd cared to admit.

Eli had apologized, of course. He'd gone down on his knees even, bringing her flowers and champagne and a ring that had once belonged to his grandmother.

He'd smiled again and Elizabeth had been caught up in it. Besides, the wedding was already paid for and her mother had already told everyone that she was marrying a handsome, well-to-do city businessman, and it had seemed too much to handle to have to explain to everyone what had happened.

Too much to handle and far too embarrassing. So Eli had promised never to do it again and Elizabeth had forgiven him and the wedding had been beautiful and exactly what she'd wanted.

Eight months after they returned from their honeymoon she'd run back to the house to pick up a sweater, the day being colder than she'd thought, and found Eli busily stripping his personal assistant in the middle of the living room.

Which was about when she really realized that she had to

settle for something. Sacrifices had to be made. She could have the perfection that she wanted on the outside to show other people, or she could have the perfection she wanted on the inside and find herself a new, less-philandering husband.

Twice more, in various different circumstances, she'd caught Eli with his pants both literally and figuratively down. Each time he'd been apologetic, distraught even. And each time she'd forgiven him.

It was only after the next time that she'd finally sat him down and set out the rules. Whoever she is, she doesn't come into my home. Whoever she is, she takes no precedence over me. And whoever she is, I never set eyes on her.

"So, you're saying that I shouldn't get caught?" Eli had asked, cautiously.

"In a nutshell," she'd answered.

And that had become the arrangement.

Eli got his fun and she… she got the perfection to show other people. The house she adored, the credit cards, the invites to the parties and everything else.

Which didn't mean that it didn't hurt. It did, of course it did. But after twelve years, hiding the pain was instinctive.

She took another glug of her wine and picked up her phone again.

Get the Aga fixed? Amanda had written in the group text they all shared.

I've got a man, Arabella had offered.

The racier, and to be fair slightly cooler, Alexandra had answered that with an emoji of a shocked face and then a laughing emoji.

Don't be puerile, Arabella had written. *I meant a repairman.*

There's nothing wrong with a little rough, Amanda had written in a rare moment of humor and actual understanding of what was going on for once. She was notoriously bad with emojis and had once understood Alexandra's innuendo laden aubergine emojis as a request for a Moussaka recipe, which she had duly provided.

Please don't encourage her, Arabella answered. *Elizabeth, let me know if you need his number.*

Especially while Eli's away, Alexandra had said, with an aubergine emoji just to be sure that they all knew what she was inferring.

She should be able to tell them. She should be able to tap away on her screen and write something like *Give me that number, if Eli gets to play then so do I.*

After all, she wasn't exactly the only woman in London whose husband played around. She wasn't even entirely sure that she was the only woman in their friend group whose husband was unfaithful. And it wasn't like there wasn't an agreement in place, it wasn't like Eli was directly lying to her.

Her fingers hovered over the screen until it timed out and went black again. She should be able to write those things, should be able to confide in them. Yet she couldn't.

She just couldn't bring herself to show them that there was rot beneath the surface, that the shiny, red apple of her marriage had worms eating away below the skin.

Wine should be sipped, she thought, as she gulped down almost half the glass in one go. It tasted better when sipped. On the other hand, it did its job far better when it was gulped. So another trade off.

She just had to remind herself of the good parts, that was all.

There were good parts.

There were holidays and store accounts and parties and all the rest of it.

She had the kind of life she'd always wanted. And if sharing her husband was part of that, well, then she'd just put up with it, as she was sure thousands of other women did.

She should be used to all this by now. She was used to all this by now.

So why did her stomach feel unsettled? Why was she considering going back to the kitchen and getting the rest of the bottle of wine? Why had she needed an unheard of two hour nap before making dinner, just to sleep off the excesses of lunchtime?

Why did this time feel different?

One blonde hair. Just one. A hair that easily could have come from someone on the tube. Not that Eli ever took the tube. Someone at an airport then. Or just someone brushing past him on the street.

She sighed, got up and headed back to the kitchen to get the wine bottle. It all felt different this time and she had no idea why.

CHAPTER FOUR

The woman in the dark coat took her coffee and sipped it immediately. She rolled her eyes to heaven and moaned. "Say what you will, you Americans make a good cup of coffee."

"Actually, I'm Canadian," Poppy said with a big smile.

"Are you, dear?"

"The clue's in the name," she said, pointing to the Canadian Coffee sign above her head.

"Oh yes, I suppose it is, isn't it?" the woman said, handing over a five pound note.

"It happens all the time, don't worry about it," Poppy said. In truth, it happened about a hundred times a day and it was her least favorite part about living in England. Well, that and the fact that every place she'd ever lived had the water pressure of a leaking garden hose.

"It's much the same though, love, isn't it?" said the woman taking her change.

Poppy didn't answer. If you didn't have anything nice to say, it was better to say nothing at all. She smiled wider as the next person in line stepped up. The queue stretched all the way to the door and she took orders as fast as she could.

"You'll be alright if I pop out for lunch, won't you?" Jeremy stuck his head through the serving hatch that separated the front of house from the back.

Poppy surveyed the monstrous line of people in front of her.

"Going to see a man about a dog," he said, with a wink.

Poppy was unsure whether this was true, some kind of euphemism, or just an English saying she hadn't heard before. She bit her lip.

"For God's sake, Poppy, I'm going to talk business with someone. Maybe someone interested in the franchise, alright?" Jeremy said, pale face flushing.

"Right, yes, of course," said Poppy, hands working at the coffee machine automatically.

Jeremy was absolutely certain that Canadian Coffee was ripe for franchising. He was sure that the business was going to take off. "We'll be bigger than Starbucks," was his frequent refrain. Poppy wanted to believe in him, and sometimes did, but she also really, really needed his help right now.

"Lisa will be in after lunch," he said, pulling his head back through the hatch.

And Poppy didn't have much of a chance to say anything really. The next thing she knew, the line was starting to dwindle and there was a knock on the back kitchen door. She looked at the chaos behind the counter. Empty milk packages, stacked steaming jugs and scoops and blender canisters littered every surface.

Then she turned her back on it all and rushed out into the kitchen.

"Bad morning, eh Pops?" Paul said when she opened the back door.

"Busy, that's all," she said, grinning. "Give me a second, I know for a fact that there's a few ciabatta sandwiches left. What do you prefer, tuna or cheese?"

"Cheese please," said Paul, waiting just outside the door.

"You can come in, Jeremy's not here," said Poppy, putting a sandwich onto a paper plate. "I'll grab you a coffee, give me a second."

She ran off as Paul let himself into the warmth of the little kitchen and then she promptly got distracted by a customer.

When she returned, Paul was whistling at the sink, a tea towel slung over his shoulder.

"Oh, you didn't have to do all this," said Poppy, looking over the sparkling kitchen.

"Singing for my supper is all," said Paul. "Besides, you looked like you could use the help."

"I kind of could."

"Jeremy's taking advantage of you, you know that, right?"

"Jeremy is working hard and trying to improve the business," said Poppy loyally. "I got you a coffee to go and a big tea as well 'cos I didn't really know what you wanted."

"I want a woman as wonderful as you to take care of me in my old age," Paul said, taking both containers.

"You'll find someone one day."

"You'd be surprised how many women on Tinder don't want to date someone of no fixed abode."

Poppy flushed. "Well, I'm sure things will work out."

"That's what I like about you, Pops, always looking on the bright side. The world could use more people like you." He picked up his dirty jacket that had been hanging on the corner of one of the work benches. "And that Jeremy is taking advantage of you, whether you want to hear it or not."

"It's fine," Poppy said. "And you'd better get out of here before he gets back. Go on."

"I'll see you later then."

"Not tonight, it's Tuesday."

"Oh, I forgot. Am-dram night, I'll see you tomorrow morning then. Thanks for the sandwich and the drinks."

"Thanks for picking up the slack back here," said Poppy. Doing what Jeremy should have done before he left, she thought, but then pushed the thought from her mind. It was unkind and unnecessary.

"Have fun doing Shakespeare or whatever it is that you've got going on," Paul said as he disappeared out the back door.

A customer rang the bell at the front counter and Poppy hurried off to help them.

THE CHURCH HALL was cold and smelled of dust and old tennis shoes, but Poppy loved it anyway. She was exhausted. Jeremy had not returned after lunch and poor Lisa was in the middle of exam season and really needed to study.

In the end, Poppy had worked the rest of her shift and most of Lisa's, closing the coffee shop down just in time to rush out to her theater group.

"Welcome, welcome," boomed Tanya, the group's ferocious leader. She swooped around in a kaftan most of the time, but Poppy suspected she had thermal underwear on underneath.

"Hello Tanya," chorused the rest of the group.

They were an odd bunch. A collection both young and old, thick and thin, shy and outgoing. Poppy had grown up watching old English detective shows on TV and knew that the amateur dramatic society was a tradition. Also, they tended to be mixed up in murders in small villages, but since she was in London rather than a picturesque hamlet in the west country or the lake district, she figured she'd probably be okay.

When she'd seen the poster in the supermarket during her first week in town she'd been overjoyed. When she'd shown up and been welcomed immediately into the company she'd been ecstatic.

The only small, tiny, little stone in her shoe was that she hadn't actually acted yet. In the four plays and three pantomimes the group had presented to the public, Poppy had been in precisely none of them.

But this season was going to be her season, she thought, thrilling with excitement.

"So, you've all had the chance to read the scripts I sent out," Tanya said, striding across the small stage.

There was a murmur of agreement.

Poppy had anxiously read the script as soon as she got it, looking for just the right part to audition for. *Murder at Marsley Manor* was exactly the kind of play she'd always dreamed of being in. A murder mystery farce. It didn't get much more English than that. Except for Shakespeare, of course, but she was pretty sure that the St. Julius Players weren't really equipped for drama of that caliber.

The local newspaper had called their *Jack and the Beanstalk* "mediocre at best with glimmers of acceptability" which suggested that *Macbeth* probably wasn't going to be included in their repertoire.

She hugged her copy of the script to her chest.

"We'll start off with a few casting suggestions," Tanya said. She was getting excited too, Poppy could tell. Tresses of graying-red hair were escaping from her turban. "Peter, darling, you'll be the Colonel, of course."

A tall, mustached man beamed with pride.

"Darling Midge, you'll take on Marjorie, I assume?" Tanya went on.

Midge, busty and smiling, owned a sweet shop and looked like she did. Poppy grinned at her, Midge was the perfect choice for the role.

"We'll hold auditions for some of the smaller roles," Tanya was saying now.

Which was her cue. Poppy stuck her hand up in the air and waved it, but Tanya was already looking in the other direction.

"With the exception, I think, of Nancy."

Poppy's heart stood still. That was the part she wanted. The part that as soon as she'd read the script she'd known was for her. It could have been written for her. Nancy, the bright, talkative American cousin.

After all, didn't she get mistaken for an American every day? She glanced around the room. There were no other foreigners here, just her and old Mr. Naipaul who'd lived in England since he was four and anyway, he always painted the scenery and wasn't in the slightest bit interested in acting. Even if someone had offered him the part of a twenty-something blonde debutante.

Tanya had to be about to call her name.

"Cheryl, my love, you can take on Nancy," Tanya said to the

company's youngest member.

Poppy was so astonished that she forgot her hand was still waving in the air.

"Yes, Poppy?" Tanya said, finally turning around. "Oh, of course, you'll be the perfect person to help Cheryl with her American accent being one yourself, won't you?"

"Actually, I'm Canadian," Poppy said automatically.

"What's that, my dear? Oh, before I forget, you will call about the rights to the play, won't you? And I'll need you to work on the rehearsal schedule. You and I can go over the logistics of that later tonight when the others are warming up. Yes, and I'll leave the organization of the coffee fund to you as well, shall I? You can start the collection, we can't put on a play without gallons of tea now, can we?"

And she was moving on, sweeping across the stage to talk to Mr. Naipaul about settings, and Poppy was left sitting with her mouth wide open feeling slightly like she'd been run over by a truck.

CHAPTER FIVE

Elizabeth was just home from yoga class and about to shower and get ready for a lunch at Alexandra's club when her phone rang.

"Darling, are you back in the country?" she asked as soon as she picked up.

"What?" said Eli. Then he coughed. "Oh yes, yes, absolutely."

"So I'll expect you for dinner tonight then?"

There was a brief silence and Elizabeth's heart pattered in her chest and she swallowed down a sick feeling.

"About that," Eli said. "Perhaps it would be best if you met me at the office."

Hmm. She considered the idea. She did like going to the big glass and steel building, she liked going there knowing that her husband was important. On the other hand, Eli nearly never invited her and she had no idea why he'd be inviting her now.

"Just wait at reception," he said, more confident and hurried now. "I'll be there at six."

"Okay—" she began, but Eli had already rung off.

Meet him at reception. Well, maybe he wanted to take her out to dinner. Or maybe he was going to tell her he'd been fired. No, that couldn't be right, not if she was meeting him at the office. Dinner it must be then. Or not.

She saw the time and hurried into the shower. She'd dress for dinner, she decided as the hot water hit her. Elegant but semi-casual, since she had no idea where Eli would take her.

THE EVENING WAS colder than she'd thought and she shivered a little as she waited in the big, glass reception area. The skylights were stories above her and the living garden made trickling noises that made her want to use the bathroom while she waited.

But she didn't wait long. Just long enough to inform the blonde receptionist of who she was, and by inference who her husband was, and to wonder if this was the woman. Blonde, but her hair wasn't long enough, Elizabeth had decided, just as Eli walked out of one of the elevators.

"Darling," she said, turning her cheek for the expected kiss that didn't come. When it didn't, she frowned. "Is everything alright?"

"Let's just get out of here," he said.

"Your tie is crooked," she said, reaching up to straighten it.

But Eli pulled away, and putting his hand on her elbow started to escort her out of the building.

"Eli, what's going on?" She wasn't going to panic. Not here, not in front of people.

"Listen, Elizabeth, I'm sorry."

"Sorry for what?"

He was already walking her down the street, but he let go of her elbow now and walked beside her, enough room between them that she couldn't smell his cologne.

He took a breath and she noticed that he looked pale. "Probably I shouldn't have done it like this," he said finally.

"Done what like what?" Don't panic.

"This like this," he said. "I mean, I should have been braver perhaps, had bigger balls."

"Eli!"

He almost smiled at that. He liked to shock her. "But in the end, I really did think this was best. In public, I mean."

She stopped now, putting her hands on her hips. "What's

best?" she asked. "What's going on, Eli?"

She was angry enough at his hesitation that she wasn't so worried about panicking anymore. Whatever this was, whatever was happening, Eli needed to spit it out and do it fast. He needed to stop being silly.

He took another breath and exhaled so hard it blew his cheeks out. "Listen, Elizabeth, I didn't want it to be this way."

She gritted her teeth. "Eli…"

"I honestly didn't." He looked at her with big blue eyes and she saw that he'd cut himself shaving that morning. There was a small dot of blood on the collar of his fresh white shirt.

She was going to say something, but she didn't. She didn't because despite what she might have said, she did know what was happening. Deep inside she definitely, certainly knew and it felt like a big pool of acid burning through her stomach.

And she was damned if she was going to make this any easier for him.

"There was just less of a chance that you'd make a scene in public," he said.

In that small moment, she hated him. Hated him for knowing her so well, for knowing that whatever she was feeling, however much she might be hurting, she would never show it in front of other people.

She was almost, almost tempted to scream right there on the street, just to prove him wrong. She didn't though. What was she supposed to scream? Did one choose a word? Or just open one's mouth and let the sound out? What kind of word should she choose? It seemed wisest and easiest in the end not to scream at all.

Eli took a step back.

It was fine, she told herself. As long as he didn't say the words it was fine.

"Elizabeth, I'm leaving."

Each word was like a physical blow.

"Leaving the company?" she asked, hopefully.

He shook his head but still didn't actually say the words.

Her legs felt funny, weak and shaky like they wouldn't hold her up for much longer and she wondered if perhaps she'd overdone it at yoga this morning. The next thing she knew, the pavement was swirling beneath her feet and Eli's hand was on her elbow again.

"Christ," he said. "Come in here, sit down."

He pushed open the door of the coffee shop that they'd paused in front of, pushing her inside, pulling out a chair for her and forcing her into it.

"Two teas," he shouted over to whoever was behind the counter.

"I don't drink tea in cafés," she said.

"Make an exception," said Eli. "You need it. Put sugar in too."

"Good for shock."

He folded his hands on the table. "Elizabeth, I'm handling this badly, that's pretty damn obvious. But I need to say this and you need to listen. I'm so sorry it turned out this way and honestly, I never set out to hurt you, truly I didn't. But I am leaving you."

"Why?" It was a decent enough question, one she had a right to an answer to, and one that she knew Eli would hate to answer.

Sure enough, he shifted in his chair. "There's someone else."

She shook her head. "We had an agreement. We have an agreement. You know that I look the other way."

"I know that... that I can't do this anymore, Elizabeth. It's that simple."

"Can't do what?" she asked.

Someone put a large mug of tea in front of her and out of habit she wrapped her hands around the cup and felt its warmth.

Eli rubbed his face. "This. Us. What we're doing. Elizabeth, I really can't. It's true that I've met someone else, but it's also true that this hasn't been working for so long. You're so... so controlling and everything needs to look perfect. You get angry when I leave my shoes by the door."

"We have a shoe stand."

"And angry when I don't fold the towels the way you like."

"Why her, why this time?"

He picked up his own tea and sipped at it, grimacing as he put the cup down. "Jesus, that's like battery acid." He looked over at Elizabeth. "She makes me feel different."

"Younger? Is this a mid-life crisis?" she asked, hating herself for the hope in her voice.

"No, no it's not." He rubbed his face one more time, then got up.

"Where do you think you're going?" she asked, finding a little of her old self.

"Away," he said. "This conversation is going nowhere and there's really nothing else to say. I'll call you about arrangements."

Then he was walking away. Just walking away like nothing had happened, like he wasn't breaking her heart and crushing the life out of her, like he hadn't just destroyed everything that she'd worked so hard to build.

She looked into her tea cup. The tea was dark brown despite the milk. She took a sip. Not bad. Not as bad as she'd thought.

"What a tosser."

Elizabeth looked up to see a short, blonde woman with curly hair and a friendly looking face looking down at her. Her eyes were deep brown and her sympathetic smile showed slightly uneven front teeth.

"A tosser," Elizabeth repeated, trying the word out. She'd never actually used it before.

"Yeah, dumping you like that in the middle of a cafe. No class." The waitress picked up Eli's tea and moved it over to an empty table. It was a tiny gesture but one that made Elizabeth swallow hard to stop her emotions taking over. "How long had you guys been dating?"

Elizabeth shook her head. "He's my husband. Twelve years."

"Fuck." The woman pulled out Eli's chair and sat down. "Shit. Are you alright?"

She didn't start on the subject of bad language. "Fine," she said.

"Ah, but you're English," said the waitress. "So that means

you're not fine at all. You only say fine when things are very much not fine."

Elizabeth looked up at her. "Well, it was a stupid question. My husband's just left me for another woman, do you really think I'm alright?"

"Another woman?" The waitress pushed Elizabeth's tea closer to her. "Drink some more."

"Another woman. After all these years. I mean, I knew he had others," Elizabeth said, wondering why she was speaking, but the words kept spilling out of her. "I knew there were dalliances, of course. But I didn't actually think he'd actually leave me. I didn't think what we had was that meaningless."

"You must be devastated." The waitress pulled out a pack of tissues from her apron and handed them over.

Elizabeth gripped the package in her hand tightly and then shook her head. "You know what?" she said. "I don't think I am. Not devastated. No..." She paused for a second and examined her feelings. "You know what I am? I'm angry."

The waitress grinned. "Nice to meet you, Angry. I'm Poppy."

Much against her will, the joke took her so by surprise that Elizabeth actually let out a bark of laughter. "Elizabeth," she said. "Nice to meet you, Poppy."

CHAPTER SIX

Poppy got up and switched the shop sign to closed and locked the door. Then she turned back to the table. Elizabeth. An appropriate name since the woman looked regal. Regal and sad and, as she'd said, pretty angry.

Still, Poppy thought that even she'd be angry in a situation like this, and she tried very hard not to experience negative emotions.

"I could kill him," Elizabeth said now, pack of tissues still clutched in her hands.

"I'm not sure I'd do that," said Poppy, sitting down again. She was closed, but she'd stay here as long as she needed to. "You're bound to get caught. I mean, what if they put Morse on the case, or Miss Marple."

"Or Poirot?" asked Elizabeth, a small smile twitching at the corner of her lips.

"His little gray cells would figure it out immediately, no matter how well you tried to cover it up," agreed Poppy. "Anyway, you don't look like the kind of woman who could kill anyone."

Which wasn't exactly true. She was attractive, tall and willowy, with long dark hair and eyes so dark they were nearly navy blue. Attractive enough that Poppy had instinctively been attracted to her. She also had a strict, severe look that did kind of make her look black widow-ish. Like she might have a couple of husbands already under the floor.

"I couldn't," Elizabeth said. "Not really. But I am so angry."

"Maybe you just need a little revenge then," suggested Poppy.

"And you don't look like the kind of person that believes in revenge," said Elizabeth, drinking more tea.

"I prefer to think of it as re-balancing karma. Besides, sometimes you need to express your feelings, it's good to get them out."

"You mean cutting all his shirts to shreds?"

"Or throwing all his belongings out onto the street."

"Or," said Elizabeth, eyes gleaming, "making sure he's never happy again and destroying everything he holds dear?"

Poppy laughed. "You're getting into the spirit of it, I'll give you that. But if you're going to go all out, then I'd probably think about doing a sort of *Strangers On A Train* thing, you know, swapping with someone else so that you don't get caught."

"So I avenge some other woman's cheating husband and she avenges mine?" Elizabeth said, thoughtfully. "But I don't know anyone else whose husband is cheating."

"I guess it doesn't have to be a cheating husband, it could be anything. You just swap revenges, that's all."

Elizabeth drank yet more tea. "What about you?" she asked. "Got anything you need avenging?"

Poppy grinned and shook her head.

"I'm sure that's not true. Evil boss, dirty stepfather, crazy ex?"

"Well," allowed Poppy, "I suppose there are a few karma imbalances."

Elizabeth finished her tea. "Mind you, most of those are probably back home, aren't they?" she said, putting her cup down. "I'm not sure I can travel all the way to Canada to avenge anyone."

Poppy laughed. "You don't think I'm American?"

"Isn't the clue in the name?" asked Elizabeth, pointing at the Canadian Coffee sign. "And you're closed. I should leave. I'm sorry, I didn't mean to impose."

"You're not imposing," said Poppy, but Elizabeth was already standing up.

"I am, you'll need to get home." Elizabeth said, tying a light rain jacket more tightly around her waist. "But thank you."

"I did nothing."

"You were here," the taller woman said.

"Well, I'm here any time you need me," said Poppy as Elizabeth walked to the door and unlocked it.

Elizabeth gave her a small, sad smile. "Thanks." She sniffed a little. "Maybe you should give some thought to who you'd want revenge on. You never know when you're going to meet a stranger on a train, after all."

Poppy grinned. "I'll have someone in mind the next time you pop in."

"I don't have any more husbands to dump me," said Elizabeth. "But thanks for the thought."

She went out into the night, bell ringing and door banging behind her, leaving Poppy alone in the deserted shop.

What a way to get dumped, Poppy thought. Poor woman. Then she looked out over the dirty tables and the floor that needed to be washed and the coffee machine that needed to be cleaned and thought that maybe, if she were ever asked again, she might quite like to avenge herself on Jeremy.

BY THE TIME she got home, Poppy was tired and her feet ached. She was pleasantly surprised to find that Mel was cooking up something that smelled amazing in the kitchen.

"Spag bol?" Mel said as Poppy walked into the kitchen.

"I don't think I've ever wanted something as much as I want spaghetti bolognese," she said, stomach rumbling.

"Then grab plates 'cos I'm almost done here. Good day?"

"Long, tiring."

"Jeremy disappear again?" asked Mel, serving pasta onto the two plates that Poppy got out of the cabinet.

"No," she said, defensively. Then she rubbed her nose. "Actually, he didn't show up at all."

Mel grunted but continued piling sauce over the spaghetti.

"And then a woman got dumped just as I was closing," Poppy said, getting forks and spoons out of the drawer.

"Poor thing."

"I know, right in the middle of a café. And he was her husband too, twelve years they'd been married."

"Tosser," said Mel.

"Exactly what I said," said Poppy. She carried plates over to the tiny table. "She was nicer than I'd be about it though. At least she wasn't sobbing her heart out at closing time. She was… collected, I guess. You know, in that way that only English people can be? Like my grandma just died but I'll still offer you a cup of tea and ask how your day was."

"It's a cultural thing," Mel said, sitting down. "We don't really do emotions in public. Well, the well-brought up amongst us don't. It's horrifically mentally unhealthy, of course, which could be why the rich are eccentric, all that angst has to come out somewhere."

Poppy wondered if Elizabeth was rich. She'd worn nice clothes, she probably had money, she decided. She was definitely better off without that asshat of a husband.

"What about the play?" asked Mel. "I didn't see you when you got in yesterday."

Poppy pulled a face.

"That bad? Did you even have a chance to audition yet?"

"Tanya gave the part to Cheryl."

"Cheryl the crying Jack from *Jack and the Beanstalk*?" Mel asked, fork halfway to her mouth.

"She only cried because she stubbed her toe on the bottom of the beanstalk before she started climbing it," Poppy said. "But yes, that Cheryl."

Mel put her fork down. "Pops, did you say anything?"

Poppy shook her head and Mel reached out to pat her hand.

"I'm sorry," she said. "I know you wanted the part." She picked up her fork again and shook her head. "You're too nice for your own good, Pops, you know that, right? You really do need to stand up for yourself a bit more."

"It's fine," Poppy said. "I'll get the next part. And I think Cheryl will do a great job."

Mel sighed. "You're too good to be true." She reached for the package of parmesan. "I've been thinking."

"Uh-oh." To be fair, Mel did have good ideas. It was just that generally they involved Poppy having to 'put herself out there' or 'stand up for herself' or 'grab the bull by the horns.' And Poppy for one wasn't about to stroke a strange dog, let alone grab farm animals by their heads.

"You should ask for a raise."

Poppy opened her mouth to argue, then closed it again. See? Mel did have good ideas.

"Look, you're doing a ton of work, you haven't had a raise for at least two years, you deserve it. And a raise would mean that you could afford a little more in terms of rent, which would mean that finding a new place would be much easier."

"You're not wrong," Poppy said carefully.

"I'm dead right," said Mel. "And you know as well as I do that it's deserved, you're not asking for something that you've not got a right to. The only person that you've got to ask is Jeremy anyway, and he's hardly intimidating."

The idea was growing on her. Maybe a raise would make her feel slightly less vengeful toward Jeremy. She grinned, thinking of Elizabeth exacting revenge for her. Elizabeth with a carving knife in hand threatening to cut off Jeremy's balls if he didn't actually show up for his shift and work the entire damn thing.

"What are you grinning at?" Mel asked.

"Nothing," said Poppy, still smiling at the thought.

"Well then, are you going to ask?"

Poppy sighed then nodded. "Yes, I will."

"Great," said Mel, getting up and pulling a bottle of wine off the shelf by the stove. It was cheap enough that it had a screw-top. "I've been looking for an excuse to open this." She looked at the bottle like it was champagne. "Let's celebrate."

"I haven't done anything yet," pointed out Poppy.

"Yeah, but you will," said Mel. "I get the feeling that there's change afoot."

"Nice word choice."

"I mean it," Mel said, fetching two jam-jar glasses to go with the wine. "Things are changing around here, just you wait and see. I've got a feeling that this is going to be your year, Poppy Robbins."

Poppy held up her jam-jar. "I'll drink to that," she said.

CHAPTER SEVEN

Eli arrived at nine in the morning which was not a good sign.

Elizabeth had debated tearing up his shirts but frankly, had been tired and empty and had finally sunk into bed for a good, long cry. She'd just gotten up, put herself together, and was debating whether a knife or scissors would do the job better and coming down firmly on the side of scissors, when the front door downstairs opened.

"Elizabeth?"

She rarely swore, even in her head, but this time she said something filthy and then clamped her mouth shut until Eli's feet pounded on the stairs and he stuck his head around the bedroom door.

"There you are," he said, as though he'd been searching for ages. "I've come for my things."

Not trusting herself to speak, Elizabeth gestured toward the cupboards on his side of the room. Eli pulled a suitcase out from a cupboard and laid it on the bed.

"I have to say," he said, as he pulled a collection of folded shirts out of a drawer, "that I'm glad we're doing this like adults." He paused for a moment and looked at her. "No screaming and shouting, I mean."

As if she would. She swallowed and watched him pack.

It hurt. Every movement that he made hurt her, like he was

stabbing her with each sweater he folded, punching her with each pair of trousers he smoothed. It was her Eli. If she held her breath she could imagine that he was just packing for one of his interminable business trips.

This couldn't be happening. This wasn't happening. She started to get angry again. This was absolutely ridiculous.

"This is absolutely ridiculous," she said, finding her tongue at last.

"What is?" he asked, pushing dark hair back from his forehead as he collected a handful of socks.

"This. All this. What are you doing, Eli?"

He stood up straight. "Packing, Elizabeth."

"But why? After twelve years have we not settled into life together? You're really planning on starting all over again? That's what's ridiculous, Eli. Why on earth would you do that?"

"Because I've found something," he said simply. "Something warm and hopeful, something that fills my heart and something that I can't live without now that I've tasted it." He put the socks in the suitcase. "I am sorry, Elizabeth. Truly, I am."

"Then don't go." She hadn't exactly meant to say that, the words had just slipped out.

"I have to go. It wouldn't be fair on anyone if I stayed," he said reasonably. "Would you really want me to stay if you knew I was thinking of another woman all the time?"

"Isn't that what you've been doing for most of our marriage?" she said, again not really meaning to speak the words aloud. She really needed to work on filtering.

"This is different. Sally is different." He shrugged. "It just is, Elizabeth. And I hope that one day you can understand what I mean, that one day you'll find someone that makes you feel the same way."

"I have a husband," she blurted out. She slammed her mouth shut and firmed her jaw. Really, she needed to think before she spoke.

But Eli was shaking his head. "No," he said. "I'm sorry, but you don't. Not anymore."

She swallowed away the pain of the words. "You should be going," she said decisively. "You should be at the office. We can talk about this when you get home."

"I'm not coming home," Eli said, the tip of his nose getting white as he got more frustrated. "And I'm not going into the office today."

Which was exactly the moment that Elizabeth understood this was real. Eli who worked all the time, Eli who took his laptop on holiday, Eli who had sat at his desk with a fever and 'flu, wasn't going to the office today.

"You're a fool."

"What?" Eli looked up from rolling up a pair of boxer-briefs.

"You're a fool," she repeated, heart growing harder by the second. "You think this little floozie will look after you the way I have? You think you can have a better life with some slip of a girl that can barely spell her own name and isn't old enough to drink?"

"Sally is well over age," Eli said, returning to his folding.

"And she's going to clean your house, make sure your suits go to the cleaners, ensure that you have laundry for your business trips and dentist appointments and all the rest of it?" Elizabeth said, voice rising.

"Maybe," shrugged Eli. "Or maybe I'll have to do those things myself."

She gave a bark of laughter. "If only you had any idea of what I do for you every single day."

Now he really looked up, blue eyes glinting. "I know that you control me," he said. "I know that you decide who we're friends with, which invitations we accept, you buy my clothes and decide which holidays are acceptable. I know that you won't let me lie on the couch in my own house."

"You have a bed," she said automatically.

"Exactly. You won't let me leave my shoes by the door, a cup on the draining board. I know that you want perfection, that everything has to look just right and be just right. And I know that it suffocates me."

Elizabeth rolled her eyes. "You? Suffocated? You've had the opportunity to screw half your office and every flight attendant between here and New York. You think you're going to get that from your precious Sally?"

He paused and shook his head.

"See?" Elizabeth said. "She's not that perfect."

"She doesn't need to be," he said, pulling the suitcase lid down. "And neither did you."

She gritted her teeth as he pulled the zipper on the case closed.

"I'll be in touch with the details of everything," he said, pulling the case off the bed. "My lawyer will send the appropriate paperwork and I suggest you get a lawyer of your own."

Her own lawyer? She hadn't even considered the idea. Having her own lawyer sounded impossibly adult, like she'd done something terribly wrong when she knew that she hadn't.

Eli hefted the case up and started downstairs. Elizabeth followed, not sure why she was going except that she either needed to stop him or watch him walk away to know that this was real and not a dream.

"In terms of the house, we'll have to discuss what we're going to do," he went on.

"Wait, the house?"

"Of course, we'll probably need to put it on the market."

"No!" Not her house, her beautiful, perfect house.

"Then you'll need to find a way of paying for it," Eli said, pulling on a jacket that was hanging by the door. "Apropos of which, I've instructed the bank to close our joint accounts and set up individual ones. You should get everything you need in the post. Your account will have a decent proportion of our savings, don't worry about that. As for the rest, well, we'll see what the lawyers hammer out, won't we?"

Elizabeth was still thinking about the house, still thinking about the kitchen she'd planned herself, the way the light hit the fireplace just right in the living room, the bed that she wouldn't have to share anymore.

And Eli was already letting himself out of the house, not even saying goodbye, just lugging that great suitcase out to his car at the curb.

She watched and then had to slam the door as something rose up inside her, tears almost choking her, pieces of her heart breaking off and lodging in her veins until she couldn't feel her feet and couldn't breathe and couldn't even keep her eyes open.

It was a long, long time before she stirred. Her bottom was stinging from sitting on the hall floor for too long and the light was fading, the early autumn evening setting in.

She'd cried until the tears had dried up. And now that they were gone and she was sticky and snotty and altogether unlike herself, she found that all that was left was the anger.

How dare he do this to her?

How dare he think that he could take her house from her?

How dare he ruin the life that they'd built together?

She itched to slap him and wished that she had.

Then she looked at the foot-marks on the otherwise pristine hallway carpet. He hadn't even taken off his shoes. And a plan started to form in her mind. Slowly the pieces began to come together and as they did the feeling came back to her legs and her heart began to beat properly again and she could breathe.

She fondled the phone in her trouser pocket, tapping her fingers on it. But no, she didn't need her regular contacts for this. The three As would be no help here. In fact, the less they knew, the better. If she was lucky then they'd never have to know about this at all, she'd never have to face them as a single woman. She could deal with this and be back to normal in no time.

But she needed a little help.

She got to her feet, feeling a little dizzy from lack of food and too much sobbing. A wash and brush up, a change of clothes, and she'd be as good as new though. Then she'd go out. She knew exactly where she needed to go.

CHAPTER EIGHT

Poppy pulled her scarf up over her chin and snuggled into it. It was a cold morning, the air crisp and bright. She'd have to remember to bring Paul a thermos, she was sure there was a spare one knocking around somewhere. He'd need a hot drink to get him through the day.

"Morning," Paul said, as she stepped out of the tube station.

"Morn—" she started, before some harried commuter pushed past her and almost knocked her off her feet.

"Oy!" shouted Paul.

But the man was already gone, practically running down the street, his briefcase knocking against his leg.

"Bastard," said Paul. He turned to Poppy. "You can stand up for yourself a bit more, Pops. He doesn't have a gun, this isn't the Wild West over here, you know."

"I thought knife crime was more in fashion here?" Poppy said, grinning at him.

He blushed. "Yeah, alright. But a tosser like him isn't going to have a knife. Most dangerous thing he's got on him is a spreadsheet and you can't do much damage with that."

"You'd be surprised," Poppy said. "I've got to run, pop in later?"

"Will do, I'll need to get out of the cold today. Brass monkeys out here."

Brass monkeys. Presumably that meant extremely cold. Poppy filed it away in her bank of British expressions as she made her way to the coffee shop. She was hoping to be early enough to catch Jeremy before he opened.

She was going to do it. She'd thought long and hard last night and Mel was right. She did deserve a raise. Even if it was just a cost of living raise. And she was going to put herself out there, man up, stand up for herself, and all those other horrible things, and ask for what she wanted.

She breathed hot into her scarf, heart beating harder at the thought of what she was about to do. But it was only fair, only right.

The lights were on, but the door was locked and Poppy had to use her key to get inside.

"Pops, that you?" Jeremy shouted from the back.

"If it's not, the burglar's got a key and you should be very worried," she answered, unbuttoning her coat and pulling off her scarf.

"Ha bloody ha, what time's the bread man supposed to be here?"

"Not for another twenty minutes," she said, walking into the small kitchen.

Jeremy was standing with his back against the counter, mobile in hand, scrolling through something. Poppy eyed the refrigerators, still firmly closed. There was milk to be restocked up front and even if the bread wasn't here yet, he could have made a start on getting sandwich stuff ready.

She cleared her throat and he looked up from his phone. "All alright, Pops?"

She nodded and cleared her throat one more time just in case the words felt like leaping right out unbidden. But they didn't, so she had to try harder. "Um, there's something I've been wanting to talk to you about," she started.

Jeremy's eyes lit up. "Oh good, me too."

Suddenly the world seemed a little brighter. Maybe she wasn't going to have to do the hard bit after all. "You have?" she said. "It's just that I've been working so hard and you know I haven't had a day off in four weeks now and, well, I don't really want to complain." There was nothing the English hated more than a complainer, except maybe a queue jumper, she'd discovered.

"Good, good," Jeremy said. "No complaints, that's what I like to hear."

Poppy's smile slid a little. She realized that she wasn't entirely sure where this conversation was going now.

"Right," she said. "It's just that, well, as I said, I've been working a lot and—"

"And don't think it's gone unnoticed, Pops, it hasn't," Jeremy broke in. "Which is why I didn't worry as much as I might have done when I let Lisa go."

"You... you what?" Poppy asked, feeling a little weak and leaning back against a counter herself.

"Well, she's not working much anyway, what with all her exams, and she was going to take off for a couple of months during uni holidays anyway, so I thought I'd save us some cash. We could use some savings the way things are going."

"The way things are going?" echoed Poppy.

He blushed a little, the color looking weird on his pale white skin. "Yeah, that meeting the other day didn't go quite as well as I'd hoped. But, you know, it's just a matter of time. We'll franchise this place before you know it and then I'll be rolling in it and I'll hire you as many lackeys as you want, how about that, eh Pops?"

It was the 'I'll' that got her. Jeremy was not only convinced that he could sell his poxy coffee shop idea, but also that it was going to make him rich. Him. The one who never worked a full shift, the one who frequently didn't show up to open in the morning, the one who dodged off for meetings with shady businessmen and couldn't make a cup of decent coffee to save his life.

"I want a raise," she blurted out, letting all the anger she was starting to feel slip out with the words.

"You... you want..." And then Jeremy was laughing, seriously laughing, so that his cheeks turned even redder and tears came to his eyes.

Poppy put her hands on her hips and straightened up, but Jeremy was already wiping tears away, still chuckling.

"Nice one, Pops." He slapped her on the back a little too hard. "Nice one. Never mind, we'll talk about a nice percentage raise once I've sold the first franchise, deal? Maybe two percent." He winked. "Three if you catch me on a good day."

Poppy opened her mouth but words deserted her as Jeremy slapped her back again.

"Now, the bread man will be here any minute, you get started on those sandwiches. I'll get out of your hair." He was pulling on a coat already. "I've got to go see—"

"—a man about a dog," Poppy finished in a mumble.

"Exactly right," Jeremy said with another laugh. "Have a good day and don't wait up."

He disappeared out the back door and Poppy took his words to mean that he wasn't planning on showing up for the rest of the day.

She stared after him for a long time, longer than she should have, because by the time she came to her senses and started unloading the fridges to make sandwiches the bread man was already pulling up outside.

"Getting quite the queue out there," he said as he climbed out of his van by the open back door. "You might want to think about opening."

Poppy swore to herself and rushed off to open the front door.

MEL APPEARED JUST as the lunch rush abated, her dark hair frizzy in the cold and her nose running.

"It's freezing out there today," she said as she came in. "It's only the beginning of October."

"If you're about to say 'so much for climate change' then I'm going to have to ask you to leave," Poppy said behind the counter.

"Let me guess, you've heard that about fifty times today already?"

"Make that a hundred," said Poppy, flicking the switch on the coffee machine to start a cup for Mel.

"So, how did it go?" Mel said, leaning her elbows on the counter and leaning in.

"How did what go?" Maybe if she pleaded ignorance Mel would forget why she came and what she was talking about.

"Asking for a raise," Mel said, rolling her eyes.

Poppy sighed. "Not well. He said no."

"No?" screeched Mel. "No? The little toe-rag."

"He said we can talk about it again after he sells the franchise," said Poppy, feeling it best to get everything out in one go.

Mel shook her head. "He's an idiot. He's never going to sell a franchise on this place." Her dark eyes turned to Poppy. "And you, my dear, need to stand up for yourself, stop letting him take advantage of you."

"Exactly what I said," said Paul, appearing from the back room, tea towel over his shoulder.

"Afternoon, Paul," said Mel. "And he's right," she said to Poppy. "You can't go on like this. You're working yourself to the bone for someone else's dream, that's ridiculous."

"What am I supposed to do?" Poppy asked. "I need this job. Anyway, I like this job. Mostly."

Mel groaned. "You're going to end up living on the streets at this rate."

"It's alright," Paul said comfortingly. "You can share my box if you like. I'll show you where the toffs throw out the good stuff, and it's not as cold as you'd think outside once you've got a bit of cardboard under you."

"Not helpful," said Mel.

Poppy exhaled and passed a coffee to Mel and then another to Paul. "It'll be fine," she said. "Stop worrying, everything will work out in the end."

THE EVENINGS CAME in quickly at this time of year, and by six, the coffee shop was empty and the world outside was dark. Poppy wiped down the tables and started cleaning the coffee machine.

It would all turn out okay in the end, it had to. Everything always worked out. She had nothing to worry about. Which didn't mean she didn't want to punch Jeremy for being an unrealistic asshole. She piled up the dirty cloths by the cash register.

It had been this way since the beginning, though she could only see it now in hindsight. Jeremy had opened a coffee shop, sure, but it was Poppy that had done all the work. She'd set the menus, she cleaned the fridges, she made the orders. Jeremy just popped in from time to time to make sure she hadn't burned the place down.

And now he couldn't even consider a raise. Even after he'd fired Lisa, who had been the only actual help that Poppy had.

Maybe she should have taken up that offer of revenge, she thought, shaking her head at herself. Maybe then she'd actually be able to afford a decent place to live.

The shop bell rang.

"We're closed," she shouted out, before straightening up and turning toward the door.

"Good," said Elizabeth. "Because I've got a feeling it would be best if no one overheard what I'm about to say to you."

CHAPTER NINE

"I'm not going to kill anyone."

Elizabeth laughed until she saw that Poppy's face was serious. "I'm not about to ask you to kill anyone," she said. Poppy still looked suspicious. "I swear."

She looked around the empty coffee shop. Her plan hinged on the waitress agreeing to help her. If only because Poppy was the only woman Elizabeth could think of that Eli wouldn't recognize. And she was sure that an arrangement could be made.

"Do you mind if we sit down?" she asked, politely.

"Um, no, I guess," said Poppy, still hesitant.

But Elizabeth changed her mind. "How about you sit," she said. "And I'll bring you a nice cup of tea. You do look like you could use one."

She also looked like the kind of person who made the tea, not the kind that got offered one, which was exactly why Elizabeth had offered. Poppy sat down obediently, a good sign, Elizabeth thought, good that she'd do as she was told, and Elizabeth went behind the counter, quickly figuring out how to boil water and where the tea bags were.

"English people always seem to be able to do that," Poppy said, watching her. "It's like you have a sixth sense for tea. I swear, you could walk into anyone's house in the country and make a cup of tea like you'd lived there your whole life."

"I'm not entirely sure that's what I want my culture to be

known for," Elizabeth said, putting a dash of milk into each cup. "But I suppose there are worse things."

She brought the tea around and placed both mugs on the table and sat down opposite Poppy. Then she took a deep breath.

"I know this is strange," she said. "But I need your help."

Poppy took her tea. "I don't know if I wanted you to show up again or not," she admitted.

"Aha, so you've had a chance to think, have you?"

Poppy blew carefully on her tea. "Maybe."

Elizabeth crossed her legs. "Alright, then let's be honest with each other. I'm here because I need your help."

"So you said."

"My husband has…" Ouch. She hadn't realized how much it was going to hurt. She hadn't actually had to say it yet.

"Left you," filled in Poppy helpfully.

"Right," said Elizabeth. "And I find that I'm rather more upset than I thought I might be. Therefore…" Again she trailed off. The whole thing just sounded so foolish.

"You thought that you'd get revenge," Poppy filled in again. Her dark eyes danced a little and she might have been hiding a smile. She sipped at her tea. "Why don't you tell me what you had in mind?"

Elizabeth took one last deep breath and then began.

"He's always been unfaithful, you see, but this time he's decided it's different. Sally, that's her name. I think she's a blonde."

"I'm not hurting anyone," Poppy said.

"That's the beauty of this, no one needs to get hurt. In fact, if you think about it, people will actually avoid getting hurt. It's a no-pain revenge plan."

Poppy sighed. "What do you want me to do?"

"Seduce him."

There was a choking and splashing sound as Poppy choked on a mouthful of tea. "What?" she asked, when she could finally speak.

"It's simple," said Elizabeth, calm and collected. "You

seduce my husband. Oh, you don't need to sleep with him, incriminating evidence will be enough. Messages, whatever. And then we ensure that Sally knows what she's getting into."

"She'll leave him and he'll come crawling back to you."

"That's the idea," Elizabeth said coolly.

"And what if he doesn't?" asked Poppy.

Elizabeth shrugged. "I haven't decided yet whether I want him to or not, whether I'd let him back or not." Which wasn't true because if Eli showed up offering her old life back right this second she'd be leaving with him faster than Poppy could finish her tea. "But that's by-the-by. The point is that he's not happy with Sally."

"Who will also be informed about the kind of man she's taken on," Poppy said. Elizabeth nodded. "That actually sounds pretty fair."

Elizabeth picked up her own mug. "Which brings us to your half of the bargain. What exactly is it that you would want in return?"

Poppy puffed out her cheeks. "Isn't this all a bit... dramatic?" she said. "I mean, I feel like I'm in one of those horrible early two thousands films where everyone has an indecipherable London accent and carries a sawn-off shotgun in the trunk of their car."

"Do you?"

"What?"

"Carry a sawn-off shotgun in your car?"

"I don't have a car," Poppy said.

"Shame, it could have been useful."

"The car or the shotgun?" asked Poppy.

Elizabeth exhaled. "We're getting off topic. There must be someone that you would like to... I don't know, not hurt, like you said. But someone who could use a little teaching, someone who has a lesson to learn."

"How do I know I can trust you?" Poppy asked.

Elizabeth looked at her. "Do I look like the kind of person who can't be trusted? I've just told you what I've told no one else in my life yet. That's how much I've chosen to trust you."

"You haven't told anyone that your husband's left you?" Poppy said. And her face was so full of pity that Elizabeth almost got up and walked out right then and there.

"No," she said firmly. "And tell me who you're thinking about… plotting against." It still sounded ridiculous.

"My boss," Poppy said, finally. She looked around as though afraid of being overheard.

Elizabeth smiled, clasped her hands around her warm mug, and settled back in her chair. "Tell me all about it," she said, knowing that she was getting somewhere.

* * *

Poppy finished her story and finally took a breath. "And that's pretty much it," she added, to show that she was finished and also because she was suddenly nervous.

Why on earth had she said anything? But Elizabeth was smiling at her in a comforting kind of way and that made her feel slightly better. It was, she thought, quite hard not to trust people with posh accents. She'd have to work on hers a little more, just in case she ever needed to become a scam artist or a con woman.

"Okay," Elizabeth said, slowly. "So you need a little revenge on your boss. That should be easy enough." She blinked. "I can't say that a plan springs to mind immediately, I might need a little time to think about this."

Suddenly, Poppy realized that this was real, that they were straying across the line of talking in hypotheticals and that Elizabeth might actually want this to happen. "But this is all going to work out," she said quickly.

Elizabeth raised a perfect eyebrow. "That's what I used to think," she said. "That what's meant to be will happen. And look at me now. You have to make things happen, my dear. You can't just sit around and wait."

"Yeah, but… But this is all a bit… crazy?" Poppy ventured.

"Is it really though?" asked Elizabeth. "Is it crazy or is it just a roundabout way of each of us getting what we want, what we deserve?"

"You know that *Strangers on a Train* does not have the happiest of endings, right?" Poppy said.

"It's been a while since I've seen the film," said Elizabeth. She scraped back her chair. "But if you really don't want to do this then I suppose that I should leave you alone."

It was dark outside and cold and it had been a long and frustrating day and Poppy wanted to get home. Really wanted to get home. And all of this was just a weird, twisted fantasy.

Elizabeth was standing up now, walking away and Poppy nearly shouted out to stop her, but then didn't.

It was Elizabeth that turned back. "Hold on a minute, did you say that you were looking for somewhere to live?"

✳ ✳ ✳

It was exactly what she needed. Poppy nodded and Elizabeth went back to the little table, sitting down again.

"You need somewhere to live and I suppose I shall need someone to help pay my mortgage. Not that I have any idea how to go about doing that or even how much it is."

"It's not hard," said Poppy. "You need to call your bank."

Elizabeth growled. "Not the point. The point is that I'm asking you to move into my house."

Poppy's mouth fell open.

"For a fair rent, mind you," Elizabeth said. "And for your handshake on this agreement that we're coming to."

Poppy recovered her wits. "So if I help you get revenge on your cheating husband you'll help me get the raise I need from my boss and give me a place to live?"

"And you'll help me pay my mortgage," added Elizabeth. "So we're completely even, all fair and square."

"You're not going to go all psycho on me and stalk me and then end up dying, are you?"

Elizabeth rolled her eyes. "I'm assuming that's what happens in the film. And no, obviously I'm not." She paused, taking in Poppy's innocent face and her big, brown eyes. "Who knows, this might even be fun," she said, though she was sure that it wouldn't be in the slightest. It was obviously what Poppy needed to hear though, something to take the seriousness out of the discussion.

Poppy pursed her lips for a long enough second that Elizabeth was sure that she was going to say no. Then suddenly she grinned and held out her hand. "Alright," she said. "It's a deal."

Elizabeth took the small, slim hand she was presented with. It was warm and softer than she'd imagined. Touching Poppy made her realize just how long it had been since the last time she'd had real human contact.

"Deal," she said.

And it was all settled.

CHAPTER TEN

The house was fancy. Not quite BBC1 Sunday night historical drama kind of fancy, but still pretty nice. Poppy looked up at the red brick facade.

"Coming to stay, are you, love?"

She looked over to see a woman standing in the next garden. Whilst Elizabeth's front garden was gravel and stepping stones, the woman next door seemed to have planted some kind of jungle.

"Sort of," she said.

"Ooo," said the woman, noting the bags at Poppy's feet and the duffel over her shoulder. "You're not moving in, are you?"

"Um, sort of?"

The woman grinned. Her teeth were crooked and a spider web of lines sprang up around her eyes and Poppy found herself grinning back. "Rather you than me, love. Mrs. Marks does like things just so, if you know what I mean."

Mrs. Marks? Presumably that was Elizabeth. Poppy wondered just what else she didn't know about the woman. A whole lot considering she was about to move in.

"I'm Mrs. Lynton. Audrey if you're feeling friendly, which it looks like you are." The older woman held out a hand over the garden wall.

"Poppy," said Poppy, taking the hand and shaking it.

"Yank, are you?"

"Canadian actually."

"My grandson lives over there. Toronto. Must be nice since he only comes home once in a blue moon. Go on then, you'd better get going and ring the bell. Nothing to be afraid of. She doesn't bite, at least not as far as I know. Drop by for a cuppa when you've got time, I'm always in."

And then she disappeared leaving Poppy looking at the glass-paned front door wondering what 'she likes things just so' was supposed to mean. There was only one way to find out, she supposed.

She dragged the rest of her stuff up onto the front doorstep and rang the bell. The familiar sound of Westminster chimes rang inside the house and then the door opened.

"Ah, you're here," Elizabeth said. She smiled, then looked down and saw the collection of bags that Poppy had put on her doorstep. "With your things," she added, looking slightly more sour.

"I don't have matching luggage," Poppy said, starting to haul things inside. "But trash bags seem to work perfectly well. I've got a few more boxes but I can pick those up later."

"Right, right," Elizabeth said. "Leave all that here and I'll give you the tour. Shoes off please." She pointed to a rack by the door. "And put them just there, that would be lovely."

The English have a way of making a direct order seem like a foregone conclusion and Poppy was taking her shoes off before she knew what she was doing.

"We don't wear shoes in the house," Elizabeth was saying. "Nor do we lie on the couch. You have a bed for lying down. You're welcome to use the living room and kitchen, of course. And your room is just up the stairs here."

Poppy followed her up the narrow staircase. When she got to the top she caught a glimpse of a large double bed through a gap in the door at the top of the stairs. Bright white linen, hospital corners, the bed looked as though it belonged in a magazine. She was beginning to understand what Audrey had meant by Elizabeth liking things just so.

"This one," Elizabeth chirped, opening up another door.

Poppy squeezed past her, getting a whiff of floral perfume as she did so. For a quick second, Elizabeth's hand brushed against her arm and Poppy felt her pulse pick up a little. It really had been a while since anyone had touched her.

"It's beautiful," Poppy said honestly, looking at the neat single bed and the view out onto the street.

"There's an en suite here," said Elizabeth pointing out the door to a small bathroom. "And you'll have all the privacy you'll need." She cleared her throat. "And uh, if you'd like to get settled, I do have tea in the kitchen."

Poppy was oddly touched that Elizabeth had made her tea. Even more so when she got downstairs and realized that Elizabeth didn't just mean the drink. The kitchen table was laid with an assortment of small cakes and sandwiches, as well as a large teapot.

"Your home is lovely," Poppy said.

It might have been the first thing that she'd said right. Elizabeth's face relaxed and her eyes turned a deeper shade of blue. "Thank you. I like it. Tea?"

She was a beautiful woman, Poppy thought as Elizabeth poured the tea. She wore a fair amount of makeup, which wasn't really Poppy's style. But she had high cheekbones and her hair was thick and wavy. She obviously worked out as well. Up close she could see that Elizabeth was older than she'd thought at first. Forty maybe. With the makeup it was hard to tell.

"So, no guests, particularly overnight ones. You'll be responsible for cleaning your own room and bathroom, as well as keeping common areas tidy and neat. No shoes in the house —"

"—and no lying on the couch," Poppy finished, taking her tea. "It all sounds pretty reasonable." She scratched her nose. "What about rent?"

Elizabeth flushed. Poppy took a wild guess that she didn't like talking about money. "I actually have no idea," she confessed.

Poppy smiled. "Why don't we start with how much the

mortgage is, that should give us an idea of how much you need to cover."

Elizabeth's flush deepened and Poppy wanted to pat her hand comfortingly but didn't. "Again, little to no idea, I'm afraid."

Poppy looked at her tea, perfectly tan in its cup, then at the plates of little cakes, and nodded. She couldn't blame the woman for not knowing how her world worked. She assumed that the asshat ex-husband had taken care of the financial side of things. "How about we try to find out after we've had this lovely tea?" she said.

Elizabeth carefully picked up her cup. "Yes," she said as though it didn't really matter to her. Except Poppy could tell that it really did.

POPPY TUGGED HER hands through her hair and looked at the papers one more time. "There's no way we can do this," she said.

"We have no choice," said Elizabeth.

"But this place is expensive," said Poppy.

"And I'm not losing my house. Eli said I get some of our savings."

"Even so," Poppy said, putting the paperwork down. "Listen, I can pay you rent, of course, but that won't come anywhere close to covering what you owe every month on the house. Not to mention food, electricity and everything else."

Elizabeth took a deep breath, then said: "I'll just have to get a job."

She said it like it was the easiest thing in the world. And what did Poppy know? Maybe it would be. Maybe Elizabeth had a law degree or was secretly a doctor or something else that could pay the massive bills that a house in this part of the city generated.

"I'll start looking tomorrow," said Elizabeth.

"Sounds like a plan," said Poppy, really hoping that Elizabeth was qualified to do something useful and well-paid.

"Speaking of which, we do have plans to come up with,"

Elizabeth said.

"I know, I know. Can we take the evening to sleep on that?" Poppy was exhausted. She'd worked at the cafe all morning and had been forced to rope Mel and Paul in to help out when Jeremy hadn't shown up in the afternoon, just so that she'd be able to move into her new place.

"Fair," said Elizabeth. She folded her arms and sat back in her armchair.

Somewhere, a clock ticked, a sound that Poppy didn't think she'd heard for years. Other than that, there was quiet. She took a breath. So, what now? Surely they weren't going to sit in silence for the rest of the evening? Maybe she was supposed to go upstairs to her room? But that felt like being a kid again.

"So, we don't know much about each other, do we?" she attempted.

Elizabeth raised an elegant eyebrow. "No," she drawled. "I suppose we don't."

"Well, um, I'm Canadian, which you already know," Poppy said. "I came here for love." She grinned. "Didn't work out. I work in a coffee shop, which you also already know. Um, my best friend is called Mel. I like watching old movies."

"I could have guessed that from the *Strangers on a Train* references."

Poppy grinned again. "And I'm a member of an amateur dramatics society."

Elizabeth gave a bark of laughter. "Really? I had no idea those existed anymore."

"Well they do," said Poppy. "And I'm in one. What about you?"

"Oh, no dramatics," Elizabeth said with a shudder. Poppy didn't rise to the bait. She couldn't imagine Elizabeth making a fuss about anything. "I'm married, I live in London, I enjoy yoga and charity work."

"Okay," Poppy said. "What about... what do you hate?"

Elizabeth pursed her lips. "Brussel sprouts?"

"You and everyone else," Poppy said. "No, something unique, what do you and only you hate?"

Elizabeth frowned, then her face cleared. "People with two first names."

"You mean like Anne-Marie or—"

"No, no," Elizabeth broke in. "Like Elton John, for example. Two first names instead of a first name and a last name."

Poppy wasn't sure what to think about that. "Okay. How do you feel about Lady Gaga?"

"A title and a last name, perfectly acceptable," said Elizabeth.

With a surprised laugh, Poppy finally realized that she was being teased and Elizabeth was joking. "You do have a sense of humor then?"

"Should I not?" Elizabeth asked, a smile playing on her lips. "What about this love then? The one you came here for. Did he dump you as unceremoniously as my husband did?"

Poppy bit her lip.

"Ah, a sore subject," said Elizabeth. "Forget I asked, I'm sorry."

"No, no," Poppy said. She took a deep breath. Might as well get this over with. "Actually, it was a she rather than a he."

Elizabeth stilled for a moment and Poppy could see her calculating this, taking it in. Then her eyes narrowed a little. "Not that I have a problem with your sexuality…" she started.

"Do you not?" Poppy asked. "Because it kind of looks like you do."

"Heavens no," said Elizabeth. "What people do in their own bedrooms is their own business. The English upper classes have known that for generations. What I am rather… bemused about is the fact that you have agreed to seduce my husband."

"You said I didn't have to sleep with him," Poppy reminded her.

"No, no you don't," said Elizabeth slowly. "But… isn't the whole thing somewhat of a problem for you?"

Poppy shrugged. "I don't think so. I mean, I try not to assume things about myself and not to set limits for things. If it becomes a problem, I'll let you know."

Elizabeth's eyes narrowed again. "We made a deal."

"I know, I know," Poppy said hurriedly. "It'll all work out, don't

you worry."
And she really, really hoped that it would.

CHAPTER ELEVEN

The day was cold and Elizabeth wished that she'd brought at least a scarf with her. It would, she thought, have slightly spoiled the look, what with her slim black dress and jacket and high heels. Still, blue lips and shudders probably weren't going to do her any favors either.

She pushed through the revolving glass door.

It wasn't that she wasn't nervous. She very much was. After all, she'd never actually applied for a job before. Come to think of it, she'd never actually, technically worked before. Not for money, anyway. But she was capable, she told herself.

And if working meant saving her house, well then, she'd just have to take the bull by the horns and get on with it, wouldn't she? Which was why she hadn't hesitated outside the revolving door.

"Good morning," she beamed at the receptionist. "I'd like to leave my resumé, if you don't mind?"

The young man looked rather taken aback. "Uh, I'm afraid we do most of our hiring online," he said.

"And yet, here I am," said Elizabeth, glad that she hadn't resorted to online applications. She was making herself stand out and that had to be a good thing in an applicant.

"Which job are you applying for?"

"Oh, um, whatever jobs you have open," she said brightly.

"It's just that… I don't think we're hiring at the moment."

"Let me just leave you my CV anyway," she said, the wind slightly leaving her sails.

She left the paper, turned on her heel and walked out.

Not to worry, she told herself. It was only the first attempt. The day was young and she had a house to save.

To be honest, she was rather in shock. Shock at just how much things cost. Shock at how quickly her life could be derailed. Shock at suddenly having someone else in her home.

Not that this was all going to last that long. Their plan would soon be afoot and then things would go back to normal. But in the meantime, well, she couldn't let the side down. And things couldn't go back to normal if she had to sell the house, could they?

She walked on, checking her phone for the next address she'd marked.

She'd noted only the best firms. And only those that she thought might be interested in her skills. A handful of PR companies, a few startups (not that she particularly knew what a startup was, but she did know that they valued diversity, and what was a never-employed over forty year old woman if not diverse?), and a couple of the better art galleries.

It was a lengthy enough list, so she sped up, heels clattering on the pavement.

THERE WERE BLISTERS on her blisters. And it was only lunchtime. She was sitting on a bench groaning with tiredness when her phone rang. She answered it without thinking. Maybe this was a job already.

"Elizabeth, darling." Amanda. Not a job then.

This did require a deep breath, so she took one and forced herself to smile just in case Amanda could hear it in her voice. "Amanda, what can I do for you?"

"Well, we were rather wondering where you are?"

Elizabeth gritted her teeth and swore in her head and then chastised herself for swearing and then didn't answer at all because it had been far too long since Amanda had asked the question.

"Are you quite alright?" Amanda asked.

What was it? A lunch? A fundraiser? She actually had no idea. "Oh," she said, spotting the opportunity. "You know, I thought I was fine but actually I think I'm coming down with a migraine, I was just about to call you."

"Really?" Amanda said. "Is that cars that I can hear?"

Elizabeth cursed again at the cars on the busy street in front of her. "I was on my way, it struck rather suddenly. I'm just taking a cab back home again. I'm so sorry."

"Poor old sausage," said Amanda. "Anything any of us can do?"

"No, no, not a thing," Elizabeth said hurriedly. "I just need to sleep it off."

Fortunately, Amanda bought the excuse and quickly hung up. Elizabeth gave a sigh of relief. This was all getting more complicated by the moment.

"YOU HAVE A degree in…" The woman's eyes drifted to the CV that Elizabeth had handed her. "…sociology?"

Elizabeth nodded.

The woman frowned. "And what exactly makes you a good fit for a role in marketing?"

Elizabeth opened her mouth then realized she didn't have any words to feed out, so she closed it again.

"As I thought," the woman said with disdain. She put the resume down and looked Elizabeth straight in the eye. "We'll keep your resume on file," she lied.

Elizabeth was pretty sure she could hear her laughing as the door closed behind her.

AS SOON AS she opened the door, Elizabeth could see that the hall carpet had been vacuumed. Shoes were stacked neatly on the shoe rack, and tidy vertical lines marked where the carpet had been cleaned.

She sniffed approvingly and smelled the scent of something cooking.

"You're home," Poppy said, coming out of the steaming kitchen with a towel in her hands.

"And you're cooking."

Poppy shrugged. Her cheeks were red from the heat of the kitchen. "It's nothing special, just spag bol, I'm afraid. I'm not up to much else. But it's warm and almost ready."

Elizabeth couldn't remember the last time anyone had cooked for her. "Er… spag bol?"

"Spaghetti Bolognese," Poppy said helpfully. She looked down at Elizabeth's feet. "Don't forget to take your shoes off."

She waltzed back into the kitchen and Elizabeth, muttering, kicked off her shoes. Just who did Poppy think she was? Ordering her around in her own house. Cooking in the kitchen like it belonged to her.

She was getting too big for her boots.

"Oh no," Elizabeth said as she walked into the kitchen. "This won't do at all."

"What is it?" asked Poppy, stirring something on the stove.

"We don't use this cutlery for kitchen supper," Elizabeth said.

Poppy looked at the table she'd set then shrugged. "Whatever you say." She scooped up the knives, forks and spoons and opened a drawer to put them away. "What about these?" she asked, holding up a fork and spoon of a different kind.

"Much better," Elizabeth said. Then she spotted something on the table. "And what is that?"

Poppy peered over. "Package of Parmesan?" she guessed.

"Pre-powdered?" Elizabeth said. She tutted and went to the fridge to get a whole block to grate.

"Sorry, didn't know we had some," Poppy said. "And you can't have spag bol without Parmesan."

"Will you stop calling it that."

"What?"

"Spag bol. What a useless deformation of the English

language. Is it really so much trouble to use the extra syllables?" Elizabeth said.

Poppy moved a pan off the stove and turned around. "I get the feeling that you're trying very hard to pick a fight with me."

"Don't be ridiculous."

Poppy raised an eyebrow and smirked. "Want to tell me what's really going on?"

Elizabeth firmed her jaw and said nothing.

"I'm in control of the food," Poppy said. "I'm not feeding you if you're not talking to me."

"It's my kitchen and my house."

"Which I'm helping you pay for," said Poppy. "And if you want my help and we're going to live together, then you have to at least communicate. Let's start with where you've been all day."

"Looking for a job," Elizabeth said grumpily.

"And I'm guessing it didn't go that well?" Poppy took two bowls and started serving food.

"It appears that I am vastly unqualified for anything," Elizabeth said, hating herself for admitting it but equally glad to get it off her chest.

"That can't be true at all," said Poppy. She handed Elizabeth a bowl. "Sit down."

"It's absolutely true. I put myself out there and either every job has disappeared or I'm hopelessly unqualified."

"You… you actually went around applying for jobs in person?" asked Poppy, taking her seat. "How… sweet. And what kind of job did you apply for?"

Elizabeth sat down. "Art galleries, PR companies, places like that."

Poppy picked up the horrible packet of Parmesan. "And… wait, do you have any qualifications?"

"I went to university!"

"Okay, okay, touchy subject. So, you're what… a lawyer? Doctor?"

"Those aren't the only jobs that require a degree." Elizabeth sniffed. "I have a degree in sociology."

"So you're a… sociologist."

Elizabeth nodded and took the package of Parmesan from Poppy simply because she was offering it.

"And that qualifies you to… socialize?" Poppy asked.

"No, it… it…"

Poppy put down the fork she'd just picked up. "Hold on, have you actually worked before?"

Elizabeth shook her head, then realized she'd poured the powdered Parmesan onto her pasta and frowned.

"Okay," said Poppy, picking up her fork again. "I think you might need to lower your sights a little. Get some experience. Work as, I don't know, a waitress, a barista, something where there are plenty of openings."

"A… waitress."

"Unless you think that's beneath you?" Poppy said sweetly. "You need some money coming in and you do seem to be a good housekeeper, so you definitely have skills."

Elizabeth looked down at her powder covered dinner and felt her heart slow down and a weight settle in her stomach. "I suppose," she said.

Poppy laughed. "It's temporary. Think of it like… I don't know, like the Blitz or something. You do what you've got to do. You're a big girl, Elizabeth, you're a strong woman, you can do this."

"You think I'm strong?" Elizabeth hadn't meant to ask, but the compliment had taken her by surprise.

"Strong?" Poppy asked. "Any other woman would be bawling their eyes out and feeling sorry for themselves right about now. You're looking for jobs and plotting revenge. I'd say you were pretty strong."

Elizabeth smiled, the weight in her stomach lifting slightly, and twirled spaghetti around her fork. "You know," she said after she'd swallowed her first mouthful. "This really isn't bad at all."

CHAPTER TWELVE

"**T**his is absolutely insane," Mel said.

"Why?" asked Poppy. "I mean, I get how it might sound at first hearing, but really, what's so crazy about it when you think about it?"

"Um, you're seducing some woman's husband so that she can either get him back or potentially ruin his life or maybe even murder him in his bed."

"She's not going to kill him."

"Or maybe you," Mel said. "I mean, you are living in her house."

"I'm renting a room because I need a place to live. And Elizabeth isn't dangerous. She's… different. I don't know. She's got that whole buttoned-up English thing going on, but I think deep down she's hurting."

"And the correct way to deal with that hurt is by helping her enact revenge?" asked Mel.

They were walking through the park, the air brisk and crisp, leaves crunching under their feet. "She's not hurting anyone," said Poppy. "If anything, she's helping out Sally."

"Who's Sally again?"

"The husband's girlfriend."

"And in return?"

"She's going to help me deal with Jeremy."

"Which involves what, exactly?" Mel asked.

Poppy sighed and shrugged. "I don't know actually. We haven't come up with a plan for that yet."

"It doesn't seem to me like you've come up with a plan for anything yet."

"What would you do?" Poppy asked in all seriousness. Mel was the one that had good ideas, after all. "If you were going to teach Jeremy a lesson, how would you do it?"

Mel shrugged. "He needs taking down a peg or two, I suppose. I mean, yes, he needs to learn that he's got a treasure in you and that you do all the work around that place. But more than that, I think he has to learn that he's not as successful as he thinks. Once he can abandon this plan of franchising maybe he'll see that he's got a nice little business on his hands and concentrate on actually running it instead of selling it."

"Good, good," said Poppy, making mental notes of all of this. "So how would you go about teaching him that lesson then?"

Mel stopped and put her hands on her hips. "Pops, I won't have anything to do with this. The whole thing is crazy and really, I think you're taking on more than you can handle. First Jeremy, now this Elizabeth character. You can't just look after everyone."

"Elizabeth doesn't need looking after. She's... she's strong. She's smart. She's slightly confused right now and needs a little advice from time to time." Poppy shuddered at the thought of Elizabeth just walking into companies with a practically empty CV. "She can be a little unrealistic and doesn't always understand how the world works."

"Yeah, she doesn't sound like she needs any help at all," said Mel, putting her hands back in her pockets and walking again.

"Oh stop being such a cynic. I'm a nice person. Okay, so maybe I am helping her. But she's helping me too. I'm not sleeping in a box with Paul, am I?"

"Okay, okay." Mel relented. She hooked her arm into Poppy's. "She's not at all attractive, is she?"

"What?" Poppy asked, the question taking her by surprise and the answer in her head taking her even more by surprise.

"It's just that, well, you haven't had a girlfriend for a while and

I'm checking that you're not blinded by lust."

"Not blinded by lust," said Poppy. "Definitely not at all even a little bit blinded by lust. I haven't even thought of her in that way."

Or she hadn't until Mel brought it up. For a quick second she imagined Elizabeth's hair splayed out on a pillow and then caught herself. Eugh. No. Definitely not. Too… too made-up, too controlled, too just not Poppy's style.

"Not attractive then?"

"She's pretty," Poppy said, trying to be both honest and fair. "But not my type."

"Hmm. I believe you," Mel said. "Either you're telling the truth or your acting skills are getting better. On which note, it's time for me to drop you off."

Poppy withdrew her arm and looked toward the church hall. "First real rehearsal," she said, stomach jumping with excitement. "I always love the first read through."

"Mmm, let's hope that next time you'll actually be reading something," Mel said. She bent and kissed Poppy soundly on the cheek. "Go on, off you go. I'll drop by the coffee shop as soon as I get a second and you can tell me what plans you've come up with."

Poppy recognized that Mel was offering her an olive branch and took it. "Thanks," she beamed and rushed off to join the rehearsal.

Mel didn't need to love the idea, she didn't need to be a part of the idea, but doing anything without Mel's backing would have made her strangely uncomfortable.

"Come in, come in," Tanya called from the stage. "Everybody in."

Poppy jogged toward the stage.

"Up on the stage, let's get going," boomed Tanya.

Poppy put her hands on the stage, ready to boost herself up, but Tanya beamed at her.

"Get the tea on, will you, Poppy? Good girl."

With a sigh, Poppy went back toward the little kitchen.

BY THE TIME she got back to the house, Poppy was exhausted. She'd listened to the entire play and discovered that Cheryl's version of an American accent basically involved just slurring her words.

"Not a problem, not a problem," Tanya had said when the fact that it was very much a problem became apparent. "I'll leave that in your capable hands, Poppy."

Poppy had given a sickly smile and wondered how the hell she was supposed to coach Cheryl in something that was patently going to be impossible for her to learn.

"You're here," Elizabeth said, standing at the front door with her arms crossed.

"Home at last," Poppy said, trying to smile.

"And late," pointed out Elizabeth.

"Am I?" asked Poppy. She checked her watch. She was no later than she normally was on theater nights. Then she realized. "Oh, I'm sorry, maybe I should have mentioned it. I had an am-dram meeting tonight. First read through." She beamed and Elizabeth stepped aside as she went into the house.

Immediately, Poppy smelled the scent of something wonderful. Oh crap. She turned back to Elizabeth.

"Did you make dinner for me?"

"Well, you did do it yesterday," Elizabeth said.

"I had no idea, I'm so sorry. Have I completely ruined it by being later than you thought?"

Elizabeth sniffed and Poppy could see that she was offended.

"No, no, come on, I'm sure it's going to be delicious," Poppy said.

"Fine," said Elizabeth. "Come and sit down then."

"Oh, let me help."

Elizabeth blushed. "Actually, I rather thought that you could sit and I could serve?"

"You did?" Poppy asked. "Why?"

"Well, if you think I should be starting at the bottom and

building experience then I thought you might have a few pointers."

"You want me to teach you to be a waitress?" Poppy asked, laughing. "It's not rocket science, you'll do just fine."

"Just fine isn't good enough," said Elizabeth, steering Poppy into a kitchen chair. "I will do this well or not at all."

Poppy shook her head but allowed herself to be sat down.

"Now," Elizabeth said, brandishing a bottle of wine. "A drink to start off with." She poured wine into a glass, finishing off with a twist of the bottle at the end.

"Um…"

"What? That had to be right," said Elizabeth. "I even twisted the bottle like you're supposed to in order to prevent spills."

"Yes," said Poppy slowly. "But you didn't actually ask me what I wanted to drink. You decided for me."

"Ah."

"Generally, your first job would be to ask what diners actually want."

"I see." Elizabeth looked over at the Aga. "Since this isn't a restaurant I haven't cooked a multitude of dishes."

"Whatever you've made will be fine," said Poppy.

"You say that but you have no idea what it is." Elizabeth started to clatter around, removing something from the oven and taking lids off pots.

"I'm sure it'll be great."

"Ever the optimist, aren't you?" said Elizabeth, starting to put food on plates. "I could be serving you dog food."

"Are you?"

"No, but that doesn't mean it's going to be good."

Poppy exhaled. "El, I'm sure it's going to be fine."

"Don't call me that."

"Sorry," said Poppy as a plate was put in front of her. "What do you prefer? Beth? You don't seem like a Liz or a Liza."

"Elizabeth," said Elizabeth firmly.

"But that's such a mouthful."

"Elizabeth."

Poppy shut her mouth.

"Can I offer you anything else?" Elizabeth said. "Pepper perhaps?"

"I'm fine."

"A little salt?"

"No, no."

"A glass of water?"

"You're trying too hard," said Poppy.

Elizabeth huffed and sat down. "I'm not sure I'll make a good waitress."

"Of course you will. You're polite, well spoken, and pretty, you'll do fine," Poppy said, picking up her knife and fork.

Elizabeth picked up her own knife and fork, cutting into a piece of fish. "You think I'm pretty?" she asked casually.

Poppy wanted to roll her eyes but didn't. Elizabeth was obviously feeling delicate, she needed a confidence boost. "Of course I do," she said. She scrambled around her brain for a more direct compliment. "I think you look like the new Princess of Wales, actually."

Elizabeth sat up straighter. "You do?"

"I do." Poppy smiled. "You've got the same little wrinkles around your eyes as she does."

"Was that meant to be a compliment?"

Poppy closed her eyes. "Maybe we should talk about something else?"

"Maybe," agreed Elizabeth. "Let's talk about getting you and Eli introduced, shall we?"

And Poppy tucked in as Elizabeth started to outline her plan.

CHAPTER THIRTEEN

Poppy put the coffee machine on because she assumed that everyone wanted caffeine in the morning. Maybe it was because she'd lived with Mel for too long. Just as the machine started to burble and hiss, she heard the sound of movement behind her.

Elizabeth was dressed in a robe, her hair tangled down her back, her face free of makeup and there should have been some kind of choir of angels singing. Perhaps a harp. Maybe a beam of sunlight should have glowed around Elizabeth like an aura.

But none of those things happened.

What did happen was that in the space of a single, solitary moment, Poppy realized that whatever she might have said, however she might have felt before, she was absolutely and incredibly attracted to Elizabeth.

She turned back to the sink, insides shaking and mouth dry. How the hell had that happened? It hadn't grown over time, it hadn't been instant, and yet it had snuck up on her in that one moment.

One second and her life was different.

One turn and her whole heart felt changed.

She gulped and turned back again, either because she was a glutton for punishment or because she wanted to see if the same thing could happen again, she wasn't sure.

Elizabeth was scowling at her. "What are you looking at?"

"Um, nothing?" hazarded Poppy, turning back to the sink, insides still very much shaking.

Elizabeth started to get breakfast cereals from the pantry and out of habit, Poppy began laying the table.

"Good girl," Elizabeth said approvingly.

Poppy almost whimpered and her insides went from shaky to liquid. "Back in a sec," she managed to mumble.

She made it to the tiny downstairs bathroom and collapsed onto the closed toilet. What. The. Fuck?

Okay, okay, Elizabeth was pretty. Dark hair, dark blue eyes, slim figure, what wasn't to like? Objectively she was a good looking woman. But this, this sudden flood of feeling, was so much more than that. It was, Poppy realized, the first time that she'd seen Elizabeth without the makeup, the expensive clothes, without her guard up.

And what was underneath that sometimes very prickly exterior was someone that for whatever reason touched her heart.

She took a breath. This was new. Not that she ever turned down new things. She took another breath. Could all this be a thing? Could anything come from it? Maybe not, probably not, Elizabeth was straight and not even divorced. Did that stop her thinking about her housemate in a whole new way?

Definitely not.

Poppy stood up and splashed some cold water on her face. This was fine. Weird, but fine. Like most gay women, she was very used to having to hide crushes and feelings, she could do this.

But as she left the bathroom an image came to her of Elizabeth without the robe and she blushed so furiously that she was still red when she got back to the kitchen.

"Are you quite alright?"

The question sounded slightly annoyed and, for some new reason, very, very sexy to Poppy's ears. Which obviously only made her flush more. "Um, yes?" she said.

Elizabeth nodded. "Good. Now sit down. Breakfast is the most important meal of the day, don't dilly dally."

In relief, Poppy sank down into a kitchen chair and then busied her hands pouring some cereal.

"So, what are your plans for the day?"

Polite small-talk. Okay, she could do this. "Work, like every day."

"Don't you ever have a day off?" asked Elizabeth. "Please pass the milk."

The cut glass accent was so perfect that Poppy was already unconsciously trying to mimic it. "Not really," she said carefully, passing the milk. "We're pretty busy and there isn't much help at the shop."

"Which I suppose I should be grateful for."

"Sorry?"

"Well," Elizabeth said, "you wouldn't be here planning revenge with me if you had plenty of help now, would you?"

"I suppose not," Poppy said, looking down at her spoon.

Rather than the cocoa puffs or honey nut flakes or frosted cereal she'd normally have, Elizabeth's pantry offered up brown cardboard like things that looked about as appetizing as, well, cardboard. Grown up cereal.

"Problem?" asked Elizabeth.

"No, not at all," said Poppy, putting her spoon down again.

"You know, you're welcome to place the market order if you prefer other things."

"Market order?" Poppy was about to question it further, then realized that of course, Elizabeth had her groceries delivered.

Elizabeth realized this at precisely the same time and her face paled. "Oh God."

Poppy felt a pang of pity and her overwhelming new need to plant a kiss on Elizabeth's plump lips faded just a little. For a second. "Mmm, might have to ditch that and go shopping like the rest of the rabble."

Elizabeth looked over at the pantry. "I think we can survive for at least another week."

Poppy laughed. "It'll be fine. I'm sure you've been to a

supermarket before. I'll go with you, if you like, we'll get it done together."

Elizabeth's face brightened again in a way that made Poppy want to smile. Surely if she made Elizabeth happy then… For God's sake. She went back to her cardboard cereal.

"We haven't talked about your plan yet," said Elizabeth, pouring a little milk into her coffee. "Jeremy, that's his name, isn't it?"

Poppy shifted uncomfortably. Talking about a plan would make things real and she wasn't exactly sure that she was ready for real. "About that…"

"You can't change your mind," Elizabeth said promptly. "You can't back out now."

"I wasn't backing out, I just…" She trailed off, not knowing how to finish the sentence.

"We don't have months to plan this out," said Elizabeth. She put her coffee down. "Have you changed your mind about who the plan should concern?"

"No," said Poppy slowly.

"Good," said Elizabeth. "Because whatever you may be able to persuade yourself to do, I'm not entirely sure I could make myself seduce your ex-girlfriend."

"Evelyn? Why would you?" Poppy asked, using the question to cover up the ache she felt at just how definite Elizabeth seemed about that. A hundred percent straight then. Not that she should have expected any different, but still, the confirmation didn't make her feel amazing.

"Who's Evelyn?"

"My ex-girlfriend."

"The one that you came to England for?"

"That's the one."

"You don't seem especially angry with her," Elizabeth said.

Poppy shrugged. "Why should I be? Things didn't work out, it's fine, that's life. Things usually happen for the best I've found."

"God," Elizabeth groaned. "It's far too early in the morning for your optimism. Can we just pretend that you secretly want to strangle Evelyn in her sleep and move on from there?"

"Fine, fine," said Poppy. She'd had four spoonfuls of cereal and was feeling full. Maybe that was the point of it. You ate just a little and it swelled up inside you like actual wet cardboard and then you didn't want to eat any more. A terrible brand marketing plan, but a solid weight loss plan.

"So, Jeremy then. Any ideas?"

"Well, Mel did have a point."

"Mel?" asked Elizabeth. "Another ex-girlfriend?"

"No, my best friend." Poppy was about to add 'you'd like her' but reconsidered because she wasn't actually sure that Elizabeth and Mel would get along that well. "She's a psychology student and, well, she knows me pretty well and Jeremy too."

"Reliable source then," agreed Elizabeth. "So what did she say on the matter?"

As they finished breakfast, Poppy explained about Jeremy and his franchising plans and his inability to face reality, and Elizabeth listened carefully.

"Alright," she said finally. "That could be something we can work with. He needs taking down a peg or two." She pursed her lips in thought and Poppy was struck again by just how kissable they were.

Poppy stood up and started clearing dishes away thankful, not for the first time, that she wasn't a man. If she had been, standing up just at that moment would have been impossible. But even though she'd turned all liquidy inside again, she still managed to put bowls and plates into the sink.

"I'll think about it," Elizabeth said, scraping her chair back. "You haven't forgotten that we're meeting this afternoon, have you?"

Crap. Yes, she had. She'd just have to hope that either Jeremy was actually at the shop or she could persuade Mel to come by and take care of things for her. "Of course not," she said brightly.

Elizabeth came up behind her, reaching around to place her dishes in the sink, her arm brushing against Poppy's as she did so.

"You set the table perfectly and now you're even rinsing the dishes before you put them in the dishwasher," Elizabeth said, her voice close enough to Poppy's ear that goosebumps raised on her neck. "Good girl."

Poppy did whimper this time, entirely uncontrollably.

"Are you absolutely sure you're alright?" asked Elizabeth stepping back. "You have been a little… odd this morning."

Poppy swallowed. "Absolutely fine," she said, scrubbing at a coffee cup. Other than the fact that she'd developed some kind of instantaneous crush on a straight woman that she had to live with and now, apparently, had formed some sort of praise kink at the same time. Yes, she was absolutely fine.

"Good," said Elizabeth. "Now is not the time to be getting ill. There's far too much to do." She hesitated. "You will… dress nicely this afternoon, won't you?"

Poppy sighed. "Yes, obviously."

"I don't mean designer clothes and the like, I just mean…" It was Elizabeth's turn to trail off and Poppy had to giggle at her tact.

"You mean dress sexy," she said. "It's all in hand, never fear."

"Good," Elizabeth said. "And don't be late."

She strode out of the kitchen and Poppy leaned against the wet edge of the sink wondering why her hormones had decided to misbehave today of all days.

Elizabeth was straight. Elizabeth was roping her into a plan to avenge her husband, for God's sake. Elizabeth wasn't even her type. All of these were excellent reasons not to be interested in her. "Just get over it," she scolded herself quietly.

But not quietly enough.

"Get over what?" asked Elizabeth, coming back in and picking up her phone that had been charging on the counter.

"Absolutely nothing," Poppy said with the biggest, brightest smile she could muster.

"Hmm." Elizabeth raised a doubting eyebrow but then backed out of the kitchen and Poppy breathed a sigh of relief.

CHAPTER FOURTEEN

Elizabeth checked her watch and sighed. Ten minutes late, she really should have known better. Next time, she told herself, she would tell Poppy to meet thirty minutes earlier than necessary. That way things should start on time.

She clutched her jacket around herself, freezing cold, and then spotted a figure jogging around the corner. Poppy waved furiously and almost tripped and Elizabeth fought not to smile.

"You're late," she said, as Poppy got close enough to hear.

"I'm sorry, sorry, sorry," Poppy gasped. She stopped, put her hands on her hips and took deep, gulping breaths. "I was on my way when I realized I forgot Paul's coffee and I had to go back and… And I'm here now."

"Who's Paul?"

Poppy exhaled. "Not important." She started to unbutton her coat. "God, I'm boiling now after running." She flapped her coat a little to cool herself then peered more closely at Elizabeth.

Elizabeth squirmed. She didn't particularly like being examined. "What?"

"You look freezing," said Poppy. She unwound her scarf. "Here you go."

Before Elizabeth could stop her, Poppy was winding the wide, multi-colored scarf around her neck. Hands brushed her skin and she could smell something spicy like incense, the smell of Poppy, she realized, as the scarf started to warm her.

"Much better," Poppy said, stepping back and beaming.

Elizabeth was going to protest but then she saw what Poppy was wearing under her coat. "That… that is some outfit," she managed.

"Like it?" asked Poppy, giving a twirl.

The short, skater-like skirt she was wearing floated out in the cool air, baring slim legs encased in thick tights. A t-shirt with a neck that was large enough to show cleavage and a baggy flannel shirt completed the outfit, and black Doc Martens covered her feet.

"It's…"

"Sexy?" supplied Poppy with a grin.

A word that Elizabeth suddenly found had a new meaning. Glancing Poppy up and down, from her gold curls to her thick-soled boots, she was struck by the thought that actually, yes, this was very sexy indeed, and she had no idea why.

"It's not quite what I had in mind," she said, pulling herself together.

Poppy looked down at her outfit. "You don't think Eli will like it?"

"I think Eli might not notice if you smile wide enough," Elizabeth said grimly. "I'm not entirely sure it's your clothes he's interested in anyway." And she had to tear her eyes away for fear of being found over-interested in Poppy's outfit.

Poppy sniffed. "I'm sure it'll be fine. Now where's he coming from?"

"Over there," Elizabeth said, pointing toward the glass and chrome building that Eli worked in. "He should be coming out anytime soon."

"What time does he finish work?" asked Poppy, rubbing her hands together in the cold.

"Hard to say," said Elizabeth, carefully watching the doors of the building. "Could be now, could be in half an hour, an hour."

"An hour?" squeaked Poppy. "It's freezing out here, we'll catch hypothermia before then."

"Then button your coat back up." Elizabeth considered giving the scarf back, but it felt nice around her neck, warm, and the smell was enticing.

"It's always freezing around here."

"Spend a lot of time around here, do you?" Elizabeth asked, sarcastically.

"Actually, yes, my theater group meets just around the corner over there in that red building you can see the corner of. Anyway, you should have told me how long this was going to take, I'd have bought a Thermos of tea," grumbled Poppy.

It was unusual to hear Poppy complain. In the space of just a couple of weeks even Elizabeth had learned that. "Trouble at work?"

"Ugh. Jeremy didn't show up. I had to get a friend to fill in for me."

"All the more reason for us to come up with a plan," Elizabeth said. "I was thinking—"

She was cut short by the sight of a blonde head appearing on the street opposite her. She held her breath. It couldn't be. But it was. A tilt of the head, the way she walked, Elizabeth's heart just about stopped.

Arabella.

How could she have forgotten that Arabella's husband worked just around the corner? They must be meeting for dinner or drinks. The blonde head started to turn and Elizabeth panicked, gripping hard on Poppy's arm and practically dragging her backwards and into the shade.

So far backwards did she drag her that they ended up hitting a pane of glass that slowly began to move.

It took Elizabeth a second to realize that they had backed right into the revolving door of the grimy building behind them. She stopped pushing, effectively trapping the two of them in the tiny compartment.

For a long moment time seemed to stop. She and Poppy were face to face, Poppy's breath was coming fast and Elizabeth realized that her own was too. For far longer than should have been possible there was silence.

She could smell Poppy's scent more strongly now, could see the way her cheek curved and how her long eyelashes swept her skin even without mascara. She could see a tiny flaw, one blonde hair in an otherwise dark eyebrow.

And for one impossible moment she considered touching that flaw, running her finger over it.

Her hand was actually starting to move when the moment was broken.

"Um, mind telling me what we're doing?" Poppy asked, breath warm on Elizabeth's face.

Elizabeth looked down. Poppy had dark eyes. Strange in a woman so blonde. But oddly, it kind of worked. She swallowed because for some reason her mouth had gone all dry. "Nothing," she said.

"Yes we are," said Poppy, stepping back as far as she could in the little door compartment. "You pushed me into a revolving door. That's not nothing. Was it because of that woman? The one you were staring at?"

"No," Elizabeth lied, the lie immediately apparent because she felt blood pouring into her cheeks.

"It is," Poppy said. "Who is she? Is that Sally? Your husband's new girlfriend?"

Elizabeth sighed. "No. No it wasn't. That was a… a friend of mine."

"But why run away and hide from a friend?" Poppy said. Then her eyes widened. "Oh."

"Oh what?"

"You haven't told her, have you?" Poppy put a hand out, laid it on Elizabeth's arm. "Have you told anyone about Eli leaving you?"

"I've told you," said Elizabeth, the warmth of Poppy's hand making her feel sticky and breathless and almost sick.

"That's not what I meant."

"I really don't want to talk about this," said Elizabeth, finally remembering where they were and pushing onwards so that the door revolved and spat them out into a dim building lobby.

"Excellent," said a voice. "You must be here for the course."

In the half-light, Elizabeth just made out a woman holding a clipboard.

"How long do we have to hide then?" Poppy asked.

"We're not hiding," said Elizabeth, getting flustered.

"Are you here for the course then?" demanded clipboard-lady.

"No," snapped Elizabeth, at exactly the same time as Poppy said: "Yes."

TWENTY MINUTES LATER they were both bending over the body checking for a pulse.

"This is all your fault," hissed Elizabeth.

"Excellent," said clipboard-lady, whose name it turned out was June. "When you've established pulse status you may then move on to CPR. Remember what we talked about. Firmness and rhythm. Let's get to it then." She clapped her hands.

Elizabeth didn't move. "Better get to pumping, or John Doe here is going to be pushing up daisies."

With a sigh, Poppy folded her hands together and started. "This isn't my fault. You're the one that pushed us into the building."

"You're the one that lied and said we were here for the course."

"Well, you're the one that needed to hide from your friend."

"I told you, we weren't hiding."

"And you're definitely not the one who's bending over a dead body in a skirt short enough to show everyone what you had for breakfast this morning."

Elizabeth smirked. "You chose to wear the skirt. And frankly, you chose to be here." She looked around at the rest of the Red Cross class participants. "Besides, nobody's looking."

Poppy huffed and lightened up on her compressions.

"He'll die," pointed out Elizabeth.

"I don't see you doing anything about it."

"I've been thinking," said Elizabeth, sitting back on her heels. "Why don't I pretend to be interested in the coffee shop?"

Poppy stopped her compressions altogether. "What?"

"If this Jeremy needs a dose of reality, why don't we give him one?" Elizabeth said. "He's obviously not listening to anyone's advice, so he's going to need some real experience. I pose as a rich entrepreneur and he woos me and I ask him questions he can't answer and just generally play him around until he realizes that he's really not ready to play with the big boys."

"Do you think that will work?" Poppy asked.

"I don't see why not. Nobody gets hurt, he learns a lesson, and hopefully he becomes a bit more realistic about his expectations."

Poppy scratched her nose.

"Ladies, ladies, your victim is dying. Now we don't want to see panic, but I would rather expect to see a little more activity around someone experiencing heart failure," June said, towering over them, clipboard still in hand.

Poppy jumped to it.

"Better," said June, grimacing and moving on.

"Alright," said Poppy. "On one condition."

"What's that?" Elizabeth asked, secretly quite proud of herself for coming up with the beginnings of a workable plan.

"We move the whole Eli thing online. I don't want to catch cold waiting for him to leave work and I definitely don't want to do another CPR class."

Elizabeth regarded her for a moment. "Fine," she said finally.

"And you take over compressions."

"Oh no," Elizabeth said. "You said one condition, that's two. Besides, you're doing an admirable job. Good girl."

Poppy's face flushed bright red and Elizabeth thought that maybe she should take over. Poppy was getting breathless herself and the last thing they needed was an actual dying body. Though, she supposed, at least they were in the right place should Poppy decide to keel over.

CHAPTER FIFTEEN

Poppy clicked 'next.' "Okay, they want a picture," she said.

"Obviously. Choose something sexy," Paul said, leaning over her shoulder.

Mel made a buzzing sound. "Wrong answer. You'd think that men were looking for sexy pictures in online dating, but actually, profile pictures with smiles and a natural look do far better. Here, give me your phone."

Poppy gave up her phone and let Mel swipe through her camera roll.

"So, remind me of why you need to do this again?" Paul said, leaning against the counter.

"Because attempting to meet men in real life is cold," said Poppy. "Besides, online meetings are all the rage nowadays."

"It's safer," said Mel, still engrossed in pictures. "Not to mention lower risk in other ways."

"Like what?" asked Paul, interested now.

"Like you don't have to spend dinner with someone to find out whether you like them. Not that most women have that problem."

Paul looked puzzled and Mel put Poppy's phone down. "Look, most of us have an instinct that kicks in pretty immediately when we first meet someone. It's not really a sixth sense, it's more like a super-fast evaluation of a million details, the way someone talks, how they look, how they hold themselves, where you are, someone's age, tons of things go into making a snap decision about someone you've just met."

"Sounds like judging a book by its cover," sniffed Paul.

Mel grinned. "It is. But oddly, we tend to be pretty spot on. Not always, but as a general rule, your first, gut feeling about a person is usually fairly accurate. So, for example, say you meet up with a woman and you immediately get a bad feeling about her, what do you do?"

"Make some kind of excuse and then leave," Paul said quickly.

"Right, a very male answer. Females, on the other hand, will tend to have dinner and continue with the date, potentially even going further than they'd planned, even if they don't like someone."

"That sounds stupid."

"No," said Mel. "That sounds safe. At least from a female point of view. If we walk out we risk offending the man in question. Which can be dangerous if you're a woman. We've been brought up not to make a fuss, not to offend, not because it's polite, but because if we're demure and pleasant to be around then there's less chance that we'll be victimized."

"Jesus fucking Christ," Paul said. "Sure you're not being over-dramatic there?"

"You have any idea how many women have laughed at your jokes not because they were funny but because they were afraid not to?" Mel asked him.

"Hey, I'm a nice guy!"

"I never said you weren't," said Mel. "But that's the problem. How are we supposed to tell a nice guy from a bad guy? There's no handbook on this stuff. It's not like the bad ones have it tattooed on their foreheads."

"You're making me extremely glad that I don't date men," Poppy broke in.

"Like there aren't predators in the lesbian community?" asked Mel.

Poppy held her hands up. "Okay, okay, but this isn't supposed to be a learning opportunity. This is supposed to be a Tinder profile."

"Then use this picture," said Mel, handing her the phone back.

Poppy did as she was told. "Okay, what about hobbies and interests?"

"Probably you should choose whatever it is that Emil is interested in," Paul said.

"His name's Eli," said Poppy.

"And you want common interests that are related, rather than identical ones," said Mel.

"Why?" asked Paul, folding his arms and starting to look comfortable.

Poppy groaned. "You know what, why don't you two make the profile? You just set it all up and I'll go with whatever you think. I've got work to do here and you two have some kind of round-table discussion on sexual politics to have."

Mel rolled her eyes, but Paul was already pulling out a seat, and with a grin, Poppy left her phone with them and left them to it. She really did have other things to take care of. The milk order coming in, for example. Especially since Jeremy was out to a long lunch and there was no one else to do things.

POPPY FLEW INTO the church hall precisely eighteen minutes late. Not that it mattered, she discovered as she shed her coat and ditched it on a stack of chairs. No one even looked up as she came in.

A read through of the first half was currently underway and when Poppy tried to make her way to the front of the hall, Tanya turned around and hushed her dramatically.

Still out of breath, Poppy dropped into a chair.

Her phone vibrated and she took it out of her pocket for lack of anything else to do.

A Tinder notification glowed in her bar. She swiped down then ignored it. Not Eli, not her problem. But before she could put her phone away again, another notification dinged. Tinder again. Ignore. A third ding.

Embarrassed, she set her phone to silent and stuck it back into her pocket. Apparently Tinder was more active than she'd thought. Straight dating looked to be a lot easier than gay dating.

"No, no, no," Tanya said, throwing down her script. "The timing is all wrong." She wafted up onto the stage, kaftan flowing behind her.

Poppy leaned on the back of the chair in front, the small movement caught Tanya's eye.

"Yes, yes, that's what we need." She moved to the very front of the stage and took Cheryl by the arm. "You, go with Poppy. She'll run your lines with you and get that accent tip-top in no time, won't you dearie?" she asked Poppy.

"Of course," said Poppy, not feeling like doing that at all.

With a sigh, she stood up and waited for Cheryl to climb down from the stage.

"Come on," she said. "Let's go over to the entrance hall, that way no one will disturb us."

"I really don't know what she's complaining about," Cheryl said as she followed Poppy to the small entranceway where two cozy chairs waited with a dying pot plant. "I think she's not hearing me properly. I mean, I've been watching *Vampire Diaries* and *Real Housewives* for weeks now to prepare for this role."

Poppy took a deep breath. Okay, how to say this nicely? "I think maybe the devil's in the details?" she said.

"What do you mean?" asked Cheryl, sitting down, her dainty nose in the air and a look of truculence on her face.

"Well, you're sort of slurring your words," said Poppy carefully. "And whilst it's true that most Americans don't have the strict diction that Brits do, it's more a matter of dropping or softening certain letters, rather than squishing all your words together at once."

"I have no idea what you mean," Cheryl said.

"It's sort of like this," Poppy said. She put a hand on Cheryl's script. "May I?"

Cheryl gave up the book and sat back, folding her arms, while Poppy found the monologue that she'd practiced to audition with. She folded back the pages and crossed her legs, taking a breath, and then launching into it.

She'd only meant to do a line or two. But once she fell into the rhythm of the words, she ended up doing the whole page, not looking up until the sound of someone clapping broke the spell.

"Very impressive," Elizabeth said, standing at the door. "Acting is definitely in your skill set. Well done."

Poppy blushed. "Actually, that's not my part. It's, um, it's Cheryl's." She handed the script back to Cheryl.

"Why on earth not?" asked Elizabeth, looking surprised.

"Because I cast Cheryl in the role," said Tanya. She looked over at the three of them. "I was just coming to see how the two of you were getting along," she said.

"I'm supposed to be helping Cheryl with her American accent," Poppy supplied.

"But you're Canadian," said Elizabeth.

"Is she?" asked Tanya.

"Do you mean to say that you have not only a real North American in your company, but also a damn fine little actress and you chose not to cast her?" Elizabeth said, turning to Tanya.

"Well…" Tanya began.

"What part do you have then?" Elizabeth asked Poppy.

Poppy blushed even further. "Actually, I'm not in this play at the moment."

Elizabeth turned back to Tanya. "Are you a fool? Or just completely incompetent?"

"Well, really," Tanya said.

"Don't 'well, really' me," said Elizabeth. "I assume you're in charge around here and if you can't see what's right in front of your eyes then you must be a fool." She shook her head in disbelief.

Tanya opened her mouth to answer back but obviously thought better of it, because instead she took Cheryl's arm. "Come with me, dear. We need you to run the scene again." She ushered Cheryl back into the hall and tutted at Elizabeth as she followed her actress.

"What are you doing here?" Poppy said, once she and Elizabeth were alone.

"You told me where you met," said Elizabeth. "And when you didn't come home on time I assumed you were here and thought I'd get a look at your acting skills. I'm assuming that you're going to be acting when seducing my husband."

"I suppose," Poppy said. Then she grinned. "Did you really think I was good?"

"Very acceptable," Elizabeth said.

Poppy's grin got wider. She'd lived in London long enough to know that that was high praise indeed. "That was pretty chivalrous of you, you know?"

"What was?"

"You, defending my honor like that," said Poppy.

"I was not."

"You were too," teased Poppy. "So maybe you're a romantic at heart, after all."

Elizabeth grunted but her cheeks started to go pink and Poppy laughed. "Come on, let's get out of here."

"Don't you have a rehearsal to finish?"

Poppy looped her arm through Elizabeth's. "I'm not sure I should be in Tanya's presence for the rest of the evening."

"Oh dear, have I got you into terrible trouble?"

Poppy's stomach contracted at the feeling of Elizabeth close to her. "No, no," she said. "Don't worry about it. She'll have forgotten all about it by next rehearsal, I swear."

"Well, since you're finished early, how about a drink? I owe you that much."

"No," Poppy said, laughing. "I'm buying. You did defend my honor, whatever you may say."

CHAPTER SIXTEEN

Elizabeth eyed Poppy over the breakfast table. It was painfully obvious that bran flakes weren't really her thing. She made a mental note to stop by the shop on the corner of the road and pick up something more suitable. One of the cereal boxes with a cartoon character on the front, she thought.

"Why today?" Poppy said.

"Why not today?" asked Elizabeth. "There's no time like the present. And there's no telling how long this will take, so we might as well get started."

"There's no telling whether or not Jeremy will be in the shop today," said Poppy. She sighed and Elizabeth wondered for the first time if this was really a good idea.

Had she pushed Poppy into doing this? Was she manipulating her? Giving her a place to live in return for doing something she didn't want to do? And what was going to happen if Eli did move back in? If all this worked?

No, not if, when. When Eli moved back in. And when Poppy moved back out. Elizabeth narrowed her eyes and tried to imagine Eli's bulk taking up the chair on the other side of the table. But it was impossible. Poppy's curly head just kept intruding.

"It's only supposed to be a random meeting. If he's not there then, well, I suppose I'll come in another day. Though that might be hard."

"Hard?" Poppy asked. "Why hard?"

Elizabeth shuffled in her seat. "I, um, have a job."

Poppy squealed. "Really? Doing what? Oh, congratulations, El. I told you it would all work out."

"And I told you not to call me that." She sipped at her coffee and tried not to look as proud as she felt. "It's nothing really, just a waitressing job at a bistro. Nothing big."

A bistro far away enough from everyone and everywhere that she should never have to see anyone she actually knew. It had been a bit of a find actually, and she'd ventured far off her normal beaten path to get there.

"Congratulations anyway, I'm sure you'll be amazing," Poppy said kindly.

"Which is why I should finagle this meeting with your boss today, I'll need to work around other things." At least for the time being. It wasn't as if she was actually going to keep this job in the long run. Once her marriage was back on track she'd hardly need it, would she?

"Okay, okay," Poppy groaned. "Fine. But just so you know, I haven't matched with Eli yet."

"But you slid left on him, right?"

"Swiped right," Poppy said with a grin. "And yes, obviously I did. I don't know what's wrong. I've had about a zillion other notifications, but nothing from him."

"Give it time," Elizabeth said, a buzz of worry starting in her stomach.

"It'll all turn out alright," smiled Poppy just as she normally did.

"I suppose I should go and get ready." Elizabeth checked the time.

"Already?" asked Poppy.

"Perfection takes time," Elizabeth said primly and got up from the breakfast table.

IT HAD BEEN a long few weeks. Avoiding social contact was harder than she'd imagined, and though Elizabeth couldn't say that she missed the punishment of her gym sessions, there were all those delicious lunches and fundraisers that she hadn't attended.

So when she checked her phone after she got out of the shower she felt a pang of guilt reading through the group text channel.

Should we be declaring mourning for Elizabeth? Arabella had typed.

Perhaps she's busy now that Eli is back in town, Alexandra had written with a winky emoji.

Elizabeth, dear, are you quite alright? came from Amanda.

Feeling awful that she'd made them worry, she quickly typed back *I'm fine, just been a little off colour. All is well now!*

Three dots immediately appeared, then a message. *So you'll be at lunch tomorrow? Hurray!* from Arabella.

Elizabeth sighed. She had no reason not to go. It wasn't even her turn to pay, so she couldn't pretend that poverty was a justification. And she should see them, she thought. Not to tell them anything, of course, but just to allay suspicions.

Fine. *Of course*, she wrote back. *Looking forward to it.*

She put her phone down and quickly dried herself off with brusque strokes of the towel.

This was all going to turn out alright, she told herself. It had to. She had a plan. And she was sure Sally would walk out as soon as she heard what a cheat Eli was. Any sensible woman would. Sally would go and Eli would realize what he'd had and come crawling back. Easy.

The biggest question still revolved around her head. Did she let him back?

Obviously, the answer would be yes. Eventually. He'd have to beg for it first. Beg for it and grovel and apologize. And then, eventually, she'd get back her life of credit cards and lunches and gym sessions and new shoes, and her house would be safe and all would be well.

All would be well but it would be Eli sitting at the breakfast table, not Poppy. The thought of which made her ridiculously sad for some reason.

"Pull yourself together," she said out loud, and selected a slim black dress from her wardrobe.

She pulled on underwear, stockings, and the dress itself then heard footsteps on the stairs. Just in time. "Poppy?" she called out.

"Yes?"

"I need a little help in here."

There was a pause before the bedroom door creaked open and Poppy stood on the threshold looking like she'd been summoned to the headmistress's office.

"Don't look like that, you're not getting a caning, I just need help with my zipper," Elizabeth said, turning her back on Poppy.

She sensed hesitation before Poppy moved up behind her. There was fumbling at her waist and then the zip began to move and just as it reached the top of her back, right between the shoulder-blades, she felt the tickle of Poppy's fingers on her skin.

She gasped, smothering the sound with a cough and pulling away as soon as the zip was done. She found that she was shaking slightly, which really was foolish. And she had no idea what to say.

"Is that what you're wearing?" Poppy asked, oblivious to what had just happened. Not that anything at all had happened.

"Yes," Elizabeth said, turning around. "Problem?"

"You'll be freezing," said Poppy. "Hold on." She went to the open wardrobe and flicked through the contents. "Here. Wear this on top. It'll look good and you won't catch your death out there."

Elizabeth looked at the jacket and nodded. "Just lay it on the bed," she said, before sitting down at her dressing table.

"So, do you have a plan?" Poppy asked, perching on the end of the bed.

Elizabeth watched her in the mirror. She really was rather pretty. With her curly hair piled up in a messy bun, her pajama pants and her baggy t-shirt, she looked all of about seventeen. Elizabeth envied her ease and casualness. Not a lick of makeup and the fact didn't bother her at all. Not that she needed makeup. What Elizabeth wouldn't give to subtract a decade or more and be Poppy's age again.

"Not particularly," Elizabeth said, pulling out a foundation brush. "I'll just improvise, isn't that what you actors call it?"

"It is," said Poppy slowly. "But you don't want more structure than that? I mean, you're not just going to walk in and say 'I'd like to think about franchising your coffee shop and then screw you over so that you learn a lesson' are you?"

"Obviously not." She patted foundation on her skin and then used the brush to blend it in.

"So what are you going to say then?"

Elizabeth sighed. "Poppy, leave it. I'm an adult who is very capable of having adult conversations. I don't need a script."

"Fine," Poppy said. But she didn't move from the bed, she looked down at her feet and Elizabeth watched her in the mirror remembering the fleeting touch of her hand on her back.

"Can I ask you something?" Elizabeth said, finally going back to work with her brush.

"Sure." Poppy looked up and those dark eyes caught Elizabeth's in the mirror.

She should not ask this question. But she wanted to. "How did you know?" she said, looking down at a collection of eye shadows because she didn't want to look Poppy in the eye.

"Know what?"

"Um, that you were, you know, I, um, I don't actually know the preferred term, gay? Lesbian?"

Poppy laughed. "I'm not big on labels. Queer is fine by me."

"Fine. Then how did you know you were queer?"

There was the sound of a sigh behind her. "How did you know you were straight? That's supposed to be the answer to that question. Which is silly of course, because straight is the default, right? You don't realize you're straight in the same way that you don't realize you're human. You assume it. Being different is, well, different."

Elizabeth watched her quietly.

"I knew always probably. I think I really truly realized one day in middle school. The girls I was friends with were talking about how great some boy in the next class up was. And I just didn't see it. One of them told me I was stupid and said if I didn't like him then who did I like? Who made me feel tingly and warm inside?"

Elizabeth raised an eyebrow suddenly extremely aware of the fact that just a couple of minutes ago just for a couple of seconds she'd felt quite tingly and warm inside. She swallowed hard.

"Then our English teacher walked in," Poppy said, with a laugh. "And I realized that Ms. Temple made me feel very tingly in all kinds of ways and, well, I kind of put things together after that."

Obviously this was all some kind of hiccup. A sort of miscommunication among nerve cells or something. Surely that happened? The Royal Mail delivered her letters to the neighbor across the road often enough, could human cells be that different?

"Thank you," she said quietly, aware of the fact that she'd asked a tremendously personal question and that Poppy had answered honestly and with grace.

"Why do you ask?"

Elizabeth looked up and caught those eyes again watching her keenly. "Oh, no reason," she said.

Because really, there wasn't a reason at all. Not one.

CHAPTER SEVENTEEN

"Have a great day," Poppy grinned as she handed over the customer's coffee. Her phone had vibrated in her pocket three minutes ago and she was itching to check it.

"Oh, I might have one of those chocolate biscuits as well," said the lady.

"Absolutely," said Poppy, handing over a plate and a biscuit.

"Let me see, I'm sure I've got change here somewhere." The woman began rooting around in her purse and Poppy's phone vibrated again.

"You know what? It's on the house, my treat," Poppy said, sliding the plate closer to the woman.

"Are you sure, love?" the woman asked doubtfully.

"Certain, consider it a Commonwealth gift," Poppy beamed and turned around before the woman could argue with her, pulling her phone out as she went.

As usual, she was alone in the shop. But the place was quiet today and besides, things were already in motion. As promised, Elizabeth had stopped by the previous morning, looking every inch the consummate professional. Ironic considering she'd never worked a day in her life.

Except the second she'd stepped through the door Poppy's

heart had grown three sizes and breathing had become a tad dicey.

A crush, that's all it was, she'd had to remind herself. Then she'd needed to plunge her hands into cold washing up water to forget the second that morning when she'd stood behind Elizabeth, breathing in her scent, and zipped up her dress. It had taken every ounce of focus that she had not to look at or touch anything she shouldn't.

Stupid crush, stupid hormones, she'd muttered into the washing up.

By pure chance, Jeremy had been in the shop, collecting the takings and primping for yet another 'business' lunch. Poppy suspected that his business lunches were actually pints at a pub that happened to have a large clientele that dressed in suits.

Elizabeth had played her part to perfection. Ignoring Poppy altogether and asking for the manager and being all strict and brusque like she barely had a minute to spare. She'd been in and out in three minutes flat, after sizing Jeremy up and demanding a meeting to discuss 'possibilities' if this really was his shop and his idea.

Jeremy had been crowing from the rooftops when she left, leaving Poppy feeling even more guilty than she had before. But when his 'business lunch' had turned into a 'celebratory lunch' and he'd disappeared yet again she'd felt slightly better.

Which meant Elizabeth had begun fulfilling her part of the bargain. Poppy pulled up her notification bar and checked what had arrived.

She'd almost lost hope. Eli obviously wasn't interested in her. And yet right there, bang at the bottom of the bar, was his screen name.

She held her breath and squeezed her eyes tight shut.

They'd matched.

It was her turn now.

❃ ❃ ❃

Elizabeth stopped in the foyer of the restaurant. Something wasn't right. She felt… different being here.

Which was stupid because she wasn't different at all. She was temporarily under reconstruction, that was all, and she had no reason to feel like she didn't belong. She straightened up and marched right into the dining room, spotting the three As the moment she walked in.

"Oh thank God," Arabella said, standing up and grasping her arms to pull her in for an air kiss. "We really were starting to get worried you know?"

"I'm fine, really fine," Elizabeth smiled.

"You can't just desert us like that," said Alexandra, quite kindly Elizabeth thought since out of the four of them she suspected she was the one that really could desert.

"Of course not," she said.

"Glad you're here, old bean. Drinkies are already ordered," Amanda said, actually brushing her cheek with a kiss.

"And desperately needed," Arabella said, settling back into her chair. "Because the twins are out on their ear again."

"Oh my dear," Amanda said. "What happened this time?"

"They put fish oil on all the light fittings in their classroom, making the whole damn place smell like a fishmonger's," said Arabella. "So they're excluded for the rest of term."

Not that Arabella would know what a fishmonger's smelled like, Elizabeth thought.

"Hugh's furious," Arabella said, clutching at her glass of wine as soon as the waiter put it in front of her.

Not that Hugh couldn't afford a new private school for the twins.

"He would be," Amanda said.

"Did you have to go into school?" asked Alexandra.

Elizabeth took her own glass and drank, meaning to sip but ending up with half the glass sliding down her throat and into her stomach.

"George has canceled the Bahamas," Amanda was saying, when she tuned back in. "Which is darned unfortunate because it was during half-term. No idea what to do with the little ones now."

Elizabeth raised her hand and the waiter came over immediately with a new glass of wine. Say what you want about fancy restaurants, the service was always amazing.

"Well, Alessandro is kicking up a fuss about going anywhere other than the house in Italy," said Alexandra.

The wine was sloshing around in her empty stomach now and she could feel the warmth of it creeping up into her chest.

"What about you and Eli?" asked Amanda. "Do you have half-term plans?"

It had only been a matter of time. Of course it had. And she thought she'd been prepared. But in the end, how could she have been? The wine didn't help, of course. Though at least when the moment came it gave her a bravery she didn't deserve.

"Half term plans for the children we don't have?" she said, the words bursting out of her.

Amanda blanched. "Oh dear, I am sorry. That was untactful of me. I just meant holiday plans."

Holiday plans with a man that couldn't spend more than one night a week a home? A man that had left her because he'd found something 'warm and hopeful'? A man that hadn't graced her bed for three years now because he was always tired and he'd 'make it up to her'?

She took another gulp of wine. This had been a terrible idea. Seeing the As had only made her realize what she was missing. Had she really changed that much in just a few weeks? Or had she always been like this, always bitchily undercutting them and their remarks under her breath, in her head?

Don't make a scene. She could hear her mother's voice now.

All three women were watching her expectantly.

Elizabeth looked at each one calmly.

What should she say? That her husband had gone? That she couldn't afford this lifestyle anymore? That she was running out of money and she was alone and she was starting to develop inexplicable feelings for her waitress lodger that she'd moved in to help pay a mortgage that was threatening to overwhelm her?

"Actually, I'm not feeling terribly well," she said, picking up her purse. "I think I'm getting a migraine."

She stood up as the three other women all began talking at once, and walked out without ever looking back.

*	*	*

Poppy turned her key in the door, stomach full of the news about Eli. They'd matched and now she needed to know what to do next. Elizabeth would tell her what to do.

The thought of sitting opposite the man and sharing air, let alone a drink, made her feel a bit sick. But she'd do it and get it over and done with and then… And then she'd be even and her life would go back to the way it had been before: happy and uncomplicated.

The house was dark so she flipped on the hallway light. But as she was kicking off her shoes, she heard a clinking sound from the living room. Frowning, she quietly put down her bag and picked up a golfing umbrella from the stand near the door.

As silently as she could, she pushed open the living room door and reached around for the light-switch, finding it with sweating fingers.

One, two, three. She flicked the switch and pushed the door open in one movement, swinging the umbrella up over her head as she did so.

"Is that your plan?" Elizabeth said, her words slurring only the tiniest bit. "To hit a burglar with an umbrella?"

Poppy lowered the umbrella. "What are you doing?"

"What does it look like?" said Elizabeth, brandishing her wine glass. "Trying to drink my problems away."

Poppy leaned on the umbrella. Elizabeth looked pale, more fragile than she'd ever seen her. "Is it working?"

"What do you think?" Elizabeth asked.

Poppy turned around, went back into the hall and replaced the umbrella before returning to the living room.

"You know there's a baseball bat and a golf club in that umbrella stand, both of which would be a far better weapon than that umbrella," pointed out Elizabeth.

"If you're going to drink your problems away, you should have company. Drinking alone makes you an alcoholic, or so I've heard." She had the feeling that Elizabeth shouldn't be alone right now.

"Feel free to get a glass and join me," Elizabeth said expansively.

Poppy did just that, pouring herself a small glass and coming back to sit on the couch.

"Though I don't know what kind of problems you have," Elizabeth continued. "You get to live in a beautiful house, you have a job you like, you have friends."

"And you have none of those things?" Poppy asked.

Elizabeth closed her eyes and Poppy didn't know if she was passing out or trying not to cry. She shuffled forward in her seat until she could put a hand on Elizabeth's knee.

"You know, it'll all turn out fine in the end," she said softly. "If it's not fine yet then it's not the end yet."

And when Elizabeth opened her eyes Poppy saw a fury that she hadn't known existed.

CHAPTER EIGHTEEN

"Has it ever occurred to you, that people might not want to hear your ceaseless optimism?" Elizabeth spat. "Have you ever thought for just one moment that someone may want to wallow in their misery, may want to experience the feelings that they're having?"

Poppy's face fell and her eyes glazed with tears, but Elizabeth couldn't stop herself. Now that the anger was coming out it was exploding, whether Poppy was an appropriate target or not.

"Just what exactly do you have to be so damn optimistic about, Poppy? Hmm? What the hell makes you so special that you can tell the future, that you know just how things will work out? What gives you the right to spout off platitudes as though they were your own?"

Poppy pushed herself back into her seat like she was trying to get as far from Elizabeth as she could.

"Well then?" Elizabeth demanded, already hating herself but in too deep now to stop. "Go on, answer the questions."

She stopped, heart pounding in her chest, eyebrow raised as though truly expecting an answer she was sure that Poppy wasn't going to give. She picked up her glass and took a long swig, ready to empty it, put it down, and stomp off to sulk in bed. But Poppy spoke first.

"Do you really want to know?" she asked, voice small and shaking.

Elizabeth shrugged, picking up the wine bottle and serving herself now that she had an excuse to stay and drink more.

Poppy shuffled forward again, gulped, blinked, controlled herself.

"My dad left when I was seven," she said, voice getting stronger. "He left after he beat my mom so hard she went blind in one eye, after he gave me this." She pushed her hair back revealing a long, ugly scar above her hair line.

Elizabeth's anger dissolved as quickly as it had appeared. "Jesus," she swore.

"He left and didn't come back and then my mom started using. At the beginning it wasn't so bad, she could still work and we still had money. Then we had food stamps and government help. But by the time I was twelve she couldn't hold down a job any more." Poppy swallowed so hard Elizabeth could hear it. "By the time I was fifteen she was dead."

"Jesus," Elizabeth said again, not knowing what else to say. "You don't have to tell me this, you don't need to... to relive things."

"No," said Poppy, sitting up straighter. "I do. Because you need to know that bad things happen. To everyone. All the time."

"But... but you're always so optimistic, so sunny, so happy."

"Because that's how we survive," Poppy said simply. "By having hope that tomorrow will be better. When today is dark and heavy and you can't continue, you go to bed and close your eyes with the knowledge that tomorrow might be lighter, could be lighter."

Elizabeth shook her head. "I don't know. I don't know how you found the strength to become the person you are, Poppy. But I do know that I don't think I can do it. My problems are nothing next to yours, yet I honestly don't think I can do this any more."

"Problems aren't comparable," Poppy said softly. "We don't measure them against each other. Hurting is hurting, it's an absolute." She bit her lip and looked at Elizabeth with big, brown eyes. "What happened today?"

"It was stupid." But the words spilled out anyway. "I was

having lunch with friends. I just… felt like I didn't belong."

"The friends that you haven't told about Eli?"

Elizabeth nodded.

"Maybe you should tell them. They're your friends, they should understand."

"They won't," Elizabeth said firmly. Then she softened. "But you do. I told you and you're the only one I can talk to about all of this."

Poppy smiled a little and she was close enough that Elizabeth could smell her incense scent again. She remembered Poppy's hands wrapping a scarf around her neck, remembered Poppy telling her to take a jacket.

Why had Eli never done that? It was as though Poppy instinctively knew how to be a partner, how to be considerate and kind and Elizabeth didn't quite know how to deal with that. Because she didn't think it had ever happened to her before.

Poppy put her wine glass down on the table and before she could stop herself, Elizabeth was tutting, picking it up and sliding a coaster underneath it.

"Sorry," Poppy said.

And Elizabeth had the sudden thought that Poppy was her best friend. Right now, right here, Poppy was probably the best friend she'd ever had. She shook her head.

"Don't be sorry," she said. "You know why Eli left me?"

Poppy nodded.

"No," Elizabeth. "Not that. He always had other women, he could have had anyone he wanted. That's not why he went, not really." She took a shuddering breath. "He left because I'm too controlling. Because I want things to look perfect on the outside. And he's right."

"There's far more to you than that," Poppy said gently.

Elizabeth closed her eyes. "I'm afraid that there's not," she said, whispering her deepest fear into the air. "I'm afraid that I don't know any other way to be."

There was silence for long enough that she opened her eyes. Poppy was watching her with a strange smile on her face.

"I have an idea," said Poppy. "Trust me?"

And before Elizabeth could answer, Poppy was jumping up and running out of the room.

* * *

Poppy flipped the switch and handed the microphone to Elizabeth who just stared at it.

"What in hell do you want me to do with that?"

"You know, you swear more when you're drunk," Poppy said.

"And you're just as irritating when I'm drunk as when I'm sober," said Elizabeth.

Poppy bit back a smile. Elizabeth was obviously getting some of herself back. She turned to the TV, switched it on, then picked up her phone and started typing.

"Who the hell has a portable microphone on hand? And what are you doing?" Elizabeth asked suspiciously.

"Looking for the right song," Poppy said, finding what she was looking for and hitting the icon to cast it to the TV.

There was a flickering and then the video appeared on screen. Poppy paused it before the lyrics started rolling across the screen.

"What?" Elizabeth said.

Poppy gestured to the microphone in her hand. "All you need to do is sing," she said. "It's easy. The words will come up on the TV, you sing along."

"I can't sing!"

"Of course you can," said Poppy. "Anyone can sing. What you mean is that you can't sing well. And that's a matter of taste. Besides, who's here to hear you except me?"

"And you don't matter?" asked Elizabeth in a way that made Poppy think maybe she did matter a little bit.

"I don't care," she said stoutly. "Just do it. Let yourself lose control. It's a cathartic experience."

Elizabeth reached for the wine bottle and Poppy pulled it

away.

"You'll get the bottle back when you've sung the song."

For a long moment they stared at each other, then Elizabeth blinked. "Fucking fine."

"Told you you swear more when you're drunk."

"I won't be drunk any more if you don't give me my wine back," Elizabeth said. "Just start the damn video."

With a grin, Poppy pressed play and the first twanging chords of Shania Twain's *Man, I Feel Like a Woman* rang out of the TV speakers.

The lyrics appeared and very, very quietly. Elizabeth began to repeat them, off key and definitely off rhythm.

"Try harder," Poppy pressed. "Don't be so controlled. You got this."

Elizabeth started to sing louder.

"Come on, move with it," said Poppy, starting to move her hips.

Very, very stiffly, Elizabeth swayed her hips too.

"Better," said Poppy, taking her hand. "But more, less control, more volume, more dancing. Come on, let's do this."

The chorus began and Elizabeth's voice got louder. The words clicked into place and suddenly she was singing in time and in tune.

"That's right," Poppy cried.

Poppy leaned into the microphone and started singing too and Elizabeth began to dance properly, her hips loosening up as they both sang into the mic, heads close together and song ringing out through the empty house.

The bridge hit and Elizabeth lowered the microphone, but Poppy took her hand and kept her dancing, twirling her around and under her arm as Elizabeth laughed.

"Watch out, the words are coming back," Poppy said, just in time for Elizabeth to pull her in to sing again.

They finished the song with a crescendo and a shout and Elizabeth started laughing so hard that Poppy couldn't help but join her.

"See," Poppy said. "You can lose control. Eli's an idiot."

And then Elizabeth wasn't laughing. She was crying, loud, heart-rending sobs as she collapsed to the floor. Poppy went down with her, pulling her in, holding her tight against her chest as Elizabeth's tears soaked through her shirt and dampened her skin.

Elizabeth clung to her and Poppy knew, just knew, that this was so much more than a crush.

She closed her eyes and wondered what the hell she was supposed to do as she cradled Elizabeth's sobbing body in her arms.

CHAPTER NINETEEN

If it wasn't bad enough that she'd cried, actually cried, in front of the woman, there were now unidentified feelings to deal with. Wonderful. Brilliant. Just what she needed.

Oh, and her eyes were swollen. Always a good way to start a morning.

She splashed cold water over her face, grabbed a cooling face mask and applied it, then sat on the edge of the bath tub waiting for it to take effect.

Alright, so she'd had a drink. Several drinks. More drinks than she definitely, certainly should have had. Enough drinks that... and she cringed internally... she'd sung karaoke in her own living room.

She could still hear the chords of the song in her head though. She could still feel those few moments of freedom when she just hadn't cared. She hadn't cared what anyone thought, hadn't cared about how things looked or what she was supposed to do. She'd just sung and Poppy had sung with her and for a few instants the world had been a better, brighter place.

Which of course led up to the last remnants of control slipping through her fingers until she was sobbing on the floor. Because that's what happened when you let things slide, when you stopped controlling everything, it all went to, well, to shit.

The mask was tightening on her face.

So there she was, sobbing on the floor, vulnerable and out of control, and what had happened? Poppy, sweet, dear, kind, lovely Poppy, had put her arms around her and held her like a child and Elizabeth? Elizabeth had let it happen. Not only let it happen, but leaned into it. Enjoyed it.

Which in turn led to the realization that Poppy wasn't just a lodger, nor solely a friend, but the best friend that she currently had.

Comparing Poppy to the three As was a little like comparing H&M to Chanel. No, that was uncharitable. Like comparing an apple to a mangosteen or something equally exotic. Except in that comparison, she wasn't entirely sure which side represented Poppy.

It was so easy, somehow, to spill things to Poppy, to let her in, to… feel things.

Which inevitably led to the absolute and final thing that Elizabeth truly remembered about the evening. The growing warmth she'd felt in her stomach, the bubbling she'd experienced, the sudden and inexplicable desire to turn her head until Poppy's lips were right there and…

And nothing, of course.

She'd been crying and covered in snot and hiccuping. Not her best look. Not that she needed to look her best in front of Poppy.

She sighed and her face mask cracked forcing her to be absolutely still again.

Look, it wasn't that she had a problem with gay people. Or queer people. Whatever word she was supposed to use. She truly didn't. She'd never really given the matter much thought, to be honest. She supposed if she had she'd have come to the conclusion that the issue didn't concern her and she would therefore have ignored it.

Wait. Was that bad? Probably that was bad. Ignoring issues because they weren't your issues was a bad thing, she had a feeling about that. Like, just because you weren't homeless didn't mean that you shouldn't care about the homeless, right?

She growled under her breath and her stomach rumbled. She was tired and half-hungover, which always resulted in her being starving. What she wanted was a good, fried English breakfast. What she would have would be muesli.

Right, so, homosexuality, something she thought she had no real opinion on other than it being none of her business. And then…

Then whatever that was last night.

It perhaps wasn't that she didn't have an opinion and more that she'd never thought it concerned her. But now it did. For reasons that she really didn't want to think about.

The problem wasn't that Poppy gave her feelings. The problem was more where did those feelings lead?

Because if she had feelings for Poppy then what about Eli? And if Eli was out of the picture then what about the house? And what then about the life she'd so carefully built and tended?

Feelings for Poppy could only lead in one direction, and that was toward a life that was totally and inescapably different from her own.

She stood up and turned the tap on, waiting until it warmed.

There might not be any feelings, of course. There was always that. She'd been drunk and upset and altogether not herself. So probably she'd just been thoroughly mistaken about whatever strange sensations her body was experiencing.

She leaned over the sink and began to wash the face mask off.

The first time she'd seen Eli, when he'd smiled over that university bar, she'd felt a thrilling inside. She'd told herself and everyone else that it had been love at first sight.

If she was being honest though, it had been something a little different, a little more complex and nuanced than that. It had been more the feeling that he was perfect. Not just for her, but for the life she wanted to lead, the person she wanted to become.

Which wasn't to say that she didn't love him, that he didn't leave her breathless and vibrating on their good days and deflated and heavy on their bad ones. She did love him. Had loved him. She wasn't sure which.

At some point, that love had morphed into something else. A sort of stiffness and un-changeability, kind of like plaster hardening on a wall. And then that hardness had begun to flake away, to turn to powder over time. And then, finally, here she was.

All of which meant that she probably didn't love Eli. Didn't it?

But then what about the house? What about her life? And what about damn Poppy with her blonde curls and her dark eyes and her inexplicably kind heart?

Elizabeth patted her face dry and then had a flashback of the evening before. She groaned.

Poppy had put her to bed.

Not only that, but she had a distinct memory of Poppy taking wet-wipes from the bathroom cabinet and carefully wiping her makeup off.

How on earth was she supposed to deal with someone as considerate and lovely as that?

Elizabeth was no fool. She knew that she was far from kind, far from nice, far from deserving of the kind of tenderness that Poppy had shown. She was brittle and strict and sensible. Not at all what Poppy should want out of life.

Not that Poppy had been untoward. She hadn't. Obviously, there was always the chance that Poppy wasn't interested in her at all.

Not that she was interested in Poppy.

She wasn't.

Probably.

Her stomach rumbled again.

But, said a little voice in the back of her head, what if she were? Would that be such a big deal?

Yes, obviously it would. What about her husband? Her life? Her house?

Mmhmm. But what about being held in those warm, kind arms again? What about feeling her heart pumping again like it was really alive instead of just marking time? What about wanting again? Feeling again? Needing again?

All massively over-rated, she told herself sternly as she pulled on her dressing gown.

SHE'D SMELLED IT from the stairs and had assumed it was her hungover brain playing tricks on her. But when she walked into the kitchen and saw Poppy holding a frying pan she couldn't help but think that the balance had suddenly tipped to Poppy's side.

If being queer meant cooked breakfasts, whispered the voice in her head…

She had to take a deep breath before she could even speak. A deep breath that let out all the embarrassment and shame she felt about the night before. She could only hope that Poppy was lady-like enough not to mention what had happened.

"You look pretty good for someone that drank countless bottles of wine," Poppy said conversationally, flipping some bacon over in the pan.

So much for that. Poppy and lady-like didn't obviously belong in the same sentence. "Thank you?" hazarded Elizabeth.

"I thought you might like breakfast," said Poppy. She turned, her face dropping. "Unless you feel too bad? Did I screw this up?"

"No, no," said Elizabeth hurriedly. "It's just the ticket. Exactly what I needed."

Which, now that she came to think about it, was Poppy all over. Exactly what she needed when she needed it. She'd been there when Eli dumped her. She had a scarf when she was cold. She had a portable microphone when she needed to lose control. Was there any situation that Poppy was unprepared for?

"Here you go then," Poppy said, placing the finished bacon onto the plate next to eggs, sausage, beans, mushrooms and toast.

"Impressive," Elizabeth said. "But I didn't think we had any of this."

"We didn't," Poppy said, taking her own plate and putting it on the table. "I went to the shops first thing."

For a second Elizabeth thought she might cry again. She blinked furiously and picked up her knife and fork. "Good girl," she said.

She caught Poppy's eye for just an instant and in that instant there was… something. A crackling, an energy between them, a connection that filled Elizabeth up and made her feel like everything was going to be okay, that last night was the beginning of something, that the future was lighter and nicer and less scary than she'd thought and then… Poppy looked away.

"So, I've got big news," said Poppy, cutting into a sausage.

"Yes?" Was there, she wondered, any tomato ketchup? She wouldn't ask. Ketchup was uncouth. She didn't want Poppy to think she was that common.

"Yes, big news," Poppy said. "Whoops, almost forgot." She got up, pulled ketchup from the fridge and passed it over to Elizabeth.

"Thank you," Elizabeth mumbled.

"Big news," Poppy said again, settling back at the table. "I matched with Eli."

CHAPTER TWENTY

"This is ridiculous."

"The idea, or the outfit?" Elizabeth said, looking down at Poppy's skirt.

"Both?"

"Frankly, I'd wear something a little more conservative."

Poppy sighed and shook her head. No way. If she had to do this, then she was going to do it her way. And she supposed she did have to do this since that was the agreement and all.

Elizabeth was bending over, plucking at the hem of the skirt and Poppy wanted so badly to stroke her hair.

It was becoming extremely apparent that all of this needed to stop. Poppy could see that. She could see that this was all doomed. Except every now and again there was a little moment when it seemed slightly less doomy and more, well, sparkly.

Holding a sobbing woman in her arms shouldn't be a highpoint in a relationship. And yet she was sure Elizabeth had leaned into her, sure that there had been a closeness there. A something there.

Right. A woman with whose husband she was about to go on a date with. Were the prepositions in that sentence correct? She had no idea. It wasn't like it was a sentence she'd ever had to say before.

"It's too soon," she said now. "We only just matched and—"

"And Eli gave you an immediate date and time," said Elizabeth sharply. "Which is more than he ever did with me. If I wanted to go out to dinner I'd get a date a month from now. So strike while the iron's hot."

"Strike while the iron's hot?"

Elizabeth nodded. "Might as well get this done."

"What exactly is 'this'?"

With a sigh, Elizabeth put one hand on her hip. "Look, you go out, you have a date, it all goes well, you charm him, and at the end you go in for a good night kiss. You don't even really have to do it, just lean in like you're going to and switch to your cheek. Just as long as it happens outside the bar so that I can get a photo of it."

"You're going to be lurking around in a long raincoat and dark glasses, I assume?"

"Don't be foolish." Elizabeth sniffed. "It's dark, I hardly require sunglasses."

Poppy closed her eyes and took a breath. Okay, okay. She was going to fulfill her part of the deal. And then? Well, then it was time to start looking for a new place probably. She knew that she should. She knew that she shouldn't be around Elizabeth with feelings like these.

But then she couldn't shake the feeling that this would all turn out for the best.

THE BAR WAS appropriately trendy and a cocktail cost more than Poppy made in a day, so she didn't order one. It seemed rude to assume Eli was paying, even if he had been the one to invite her.

She crossed her legs and felt uncomfortably out of place in among the business suits and jackets and stockings.

She was just about to take out her phone when a tall, elegant man slid into the booth opposite her. She blinked before she recognized him as the man who had dumped Elizabeth in the coffee shop what felt like a year ago.

He's a serial cheater and an asshat, she reminded herself, as she painted on a big smile.

"You must be Poppy," he said, holding out a hand and grinning.

There was something very disarming about his smile, like you were the focus of his world, the most beautiful woman in the world. Suddenly, Poppy could see just how dangerous he was.

"Thank you for agreeing to meet me so quickly," he said, looking around and then raising his hand for a waiter. "I'll take a scotch on the rocks, what would you like, Poppy?"

"Uh, um, a Cosmopolitan?" She had precisely zero idea what that was, but it sounded classy, so she went with it.

It was clear right now that she was hopelessly out of her depth. Just have a date, that was all. Treat Eli like she would a woman she was interested in. Which was easier said than done when she saw his wife every time she looked into his eyes.

She cleared her throat. "So, um, this is a nice place."

He rolled his eyes. "It's pretentious, but it's close to the office so it's convenient." He smiled again. "And I was so anxious to meet you that I didn't want to wait. Is that terrible? I mean, that must be a bad sign, mustn't it?"

"A bad sign?" asked Poppy.

"I know, I know. I shouldn't come across as desperate. But it's so difficult not to."

"Desperate?" Poppy had the swirling feeling that she wasn't quite up-to-date with this conversation.

"Mmm. I assume most men you meet are fairly desperate, aren't they?" he said, his smile faltering a little. "Unless, well, I mean, I can't be the only one, can I?"

Poppy frowned. There really was something odd going on here. This was not like any date she'd ever been on and she knew that straight people could be weird at times, but this was going too far. "Most men?" she echoed.

"I'm not the only one then," he said, sitting back and seeming relieved.

"Your drinks," said a waiter quietly, sliding glasses in front of them.

"Thank you," said Eli, clutching at his glass. "It's just that, well, I assume you're terribly busy and you're probably seeing a lot of men, a woman like you doesn't come along particularly often, and I'm grateful that you fit me in."

Poppy frowned harder and took a long suck at the straw sticking out of a cocktail that turned out to be shockingly pink. She swallowed and then began choking. The sourness of the alcohol took her by surprise and she was coughing so hard that tears came to her eyes.

"Here," said Eli, passing her a handkerchief.

"Jesus," said Poppy, dabbing at her eyes and getting her breath back. "I didn't know anyone carried handkerchiefs anymore."

"My wife makes me," said Eli. "Made me," he corrected, taking back the square of fabric. "Which is kind of the problem."

"Your wife?" Poppy said. "You're married?"

Now she wasn't completely in touch with the modus operandi of cheating spouses, but she was pretty sure that they generally didn't just spout out that they were married.

"Sort of," Eli said. He turned his glass around in his hands. "I think we're getting divorced. No, we are getting divorced."

"Oh," said Poppy, back on firmer territory. "I'm sorry?"

"Don't be. I wasn't happy. I mean, I'm sure she wasn't either," Eli said. "But we did have a good life together. Better for me than for her, I suppose. I shouldn't talk out of school, but she let me have other women, she was understanding, it was all… It was what a man like me is supposed to want, I suppose."

"A man like you?" said Poppy. Any minute now she'd come up with an original sentence all of her own. But she was trying so desperately to follow what the hell was going on here that she thought it was smarter not to prompt Eli in any particular direction.

"I thought I was a cad. A cheater. A lying, lousy husband," said Eli. "But then I met someone else."

"Many someone elses," Poppy couldn't help but put in.

"Indeed. Many. But then one. Sally's her name. And she made me realize that I just wasn't happy. See Elizabeth, that's my wife, she's controlling. But that's not really the problem, I think. It's more that we weren't good for each other. Oh, the idea of us was good, but in reality it just didn't work. Sort of like communism, I suppose."

"Communism?" said Poppy, losing the thread of the conversation all over again.

"I wanted, needed, someone to come home to. Someone who loved me, wanted me, someone who warmed me, if that makes sense? Elizabeth wasn't that for me. And I don't think I was that for her either. I don't think we ever really loved each other, we just sort of loved the idea of what we represented. A wealthy, attractive, young couple."

"I see," said Poppy, actually understanding. "Have you explained this to Elizabeth?"

Eli sighed. "She wouldn't understand. All she sees is the big house and the money and what people will think of us. She's so unhappy I don't think she understands what happy is supposed to be."

He took a sip of his drink.

"I thought I could change her," he said. "I know that sounds stupid now, but I did. She was so beautiful, her smile was heartbreaking. I thought that I could show her happiness and she'd change, she'd realize what she wanted. But I wasn't enough. I suppose she thought she could change me too."

"And now?" Poppy asked, sitting forward a little in her seat.

"And now I've finally found someone that makes me happy and I hope for Elizabeth that she can find the same, I just don't know if she can change enough to make herself see that she needs more than just an outwardly facing perfect life. She deserves an inside perfect life too."

Poppy gave up and pushed her drink away undrunk. "Which begs the question of why exactly you're sitting here with me?" she said. "If you're so happy with your new girlfriend, that is."

"You're right," Eli said surprisingly. "Totally right. Yes. Yes, I should concentrate on what I have, work on building a better life, a happier life, not be bogged down by my past. You're completely right." He beamed at her. "Thank you."

"Thank you?" Poppy asked, once again back at sea.

"I was about to delete my Tinder profile. Obviously, I will now, I don't want Sally thinking I'm up to anything. But I am glad that I saw you first. This was an opportunity that I really couldn't pass up and I'm truly grateful."

He took out a bunch of cash and slid it under the menu. "For your time," he said. "And for the drinks. Thank you, thanks again."

And he was walking out, leaving Poppy thoroughly and completely confused.

"Anything else, ma'am?" asked the waiter, swooping down on the table.

Poppy pulled Eli's half-drunk scotch to her. "Just the bill please."

What exactly had just happened? If this had been a date it had been an awfully strange one. Something was niggling at the back of her mind.

Eli had not been what she'd expected. In fact, he'd been reasonable and self-aware, not at all the asshole that she'd thought he'd be. He seemed to have a sense of what had happened, his own part in it, and what he wanted for the future.

It had, in fact, been kind of difficult not to like him as odd as his behavior was.

And yet…

She groaned and pulled out her phone, opening up the dating app and heading straight for her profile. The profile that she hadn't actually written. The profile that Mel and Paul had taken care of for her.

There it was, right at the top, just under 'bubbly fun Canadian'. She squinted and the words resolved in front of her eyes. 'Communication is my game. I'm an active listener and happy to give advice on women. Talking is key to relationships and men have been silent about their emotions for too long.'

Mel.

It had to be Mel. With Paul nodding along in the background, of course.

And now... She thought back to all the Tinder notifications she'd received. Now every straight man in London thought she was some kind of relationship guru. Including Eli.

She groaned and drank back the rest of Eli's drink. He hadn't wanted to date her, he'd wanted her to listen to him, advise him. And now she'd blown everything. He knew her face, there was no way she could seduce him now.

Which meant Elizabeth was currently waiting outside the bar, in the cold, very, very angry having seen her husband walk out with no Poppy.

Poppy pulled on her coat, grabbed her bag, and rushed out.

CHAPTER TWENTY ONE

Elizabeth carefully placed the plate on the table.

"Is this gluten-free?" asked the woman.

Elizabeth looked at the cheese toastie sitting on the plate in front of the woman and raised an eyebrow. "I doubt it," she said.

"Well I'm gluten-free," said the woman.

"I see," Elizabeth said carefully, desperately wanting to ask the woman what on earth had inspired her to order what was essentially cheese on toast if she was, indeed, gluten-free. "Would you like something else?" she asked, swooping the plate away from the woman.

"Yeah." The woman frowned. "What about a ham sandwich, that'd go down nicely. And one of those brownies I saw in the case on the way in."

"Ah," said Elizabeth, looking at the revolving cake display by the door. "I'm afraid you'll find that both those things have gluten."

"Yeah, but that's the good kind of gluten. I can have that kind."

"Yes, but, you see, there's really only one kind of gluten and—"

"You think I don't know what I'm talking about?" the woman interrupted. "You think I'm an idiot? Bit condescending, aren't you? What happened to the customer always being right, eh?"

Elizabeth bit her tongue and forced herself to smile. "Of course, yes, right away."

She bore the cheese toastie back off to the kitchen and strained to keep her patience.

This was her third gluten-free customer and the second that had ordered something blatantly gluten-containing, not to mention the fifth person that had found her in some way 'condescending,' 'patronizing,' or a 'know-it-all.'

As if the day wasn't bad enough as it was.

Poppy had royally screwed things up last night. Not that Elizabeth knew exactly what had happened.

As soon as she'd seen Eli come out of the bar alone she'd known that Poppy had somehow let her down. And she'd stormed off in a rage, not wanting to make a scene in public. She'd stormed all the way home and then, in a fit of sensibleness, had ignored the wine bottles that needed to be drunk and locked herself in her room.

She had had to get up early for work. Her first day of work. And she hadn't wanted to do that with a hangover.

But without the warmth of alcohol to send her to sleep, she'd been wide awake when Poppy got home. Awake enough to hear her creep up the stairs and listen at her door. Awake enough to hear her whisper 'Elizabeth' so quietly it was almost inaudible.

And angry enough not to answer.

Whatever it was that Poppy had done or not done, she was just going to have to fix it, that was all. The plan had been simple enough and if Poppy had ruined it then it was up to her to come up with something new.

Which hadn't made falling asleep any easier at all. In the end, Elizabeth realized that probably she should have just spoken to Poppy and gotten the full story. Because by four in the morning when she was still sleepless her addled brain had come up with at least four scenarios for what had happened between Poppy and Eli and none of them were nice.

"Order sent back," she said as she went into the kitchen.

"It'll come out of your wages," said the tall, dark faced cook as he wiped his nose on the back of his hand. "Sondra will make sure of it. Best throw it away and pretend it didn't happen. I won't say a thing if you don't."

Elizabeth tipped the toastie into the bin. "One ham sandwich."

"On it," said the cook.

She leaned on the counter and waited while he pulled out a loaf of sandwich bread.

What if Poppy had told Eli the truth, for example? That she was desperate and that Poppy was bait to break up his new relationship?

Or maybe Poppy had been attracted to him, something not out of the realms of imagination. Maybe she'd fallen for him in those few minutes and hadn't been able to pull it off.

Or maybe, perhaps, Eli had already gotten what he wanted. Maybe they'd… done things… She had a hazy idea of how this sort of thing worked, but she was fairly sure that there were people who needed sex badly enough that they would do it in toilets and all kinds of awful places.

She blushed just thinking of it.

Then she blushed harder when she realized she was thinking of Poppy pushed up against a tile wall, her mouth open, her eyes closed, her skin flushed and her breath coming hard and…

"You alright?" asked the cook, sliding over a sandwich on a plate. "Only you look like you're coming down with something."

"I'm fine," said Elizabeth, crisply, picking up the sandwich and stalking out of the kitchen.

"Here we go," she said politely to the gluten-free woman, placing the sandwich in front of her.

"Don't forget that brownie."

"I won't," Elizabeth said through gritted teeth.

"Drinks up," said the barman as she walked past the small wooden bar.

"Thank you." She picked up the tray laden with glasses and carefully carried it to the large table by the window.

"Oh dear, that looks heavy, let me help you," said the man at the head of the table.

Before she could stop him, he picked up the two glasses closest to him, unbalancing the tray and sending everything else sliding down onto the table and crashing to the floor.

Elizabeth just stopped herself from calling him stupid. "Let me get a cloth," she was able to mutter before she practically ran back to the kitchen.

"You look all done in," the cook said as she went back in. "You should take a break."

It was tempting, very tempting. Her feet hurt, her back hurt, her face hurt from fake-smiling. She could just walk away right now, just go and not come back. It was so tempting that she could see herself stepping onto the bus, could feel the soft carpet of home under her feet.

"No," she said. "I just need a cloth, that's all."

She had a job to do and god-damn-it she was going to do it.

SHE COULD HAVE crawled through the front door.

But then Poppy would have known there was something wrong and… and she really didn't know how to handle Poppy just at the moment.

She'd been so angry with her, and then she'd started to mellow and been less angry, and then she'd realized on the bus on the way home that she wanted to see Poppy, that Poppy was the only person she wanted to see after such an awful, terrible day. And that had, peculiarly, made her angry all over again.

So angry that she almost didn't want to go home.

Except home was the only place she did want to be.

And then she got even angrier at herself for being indecisive and confused and tired and just herself.

Sometimes being herself was so exhausting that she didn't know how she did it.

She was going inside. It was her house, after all. She was going inside and she was going to march straight up those stairs and get into a long, hot bath, after which she very well might just put her pajamas on and get straight into bed.

The only, singular high point in her day, and calling it high was a stretch, was that she hadn't actually been fired.

Once the breakages and returns had been deducted from her pay she wasn't entirely sure she came out ahead, but she hadn't lost the job. She'd leave that joy for her next shift, it could only be a matter of time.

She just wasn't cut out for work.

Maybe she should face it, maybe she should go back to Eli and beg him on bended knee to take her back. Maybe she should just become a damn nun and be done with it. Nuns didn't have to waitress. Nor, she thought, did they need to deal with men.

She was thinking so hard about being a nun that she was inside the house before she knew it, slipping her shoes off, heading directly for the narrow staircase. She was so intent on getting upstairs and into the bath that she didn't realize that Poppy was running downstairs until it was too late.

She just had time to turn sideways as Poppy barreled toward her.

And then there they were, face to face in the darkened stairwell, so close that Elizabeth could feel Poppy's breath on her face.

"El, I need to talk to you," Poppy said. "I'm sorry, but—"

"But nothing," said Elizabeth. "I don't want to talk about this. Not now. I'm tired. Fix it. Whatever it was that happened last night, just fix it."

"It's not that," Poppy said.

She was so close that Elizabeth could see where the dark of her eyes faded into the black of her irises. So close that, she only just realized, she could feel Poppy breathing, feel the rise and fall of her chest.

A warmth started to spread inside her. A warmth that was familiar and unfamiliar all at the same time. Before Elizabeth knew what she was doing, she was raising her hand, contorting so that she could put her palm up, hesitating only when she was millimeters from Poppy's cheek.

Poppy stopped talking. Whatever she'd been gabbling on

about suddenly unimportant in the face of... this.

It was like a thousand pins had been shot into her body stimulating a thousand nerves, and a thousand tiny ropes tied to those pins pulled her toward Poppy. It was as if the sensible, smart voice inside her head had been bound and gagged by something far bigger and more powerful.

Elizabeth moved, deliberately and slowly letting her hand close in on Poppy's cheek, letting the soft warmness of her leak into her own skin, letting her thumb rub gently across a high cheekbone. And far from pulling away, Poppy leaned into her, as Elizabeth had known she would. As felt right and natural.

Then Elizabeth was tilting her head, not at all wondering what she was doing, because she knew what she was doing, she knew as though she had been preparing for this her entire life. She knew and she was ready and any doubts she might have had were exploded into smithereens by the simple thought that she was going to kiss Poppy.

It should have terrified her, it should have made her anxious and sick, it should have felt wrong and yet it didn't.

Poppy's lips parted and Elizabeth leaned in just a fraction and her heart stopped beating and the world shrank down to a tiny bubble that contained just them and then...

The doorbell rang.

CHAPTER TWENTY TWO

Poppy pulled herself away and it physically hurt, like peeling off a band-aid. So close. So close that her heart was still pounding and her mouth was dry and other areas of her body were… not dry. She gulped. "Who's that?"

But there was already a rattling of keys and Elizabeth's face paled. "Eli, he's the only other person with keys."

"Shit."

"Language."

Poppy turned around. "I'll hide up here."

"Keep quiet," warned Elizabeth. "One sound and he'll know something's up. He can't find you here."

"No shit," said Poppy. "He just had a therapy session with me, I don't think it'd be great for his mental health to find me in his ex-wife's house."

"A therapy session?" Elizabeth asked.

The key scratched into the lock. "I'll explain later," Poppy said hurriedly. "Um, yell if you need me, I guess?"

"Why should I need you?" Elizabeth hissed.

But Poppy was already fleeing up the stairs to her room.

She heard Elizabeth greeting Eli and then the lull of their voices as they went into the living room and then silence as one of them closed the door. Carefully, she climbed up onto her bed and lay back.

What the fuck?

She had to be crazy, right?

There was no way in hell that Elizabeth had just nearly kissed her right there on the stairs.

No way.

Except she had the sneaky feeling that she kind of had. Which made no sense at all. No sense at all because Elizabeth was sitting downstairs right now with her almost ex-husband. Poppy had to smile at that.

Eli wasn't as bad as she'd thought, she'd judged too quickly. Now he was as good as his word, explaining things better to Elizabeth. Which wiped the smile off her face again because there was no way Elizabeth was going to take this well.

Poppy turned over, the bed creaking slightly in ways she hadn't noticed before she'd been trying to be quiet.

She was feeling lost, an unfamiliar feeling. She truly did believe that things turned out for the best, but even she had to admit that there had to be some human intervention at some points. Like right now.

Let's just say, hypothetically, that Elizabeth had been about to kiss her. As much as Poppy would like that to happen, would that really be the best thing for Elizabeth? Heart-broken, confused, and vulnerable didn't make for good life decisions.

So maybe Poppy needed to be the grown up one. Maybe she needed to nip this in the bud, as much as she'd rather watch the flower grow.

She gritted her teeth and wrinkled her nose and tried hard to persuade herself that she actually was an adult and she could do things for other people and realized... that she really, really needed to pee.

Crap.

She'd had at least a liter and a half of iced tea when she got home. The Brits didn't much like it, preferring their tea hot and strong enough to strip the paint off a double decker bus, which meant there was always plenty left over at the end of the day.

And Poppy was always happy to take it home rather than waste it.

She shuffled uncomfortably on her bed.

She strained to hear, but not a sound came from the living room. Maybe they were… making up? The thought made her feel a little sick. Whatever might have happened, and there were definitely two sides to every story, the one clear thing in her mind was that Eli and Elizabeth did not belong together.

Apart from anything else, their names were just too similar, which was weird.

For a second she wondered if she could date another Poppy.

What about if Elizabeth's name was really Poppy? Would she still be interested?

The distraction didn't really work though, she still had to pee.

Okay, she could be quiet. She just had to remember not to flush. And the bathroom was only a couple of meters away, it wasn't like she couldn't creep there in just a few seconds.

Given the choice between wetting her bed and very, very quietly going to the bathroom, Poppy was pretty sure she knew which option Elizabeth would prefer she took.

Slowly, slowly she uncurled herself from the bed, standing up in stages until she was fully upright. Then she took careful steps, standing only on the edges of her feet. She'd read an article once about a burglar and he'd said that was the secret to not creaking the floorboards.

She wobbled her way to the toilet and lowered herself gratefully to the seat.

Huh. Except maybe the burglar had said that walking on the edges of the stairs was the secret to no creaks. Actually that made a whole lot more sense.

Done with her business, she quietly closed the lid and crept back into her bedroom, not bothering to walk on the edges of her feet now that it seemed so ridiculous.

She was just about to reach her bed and safety when she felt something pull her back to the bathroom. She panicked, yanking herself, and by extension her sweater that had been caught on the door handle, forcefully toward the bed. The sweater freed itself and Poppy found herself on one foot, trembling, shaking and finally, thankfully, steady again.

"Close one," she mumbled to herself, turning around and promptly knocking the bedside lamp over with a crash so loud she could hear it echo in the stairwell.

For a second there was nothing, then she heard the living room door open. "I'm sure it's nothing," Elizabeth said.

"Let me check," said Eli, sounding macho.

Thinking quickly, Poppy grabbed her phone and opened YouTube.

"There's really no need," Elizabeth said from downstairs.

Poppy turned the volume way up and did a quick search.

"Let's be sure," said Eli, his foot hitting the bottom stair at the same time as Poppy hit Play.

A loud miaow followed by a screech came from her phone before she hurriedly hit Pause.

There was a long, slightly confused silence from below.

"It was, er, just the cat?" Elizabeth ventured, finally.

Poppy breathed a sigh of relief.

"A cat?" said Eli.

"Yes, and you don't want to irritate your allergies, so come back down."

"You have a cat?" Eli said in disbelief.

"It appears so," said Elizabeth dryly.

Poppy heard them go back into the living room and the door close behind them. She carefully sat back on her bed. She wasn't going to move a muscle until Eli left.

"A CAT?" ELIZABETH shrieked, coming into Poppy's room without knocking. "A cat? Seriously?"

"It was the best I could do," said Poppy. "I had to pee and then I got caught up and then the lamp fell and—"

"Enough." Elizabeth held up her hands. "I really can't deal with this right now." She turned to walk out.

"How did it go with Eli?" asked Poppy gently.

"Fine," said Elizabeth. "Absolutely fine." She turned back. "He explained that he'd met with some female relationship therapist and she'd told him to talk to me and explain things better. Which he somewhat did, I suppose. Though what I'm unclear on is how you ended up being a therapist. I assume that was you?"

"It was a misunderstanding," began Poppy.

"I don't need to hear this now." Elizabeth turned back to the door.

"What about you?" Poppy asked, keeping her voice calm. "Are you okay?"

Elizabeth's shoulders shook but she still said "Yes" like she was completely fine.

Poppy jumped up and pulled her into a hug. "Oh, El, it can't be that bad."

"It is," sobbed Elizabeth. "It really is. It's all over. We were never meant for each other. I can see that he's right, I can see that he doesn't mean to hurt me. But that doesn't make it not hurt."

"I know," Poppy said. "I know."

"And now everything else is going to crumble. The house will need to be sold and I'll have to get a new job and everything will be different."

Poppy pulled back just slightly. "I thought you had a job?"

"They're going to fire me for not being gluten friendly enough and spilling drinks because of idiots taking things off my tray and being condescending and patronizing," wailed Elizabeth until Poppy pulled her back into a hug again.

So much for leaving. She should do the right thing and walk away from what was becoming a crush that she really couldn't handle. She should let Elizabeth live her life, good or bad, in peace, without adding complications to it. But how could she when Elizabeth was so upset, so unprepared to take care of herself?

Poppy held her tight, trying desperately to ignore the feelings that holding the woman gave her. If she really tried, she thought, she could bury these feelings, she could ignore them, she really could. She'd have to. Because she couldn't leave Elizabeth right now whether she wanted to or not.

"Come on," she said softly. "Let's get you to bed."

Elizabeth snuffled and nodded and Poppy led her across the landing to her bedroom. It took ten minutes of alternating crying, nose blowing, and kind but strict guidance from Poppy, for Elizabeth to get into her pajamas and crawl into bed.

"Shall I bring you something to eat?" Poppy asked, once Elizabeth was tucked in. "Or a nice cup of tea?"

Elizabeth shook her head, her eyes heavy with sleep. "I think I'll just go to sleep," she murmured. "I'm so tired."

Poppy smiled and turned off the bedside light, her heart aching at the sight of Elizabeth so crumpled and beaten. She was about to go when Elizabeth clutched at her hand. Poppy turned to see bright blue eyes wide open again.

"I almost kissed you," said Elizabeth.

Then her eyes closed and her hand let go and she was drifting into sleep and Poppy was wondering just what the hell she was supposed to do with that information.

CHAPTER TWENTY THREE

"And then she said that she tried to kiss me," Poppy finished up.

She was wiping down the counter at the coffee shop and Mel was on the other side, finishing up a brownie and picking crumbs off her plate with a wet finger.

"Is this a great idea?" Mel asked, cocking an eyebrow.

Poppy shrugged. "I know in my head that probably it's not. I mean, she's vulnerable, right? She's just split up with her husband, she probably doesn't really know what she wants. I just…"

"You just want it to be more than it is currently."

"Yes, right. But obviously I'm not going to push for that." She tossed the wet towel into the sink.

"Why not?" asked Mel, pushing her plate away.

"Um, for like a million reasons, not least what I just said. Plus, I don't know if you noticed, but up until last night she was straight."

Mel exhaled through her nose. "Sexuality is a spectrum, Pops, you know that."

"Yeah, but she's jumping from one end to the other without a stop in between."

"How do you know?" Mel folded her arms. "For all you know,

she dated solely women before she got married and this Eli character was her one exception."

Poppy arched an eyebrow. "Do you really think my gay-dar is that bad?"

"I really think your communication skills are that bad."

"Sore subject," Poppy said. She still hadn't completely forgiven Mel and Paul for the dating profile they'd written.

Mel pulled a face. "Sorry, I got carried away."

"You think? You almost ruined the entire plan."

"I should hope so. Revenge is a childish and immature game and you should know better," scolded Mel. "And agreeing to help Elizabeth in this ridiculous plan was your first big mistake."

"First?" Poppy asked, dreading to think what the others were.

"Well, your second was apparently falling for her." Mel sighed. "You're handling this all wrong, Pops. You're second guessing and putting thoughts and desires into her head that might not even be there."

"She literally said she almost kissed me," protested Poppy, shutting off the coffee machine.

"And you did what? Run away?"

"She fell asleep!"

Mel put on her 'incredibly patient because I might actually be talking to an idiot' voice. "You. Need. To. Communicate."

"I. Am. Communicating," Poppy responded.

"By pretending to be a cat?" smirked Mel. "Listen, you're not getting what I'm talking about. What I mean is that you're assuming Elizabeth feels a certain way, has certain experiences, and that's not fair. There's no way in hell you can know whether she's really interested in you or not unless you ask."

"But is it really fair to ask?" Poppy said, leaning on the now clean counter. "I mean, I could just screw all this up and then she won't have anyone to lean on and—"

"And you're over-thinking things because you don't want to actually ask for what you want, Poppy Robbins," Mel said sternly.

Poppy sighed. "It's not that. It's that I'm afraid." She bit her lip. "I don't want to let her go. I've got a feeling that there's a lot more here and I want that, I want more of her. Heaven knows she's irritating and stern and controlling and all the rest. But that's just a façade, a shell, underneath she's soft and lovely, I can just tell."

"Like you could tell with Evelyn?" asked Mel.

"Evelyn *was* lovely."

"Evelyn made you move half-way across the world and then took a job in Los Angeles," Mel said.

"But she was lovely and felt terribly bad about it."

Mel shook her head. "You're being a fool, Poppy. I don't know what you've gotten yourself into here, but I do know that there's only one way out of it, and that's to speak your truth and let Elizabeth speak hers. Any other way just isn't going to work. You can sit around waiting for the best to happen until the cows come home, but sometimes you just have to act."

Poppy wrinkled her nose and then gasped. "Act. Shit. I almost forgot." She looked at the time. "I'm going to be horribly late," she groaned.

Mel sighed and jangled her car keys. "That's why I'm here, remember? I'm supposed to be taking you to rehearsal. You just got all caught up in dreamy imaginings and forgot that you've got a little extra time."

"Right," said Poppy. "Time that'll be gone if we don't get our skates on."

"Or what?" asked Mel. "You'll be late for making the tea? Honestly, Pops, you do let people take advantage of you." She got down off her stool. "Speaking of which, what about Elizabeth's part in this silly bargain you made? When is she supposed to be poisoning Jeremy or whatever it is?"

"Not poison," Poppy said, pulling on her coat. "And I'm sure she's got it all in hand. She always does. She's very efficient."

"Can't say that that would be a bad influence on you," Mel said as she held the shop door open for Poppy to leave. "Efficiency and cold, clear logic could have a good effect on you."

"You love me just the way I am," grinned Poppy, scooting past her.

Mel laughed. "You're right, I do."

THE CHURCH HALL was chilly and Poppy switched the central heating on next to the kitchen as the rest of the members trooped in out of the sleet.

"Best get the kettle on early, Poppy," Tanya said as she swept past the serving hatch. "It's a cold one today."

By the time Poppy had filled the kettles and filled the tea urn, warm ups were over and it was obvious that there was a problem.

"We can't do it without her," Peter was saying as he stomped around the stage.

Midge had taken up her knitting and was calmly sitting in a corner of the stage as the other cast members milled around and Tanya chatted worriedly on the phone. Poppy's interest was perked.

"What's going on?" she hissed to Mr. Naipaul who was standing off to one side.

"That young one didn't turn up," he said back. "Always a mistake trusting the young ones like that. They're like as not to flit off somewhere else doing some dancing or raving or whatever they call it, if you ask me."

Poppy was about to tell him that raving was a kind of dancing, but one that hadn't been done for at least a couple of decades in seriousness, when Tanya clapped her hands to get everyone's attention.

"Darlings, I'm afraid Cheryl won't be joining us this evening." Her kaftan wafted as she turned and then spotted Poppy. "Poppy, you can fill in Cheryl's lines, can't you? God knows you practiced with her often enough."

"Of course," Poppy said, her stomach jumping with excitement. She didn't even need the script.

"At least you won't have a problem with the accent, being an American yourself," Tanya said.

"Um, I'm Canadian?"

"Oh, are you dear? That's nice." Tanya clapped her hands together again. "Very well then, chip chop, let's get on with things. We don't have all night now. Poppy, get up here on stage. Don't worry about blocking, just read through the part. Do you have a script? Somebody get Poppy a script."

"I don't need one," Poppy said, vaulting up onto the stage and grinning at Midge who was still clicking her knitting needles.

"Of course you do, don't be ridiculous," said Tanya, thrusting a script into her hands. "And Midge, will you put that damn knitting down for a moment. Come on, come on, we've got theater to make."

POPPY WAS TIRED but happy when she finally put her coat back on. She'd done Cheryl's lines perfectly, without the script just as she'd said. She'd moved when and where necessary, and frankly, thought she'd done an excellent job.

It had been fun. The kind of fun that she'd joined the group for in the first place. Not that Tanya had said anything. When the rehearsal was over, Tanya had simply dismissed them and begun to wind an endless scarf around her neck.

"You know, you weren't half bad, Poppy," said Peter, putting his hat on. "Quite impressive in fact. Knock that young Cheryl down a peg or two anyway." He sniffed and eyed Poppy carefully, his mustache twitching. "You might want to think about auditioning. Hells bells, you might even just take the role from that youngster. Her accent is Albanian most of the time."

"Oh no," Poppy said, blushing. "The part's Cheryl's. I'm sure she'll be back by next rehearsal."

"I wouldn't bank on it," Midge said, moving her ear muffs to one side so she could hear better. "I heard she's going to need an operation." She winked at Poppy. "Learned to lip-read in school, always thought it was a useful skill. Let's me see what the shoplifters are planning in the back of the shop before they nick things."

Poppy laughed. "I'll keep that in mind and be careful."

"Tanya was definitely saying something on the phone about an operation," said Midge. "You should put your name in the ring. Tell her you'd like the part."

Poppy blushed even brighter red. "I don't think I need to do that. I'm sure Tanya will think of it. That's if Cheryl really is out for the rest of the season."

"Please yourself," Peter said. He held out his arm and Midge took it. "Fancy coming down to the pub for a quick one?"

Poppy looked at him then looked at Midge's face and the way Midge clung to his arm and grinned. Three would very obviously be a crowd right now, especially given the way Midge was glaring at her.

"No, thanks, it's been a long day. I'd better be getting home."

"Please yourself," Peter said again and led a grinning Midge off into the cold night.

Poppy sighed. She was exhausted, but in a good way. She was looking forward to an early night. Life had been too complicated recently. She needed some sleep and a little no-thinking time. Providing, of course, that Elizabeth wasn't around when she got in.

CHAPTER TWENTY FOUR

It wasn't as though she had anyone to talk to about all of this. Ordinarily, she would have talked to Eli. He wouldn't have listened, of course, but the act of putting things into words would have been enough to tell her what she needed and wanted.

There were the three As, but she'd muted the group chat after the disastrous lunch and she couldn't quite bring herself to turn it back on. What was she meant to say? She'd finally accepted that her marriage was over and, by the way, she was half-way to falling for her new female lodger? Hardly the sort of thing you mentioned casually over WhatsApp.

So in the end, she'd taken herself for a long walk on Hampstead Heath and watched the families playing and the old people talking on benches. She'd rescued a tennis ball and thrown it for an over-eager retriever, and wondered how she'd gone from having the kind of life where a retriever was a real possibility to the kind of life where she had a fake cat in the upstairs bedroom.

Eli had been honest and kind and more real than she thought she'd seen him be for a very long time. They'd talked honestly and openly and Elizabeth could see now that he was right. The idea of them together had been nice, the reality had been detrimental to them both. She wasn't entirely sure about his communism comparison, but she'd let it slide.

And it hadn't hurt as much as she'd thought it would.

This final ending, this final acceptance that all would not be well again, could not be well again, it felt less tragic, less painful than she'd expected. It was, she realized, because this was the end of a long process. She'd been hurting for a long time, mildly maybe, but still, and perhaps the accumulation of hurt added up to a lot. But this? This was just the end, the final unwrapping of a bandage, the final tearing off of the last plaster.

In a way, she supposed, it was a relief. She felt lighter though she hadn't realized just how much weight she'd been carrying.

Because what Eli had said was true. This wasn't just an ending, it was a beginning. And she could begin anything she liked.

The leaves crunched under her feet and the sky darkened and before long, sleet was streaking down through the air. Elizabeth shivered inside her jacket and put her hands deep in her pockets.

It was gone, over, all of it. The perfect life, the husband, the credit cards, the lunches, the perfect picture that made people envious, all of it was over. The house would go, in time. And yes, she hated that all that was gone.

She also felt a kind of relief that it was all gone.

There was no one to impress anymore. No need to paint her face or wear the latest fashion or listen genteelly while the others discussed schools and half-terms and all the rest.

Eli had broken her, she wasn't going to deny that. He'd shattered everything that she was, but that was a blessing, not a curse. Because something that was broken could be re-built. But this time, maybe she could build in a different way.

This time she could be something, someone else.

Which needed to begin immediately.

Gods, it was cold. She shivered again and turned back to where she thought she'd come from. She was going to make a new Elizabeth. And this one might not be better or richer or more perfect. But it would certainly be a happier one.

And happiness, for now, was going to start with Poppy. Whether she liked it or not.

HER PHONE RANG and she saw Jeremy's name on the display. She silenced the thing and slid it under a cushion on the couch. She didn't want to be interrupted.

She did need to talk to him. She wasn't about to back out on her part of the plan, particularly now that Poppy had enacted her part.

Not that Poppy had done as she was told, but, well, maybe for once Poppy had been right. It had all turned out for the best. She could understand now why Eli had gone, she could understand that he'd found some goodness in his life and she wanted only the same for herself.

She definitely could not talk to Jeremy right now though. She had everything she wanted to say all stored up in her mind and she couldn't run the risk of letting another conversation interfere with her prepared script for this evening.

She put one arm up on the back of the sofa, trying to look casual. But it felt strange, so she took it down again and tried crossing her legs. No, too formal. She cleared her throat and attempted to lounge.

It was harder than other people made it look.

Lounge too little and it just looked like she was sitting with a brick behind her. Too much and she was at great risk of sliding off the sofa altogether. She sighed, got up and went to the armchair instead. Better.

She looked around. She'd done well, she decided. The magazines weren't quite straight on the coffee table. The couch cushion had a slight dent in it. There were no snacks laid out and no drinks pre-prepared. No, everything was... relaxed, uncontrolled.

With a gasp she stood up, hunting in the couch cushions for the remote, finding it and clicking the stereo on.

Okay, most things were relaxed. But there had to be music,

right? They couldn't just fill the air with their voices. And maybe, if she was lucky, there might not be voices later, there might be actions, and a soundtrack would definitely be called for. And then—

Poppy's key scraped in the door.

Elizabeth's heart leaped up into her mouth.

She was going to do this. She was going to be happy. What other people think, be damned. She'd come so close to kissing Poppy and she was certain that for whatever reason she really wanted to do that again.

So she was going to explore, going to find a new life, a new thing to build herself into.

"What are you doing?" Poppy asked, coming into the living room.

"Just… relaxing," Elizabeth said, feeling her script leaking out of her head. She kicked one leg over the arm of the chair, trying to look a lot more relaxed than she felt. She slowly started to fall off her chair.

"Jesus," Poppy said, coming to the rescue and catching her arm. "Careful there."

Which was the exact moment that Elizabeth gave up.

Fuck it. Not a word that she said out loud and one that she rarely even thought. But now was the moment for it.

Fuck being polite and nice and perfect and everything else. Fuck all the plans and all the scripts and doubts. Fuck it all.

She stood up, Poppy's hand still on her arm, the warmth of it traveling along her limb and into her core.

She stood up, reached for Poppy's face, cupped her cheeks in her cold palms and pulled her in. She didn't hesitate even for a moment.

Poppy's lips were ripe and red and her cheeks were pink with cold and as Elizabeth ignited the kiss she could taste autumn and damp, cookies and coffee, and her heart went back to its usual place and started beating again and Elizabeth knew it wasn't just marking time for her. It was propelling her forward, pushing her into this new experience.

She closed her eyes, feeling Poppy's lips begin to part. She let her hands move down to Poppy's shoulders and let her tongue slowly, gently, tease Poppy's lips. And she let herself press her body against Poppy's, let herself just feel, just be.

Until Poppy pulled back.

"What are you doing?" she asked, hoarsely.

Elizabeth swallowed. "I'm sorry. I've been wanting to do that for a while, I think. I did, um, have a whole speech prepared but then, well, you touched my arm and the words kind of disappeared."

Poppy's mouth twitched with an almost-smile. "I'm not sure this is a good idea," she said.

"Why not?" asked Elizabeth. "I like you, Poppy Robbins. I'm not sure that I should. But hell, look what happened last time I did what I was supposed to do. I get that this is sudden, and I understand if you're not at all interested, but I need you to know that I am. Interested, that is."

"Why?"

Poppy took a step back and Elizabeth let go of her. "Why?" She thought for a second and then decided just to be honest. "Because you cook me breakfast and wrap me in a scarf when I'm cold. Because you let me cry and make me sing. Because, believe it or not, you're beautiful Poppy and I can't pretend that I know where these feelings come from, or that they don't scare me, but I know I have them and I'd really, very much, like to find out where they're going to lead."

She reached out again, pulling Poppy closer until her lips were tantalizingly near. "You keep doing that and the only place this is going to lead is the bedroom," Poppy said, obviously joking, but Elizabeth didn't laugh.

"So?"

"So?" echoed Poppy. "So, you're not even divorced yet and as far as I know you've never been with a woman before and this is all so sudden."

"I'm tired of doing things the way they're supposed to be done," Elizabeth said. She could see the soft down on Poppy's cheeks. She took a breath and pulled back a little. "Unless you're not interested, of course?"

"I didn't say that," said Poppy, voice hoarse again.

Elizabeth smirked. "Good girl."

Poppy shivered a little in her arms. "Elizabeth…"

"No, don't 'Elizabeth' me."

"El…"

Elizabeth shook her head. "If you don't want this, just say the word and that's fine. But I've wasted enough time, Poppy. I've spent enough time doing everything the way I was supposed to and just this once, just right now, I'd like to do something simply because I want to. Just for me. And for you."

Poppy bit her lip and Elizabeth almost kissed her again. "Okay," she said. "Okay. If you're sure this is what you want."

Elizabeth nodded and took Poppy's hand to lead her upstairs.

"Oh no," said Poppy. She was grinning now, a naughty smile that made Elizabeth's insides turn to liquid. "If there's one thing that you're not going to control, Elizabeth Mary Marks, it's this."

Elizabeth frowned. "How do you know my full name?"

"Read it on your mail," laughed Poppy. "And you're coming with me."

Elizabeth hesitated only for a second, then she let Poppy pull her toward the couch.

CHAPTER TWENTY FIVE

Half of her was afraid to even touch Elizabeth, afraid that she'd break or fall apart or change her mind. The other half wanted to jump her right now before she had a chance to come to her senses. Poppy held her breath and just looked for a second.

"What?" Elizabeth said.

"You," said Poppy honestly. "You're beautiful and..." And she ran out of words so she leaned in on tip-toes and kissed Elizabeth soundly instead.

Immediately, Elizabeth's hands were on her waist, pulling her in, and Poppy laughed. "Relax, slow down."

Obediently, Elizabeth removed her hands and Poppy realized she was going to have to be very careful about what she said because Elizabeth didn't know what she was doing and her perfectionist side would be crying out for more instruction.

"Okay, sit down," Poppy said.

Elizabeth sat on the very edge of the couch. Poppy perched next to her and put an arm around her, thumb stroking the soft skin at the back of her neck until Elizabeth turned and they were kissing again.

For a long time, this was enough. The careful exploration of each others' mouths, the wandering hands. Elizabeth's breathing was coming faster and Poppy was trembling. She could hardly keep control of herself.

"Lie back," she said hoarsely.

Elizabeth relaxed just a little and with careful fingers Poppy began to unbutton her blouse. This was all so… so unreal. She couldn't believe she was here, couldn't believe Elizabeth was real and she was doing this, she was just waiting for the bubble to burst.

At the same time, it was stilted and unsure and awkward and she didn't know what to do about that. First times were always a little off, but this… She swallowed as she reached out and stroked the curve of Elizabeth's waist. Slowly, slowly, she let her hand drift upward and Elizabeth's eyes closed just like they would in a movie. And Poppy stopped.

"What?" asked Elizabeth, opening one eye.

"Nothing," said Poppy. She flushed. "Just, um, well, this is a bit… A bit awkward? Maybe?" She couldn't believe she was saying that, couldn't believe she was about to ruin this opportunity.

Elizabeth sighed then nodded. "Yes, I suppose it is. Um…" She ruffled her hair, thinking, and Poppy's heart exploded.

Right then she knew what needed to happen. Elizabeth's non-perfect hair was sticking up and Poppy leaned in, kissing her long and hard and deliberately smearing her lipstick. And then she was standing up, kicking the coffee table to one side so that the magazines slid off and pulling Elizabeth to the floor.

"Poppy!"

"Go with it," Poppy said, lying down next to Elizabeth.

A light grew in Elizabeth's eyes, and before Poppy knew what was happening, Elizabeth was rolling over on top of her, pinning her down as she peppered hot kisses along Poppy's collarbone. Poppy squirmed as her core started to melt.

Elizabeth growled at Poppy's movement and Poppy was about to laugh until Elizabeth's hands clutched at her hips again, pushing their bodies together until Poppy was crushed against Elizabeth's thigh. The laugh turned into a gasp and Elizabeth grinned, an evil little smile that made Poppy moan.

"Let me," said Elizabeth, yanking Poppy's t-shirt over her head as Poppy wriggled to get out of her bra.

"Wait," said Poppy. But Elizabeth was already taking one breast into her mouth, suckling and teasing with her tongue until Poppy cried out.

She was breathing fast, her blood pumping through her veins, and she could see that Elizabeth wanted this, that Elizabeth was in control and something clicked in her head. It couldn't be like this. Not if this whole thing was going to work.

Poppy tensed herself and then in one movement rolled them both over on the rug until she was on top and Elizabeth was panting beneath her. It was her turn to grin now. "Go with the flow, El," she said.

"Don't call me that," said Elizabeth, but her voice was a cracked whisper as Poppy was pushing up her bra and circling one pink nipple with her tongue.

She was still grinning as she moved downward, kissing the central line of Elizabeth's torso, reaching the button of her sensible pants and then pausing only long enough to flick it open and pull down the zip.

"Off we come," she said, tugging at the pants.

"When you're still dressed?" grumbled Elizabeth.

Poppy arched an eyebrow then quickly stood, shucked her pants off, and knelt back down again. "Your turn, boss," she said.

Elizabeth swallowed and then slid her pants off, leaving only plain white, cotton underwear behind. Poppy's heart was in her mouth and it was all she could do not to lie right back down and demand that Elizabeth take her right there.

With trembling hands, Poppy toyed with the elastic on Elizabeth's underwear and steeled herself for what was to come. She knew what she was doing, she was good at this, she told herself. But this was Elizabeth and somehow that made it different.

"What?" Elizabeth asked again, her blue eyes wide and her cheeks pink with wanting.

Poppy smiled. "You're beautiful. It's intimidating."

Elizabeth rolled her eyes. "You'd better be damn sure I'll intimidate you if you don't—"

She didn't have a chance to say more as Poppy maneuvered between Elizabeth's long, slim legs and slithered down so her belly was on the floor.

"Oh," Elizabeth said as Poppy kissed the delicate skin inside her thigh. "Oh…" with more understanding as Poppy ran a finger under the elastic of her underwear. "Oh," she was starting to panic as Poppy pulled her underwear to one side.

Poppy propped herself up on an elbow. "Is this okay?" she asked, concerned.

Elizabeth blushed. "It's just that, well, I haven't, uh…"

"You've never done this before?" asked Poppy, surprised.

"Once," admitted Elizabeth. "It didn't, um, it didn't work though."

Poppy laughed. "Give me a chance," she said.

And before Elizabeth could say more she was tugging the white underwear aside and inhaling the scent of her, bending her head down to put soft kisses on the wiry hair there, and then carefully, slowly, tenderly using her tongue to open Elizabeth up.

"Oh," Elizabeth said again. And then: "Oooohhh."

Poppy snorted with laughter and let her tongue drift upward, circling around Elizabeth's center as Elizabeth's thighs started to clench around her ears and her body started to shake.

Poppy couldn't help herself. Her hand drifted down between her legs even as she was still tasting Elizabeth, even as Elizabeth's hips were straining up to meet her tongue, as Elizabeth was crying out partially in surprise, partially in desire.

The bitter-sweet taste of her was still on Poppy's lips as Elizabeth began to shake and then slowly, slowly to still and then to completely and totally relax.

Poppy waited as long as she could, waited until Elizabeth was breathing steadily until she snaked up beside her.

"Are you… are you touching yourself?" Elizabeth said, her voice cracking as she even asked the question.

Poppy whimpered.

"Naughty girl," whispered Elizabeth.

And Poppy took her hand, guiding it down to her wetness, letting Elizabeth's long, deft fingers take over the work so that she could close her eyes and get lost in the colors and sensations and scents of the moment.

"I THINK YOU should move out."

Poppy's head shot up. "What?" Whatever she'd been expecting Elizabeth to say, it certainly wasn't that.

Elizabeth cleared her throat. "Hear me out, please."

"Okay," said Poppy, slowly, propping her head up on one hand. "But this isn't a promising start."

"That's the whole thing. It kind of is," said Elizabeth. "There's only two ways this can go. Either this was a one night stand, in which case I enjoyed myself very much, thank you, but obviously you can no longer live here."

"Or?" Poppy asked, heart rate slowing a little as she realized she wasn't necessarily being thrown out.

"Or this is the beginning of something nice, special, in which case, living together immediately probably isn't the best way of nurturing whatever this might be."

"I see," said Poppy. And actually, she did see. The pressure of being constantly together wasn't great for a new... a new relationshipy-thing-whatever-this-was.

Elizabeth took a breath. "The house is going to be put up for sale anyway," she said. "Eli booked an estate agent to come around this weekend. So we'll both be moving. I don't think that's a bad thing. It's a new start."

"Okay," said Poppy, coming around to the idea.

"Do you have somewhere to go? I could help you find a place," Elizabeth said, looking both embarrassed and worried.

"You have to find yourself a place," pointed out Poppy.

"Ah, yes."

Poppy shook her head and laughed. "This isn't the greatest

after-sex conversation I've ever had. But I see your point. We'll both need to move anyway, so, yes, I agree."

"I'm not saying you should go tonight," protested Elizabeth.

"Oh good," said Poppy, her smile widening. "Because I wasn't quite done here."

"You weren't?"

Poppy shook her head as her hand started to slide down over Elizabeth's stomach. "Not quite. You've had your sensible moment, and I agree, your logic is sound. I'll find somebody's couch to sleep on while we get everything figured out. But right now, I need your sensible side to take a hike. I need more of wild, out of control Elizabeth, please."

"That's a shame," Elizabeth said, starting to wriggle down the side of Poppy's body. "Because my sensible side was rather anxious to learn whatever it was you did with your tongue to me."

"Oh," said Poppy. Then: "Oooohhh," as Elizabeth slid between her legs, long dark hair hanging down and tickling her thighs. "Well, I never turn down the opportunity to educate."

"Sure?" asked Elizabeth, eyes wide with innocence. "Because I could definitely get that sensible part to, um, what was it? Take a hike?"

"Oh no," Poppy said, closing her eyes as Elizabeth's head bowed down lower. "Let's keep Miss Sensible around for a few minutes longer, shall we?"

CHAPTER TWENTY SIX

Elizabeth stretched and yawned, feeling each aching muscle as she wriggled in the empty bed.

It took a second to identify the weird feelings she had. A whole minute, in fact. Then the sun broke through the curtains and she realized that she was… happy. Actually happy.

Okay, so this wasn't the life she'd ever imagined for herself. But now, in the warmth and light of the morning, it was a life that she could imagine for herself.

Her and Poppy. A little cottage somewhere maybe. Perhaps they'd actually get that cat.

She laughed at herself, laughed at the idea of one night leading to thoughts like these. Except they were thoughts that she was actually having.

It was like Eli had given her permission to be different, to be new, and suddenly she was realizing that she quite liked that idea.

What she didn't want was for Poppy to be there to see the end of the old Elizabeth. She probably shouldn't have blurted out that news immediately. Telling Poppy she needed to move out could have been handled more delicately.

She'd told the truth about it being a good decision, she was sure of that. Jumping into something, if this was going to be something, when they were already living together did not seem like a wise move. She worried that she was being too controlling pushing Poppy out like this.

On the other hand, she didn't want Poppy to be a witness to the end of the old Elizabeth. Which made no sense, other than to say that Elizabeth had always been an intensely private person. And the kind of person that hated being wrong. And that packing up the house, packing away the dreams she'd once had, was something that she wanted to do alone.

She pushed the thought from her head. She was happy. Happy that something so unexpected and beautiful had come into her life. Happy that she had given up control, had let these feelings lead somewhere. She didn't know where else they were going to lead, but she was willing to take a chance and find out.

Even if that meant giving up complete control, giving up the picture perfect life she'd thought she'd wanted.

Her phone beeped on the nightstand and out of habit she picked it up.

Jeremy.

She grinned.

Alright, this was definitely part of the new life. Ordinarily, she'd never make a phone call in bed unless she was deathly ill. But things were different now.

She let the phone ring and then it was picked up and Jeremy's slimy voice came over the line. "Hi, Elizabeth. So glad to hear from you, you know I was beginning to think that you were avoiding my calls." He laughed as though he knew that couldn't possibly be true.

Elizabeth reminded herself that she was supposed to be a busy entrepreneur. "Let's meet," she barked down the phone.

"Oh, oh, yes, of course," spluttered Jeremy. "Lunch okay? Or I could make a dinner reservation tonight?"

She bit back a laugh. He was definitely eager. She was enjoying herself, maybe Poppy had a point with this whole acting business. Maybe her new life would include taking a few classes too. "No time today," she said. "Tuesday works. At two."

"Right," Jeremy said. "I'll make a res—"

"There's a restaurant on the corner of your street, Italian, I'm sure you know it. I'll be there at two. Don't be late." Elizabeth hung up the phone before she started to giggle.

Gosh, this really was fun. Jeremy patently didn't like to be ordered around by a woman, which meant she was going to thoroughly enjoy herself.

Only then did she see the time. After ten. She couldn't remember the last time she'd stayed in bed so long. She rolled over, smelled Poppy's scent on the pillow and closed her eyes thinking about the night before.

Thinking about the way Poppy's fingers had touched her, the way her skin had felt and her hair had smelled and every single detail that she could conjure up. Until she felt warm and wet and without even thinking her hand snuck down between her legs.

Halfway there, she stopped herself. Honestly. What was she doing? She was a married woman and— Except she wasn't really married anymore, was she? And she wanted this. And she was building a new life. And this, along with a million other things, could be a part of it.

She sighed as her hand moved lower and she remembered the things Poppy could do with her tongue and shivered in delight.

ROAST CHICKEN WAS hardly the most challenging of dishes. But after lazing in bed all morning, she'd decided to brave the supermarket and had found the experience quite liberating. She hadn't realized just how many choices she'd have, and after careful consideration she'd ended up spending far more time than she'd intended.

Which meant dinner would have to be something fast if she was going to have it ready by the time Poppy got home. No, not home. This wasn't home. Not for Poppy and not for her anymore. There was going to be a new home. New homes even.

The thought stung a lot less than it would have done a week ago. The thought of Poppy's blonde head bent over a book by the fire, or her curvy figure outlined by the sink doing the washing up, was enough to make any place seem like Elizabeth would want to live there.

Her phone rang as she was basting the chicken and she picked it up with one hand and slammed the Aga door shut with her hip.

Amanda.

Again.

Her heart thudded in her chest and she put the phone down, not answering the call and not dismissing it either.

Okay, there were parts of this plan that she hadn't thought through. Building a whole new life, becoming someone else, was one thing. But what about all those remnants of her old life, her old self?

She'd supposed that at some point the three As would give up and realize that she was no longer part of their world. Not that she ever had been, not really.

Oh, at the beginning, things had been fine. When they were all young wives, before the children had come along, when they'd all been on the same boards and attended the same fundraisers. They'd all gone to the same kind of minor public boarding school, come from the same background, and that had held them together.

But over time, things had become different. The others had had children, and Elizabeth had become more and more of the outsider. She couldn't think of much that would make her more of an outsider than this though.

It was bad enough that her husband had left her. Throw in a lesbian lover and Elizabeth found herself chuckling a little at the thought of Amanda's horrified face.

The front door opened and she could feel a rush of cold air before it closed again. "That smells amazing," Poppy shouted from the hall.

Elizabeth could hear her taking off her shoes and putting them on the shoe rack. That damned shoe rack. Her new place, she decided, wouldn't have a shoe rack at all. It would have a messy pile of shoes by the door that you had to fish through to find a pair.

"It's just chicken," she said as Poppy came through into the kitchen.

Poppy's smile almost split her face in half and in that one second Elizabeth's heart stopped and the world was perfect. Poppy moved in and brushed a kiss on her cheek and Elizabeth's heart started again, but far faster than it had been beating before.

"Good day?" Elizabeth asked, voice none too steady.

Poppy nodded. "And before anything else, I want you to know that I've found a place to stay. Midge from am-dram has a spare room at her place and she's happy for me to stay there in return for helping her close down the shop every evening. She's had problems with vandals and she can't handle those big metal shutters by herself, so it works out for the best for everyone."

Elizabeth took a breath. "You, uh… I don't want to force you to leave," she said, realizing that she'd been worried about this all day.

"Yes, you do, I'll move my stuff out tomorrow and then come back and cook you dinner as a thank you for letting me stay in the first place," Poppy said firmly.

"No, I'm not controlling you, I just—"

"You just don't want me around while you close down an old chapter of your life," said Poppy. "I get that. You've got personal things to work through, and that's good, healthy. And you're right about it not being a great idea for us to live together like this."

Elizabeth breathed out a sigh and relaxed, smiling. Poppy really did get it. Poppy always got it. Which was part of what made her so appealing.

Poppy moved her hands until they were around Elizabeth's waist and Elizabeth could feel herself start to respond. Which was the other part of what made Poppy so appealing. Unable to help herself, she lowered her head, kissing first Poppy's hair and then her upturned face, her forehead, brushing her lips against

Poppy's.

With sudden urgency she wanted Poppy. Here and now. On the floor again if necessary.

Poppy pulled back. "How long until that chicken's done?" she asked.

Elizabeth darted a glance at the clock. "About half an hour."

Poppy came back until her lips were tickling at Elizabeth's neck. "Oh, that's plenty of time," she murmured as goosebumps snaked across Elizabeth's skin. "More than enough time."

"If my chicken burns, I'll…" Elizabeth began, trying to retain some semblance of control but losing once Poppy began to nibble at her neck.

"You'll what?" asked Poppy. She pulled away far enough that Elizabeth could see a glint in her dark eyes. "Spank me?"

A little thrill went through Elizabeth, one that she couldn't identify but knew that she liked. "That could be arranged," she said, almost afraid of herself for saying it.

"One thing at a time," said Poppy, going back to her nibbling. "Unless you'd rather sit around and wait for that chicken to cook?"

CHAPTER TWENTY SEVEN

Mel picked up the dish towel and shook her head. "You know, it's really difficult to persuade you that you can't just sit around hoping that things will turn out for the best when you literally sit around hoping and things do turn out for the best."

Poppy grinned. "I'm thinking about writing a self-help book, or maybe starting a cult. You can bash it as much as you want, but you can't deny that things *have* turned out for the best."

"I'll reserve judgment on that one," Mel said. "Given that I haven't met the woman in question yet." She sighed and shook her head again. "I can't believe that even her throwing you out has turned out for the best."

"You should try it," Poppy said. "It's a whole lot less stressful than you're whole 'you have to act to attain your goals' speech." She grinned again. "And a lot more relaxing as well."

Mel grunted. "We'll see," she said. "I'll meet this Elizabeth first and then I'll decide."

"Soon," Poppy said. "Promise." She looked at the clock on the wall. "I'd better be going if I'm going to get this all done before El comes home."

"You know the problem with making your best friend take over your shift?" Mel asked.

"What's that? And don't think that I'm not eternally grateful, I truly am."

"You don't have anyone to help you move," said Mel. She pulled a note out of her pocket. "Here."

"Um, I think I'm supposed to be paying you for being here, not the other way around."

"Take it," Mel said. "It's for a cab. It's the least I can do. It'll take you half the time to taxi your stuff around rather than taking it on the Tube. Go on, off with you."

Poppy pocketed the money and wondered just what she'd done to deserve someone like Mel in her life. "Ta," she said.

"Oh, don't forget this." Mel handed over a large thermos. "Paul said he doesn't need it, but you know him. You can drop it off on your way home."

"Cheers," Poppy said.

She bounced out of the coffee shop. The sun was shining, though it was still bitterly cold, the air was as fresh as it could get in the city, and her heart was light.

She couldn't believe her luck, couldn't really believe that all this was working out, despite what she said about things always happening for the best. The last two nights with Elizabeth had been… incredible. Not in a 'mind-blowing, leg-shaking sex' kind of way, though they'd definitely begun to improve. But more in a 'starting to make a real connection and build something' kind of a way, that a week ago she wouldn't have expected.

And if she needed to spend a few weeks in Midge's spare room in order to help foster a healthy relationship and help Elizabeth start to move on from her old life, then she was happy to do so. It seemed like a small price to pay.

PACKING TOOK HER all of about fifteen minutes. Shoving stuff into trash bags and her duffel, making sure she hadn't forgotten anything. Cleaning up took a lot longer.

Clean and tidy was important to Elizabeth, she got that. Having things just so, the carpet vacuumed properly, the pictures straight on the wall, was something that mattered to Elizabeth. Therefore, they were now things that mattered to Poppy.

She wiped sweat from her brow as she curled up the wire to the vacuum. The spare room looked as perfect as it had when she moved in. Exactly as Elizabeth would like it. She grinned to herself and started to put away the cleaning stuff.

She didn't want to jinx things, but she couldn't help but think about how this would all work out. She rather saw the two of them living in a little village somewhere, maybe the kind of place that had lots of murders on the BBC but none in real life. A place where the am-dram pantomime was the high point of the year.

She quite fancied playing Cinderella or Peter Pan.

She whistled through her teeth as she made sure everything was spic and span, then checked and double checked before noticing the time.

"Gotta get my skates on," she said to herself. She still needed to do some shopping for her and Elizabeth's celebration dinner. She'd do that on her way back from Midge's, she decided.

She called for a taxi then began moving her bags out onto the front step. She was still whistling, still full of joy and new beginnings and excitement when the taxi came around the corner.

The driver honked his horn as he pulled up outside the house, then leaned out of the window.

"Poppy Robbins?"

"That's me," she said cheerily.

"Let me get some of those bags for you, love," he said, getting out. He loped down the garden path and picked up two big trash bags before Poppy could stop him, carrying them easily over his shoulders and then depositing them in the trunk of the cab.

He turned around to come back for more, Poppy was already struggling down the path with her duffel, when his face turned a shade of white that Poppy didn't think she'd seen before.

"Good grief," he said, pointing to the garden next door.

There was something in the way he said it that urged her into action. Poppy dropped what she was carrying and sprang over the low dividing wall to find a woman lying on the tiny lawn between tended flowerbeds. The bushes were so high, Poppy hadn't been able to see her from the house.

She looked down, recognizing the neighbor she'd met when she'd moved in, and tried very, very hard not to panic.

She took a deep breath and remembered June, June the clipboard lady. What had she said? "We don't want to see panic, but I would rather expect to see a little more activity around someone experiencing heart failure," that's what she'd said. And Poppy had wanted to laugh and Elizabeth had been so cross.

And she had to act.

Now.

She got down on her knees, clasping her hands together.

"I'll call an ambulance," said the cab driver, coming into the garden.

"My mobile's in my right coat pocket," said Poppy, feeling him reach in for it as she started to press on the woman's chest.

What was her name?

Audrey. That was it. Audrey something. She'd introduced herself and seemed quite lovely. Now she looked grey and white with cold and Poppy pushed down on her chest until she remembered that she was supposed to be making a real effort, she was supposed to press "firmly down by at least two inches," June had said.

"Five centimeters that is," Elizabeth had hissed back as they both leaned over the stupid CPR dummy and Poppy had been worried about how short her skirt was.

She pressed harder and as she did so she heard a choking sound then a spluttering then a coughing. She snatched her hands away quickly.

It occurred to her that she probably should have paid a little more attention in that Red Cross class. Because she'd only just remembered that the very first thing she was supposed to do was check for a pulse and breath sounds, neither of which she'd done.

"Audrey?" she asked.

"Where am I? What happened?" The elderly woman struggled to sit up. "Who are you?"

"I'm Poppy, from next door? Stay lying down a minute, it looks like you've had a fall maybe, or fainted."

"Did I?" Audrey lay back on the cold ground and Poppy pulled her coat off, folding it into a pillow.

"Ambulance is on its way, love," said the cab driver, coming back into the garden.

"Oh, don't leave me, will you Poppy?" Audrey said, reaching out and taking Poppy's hand.

Poppy looked at the cab driver, then down at Audrey. "No," she said. "No, of course I won't leave you."

"Gimme a minute, love," the driver said, disappearing again.

"Does anywhere hurt?" Poppy asked.

"No, dear," said Audrey. "I just feel a bit off color, that's all. I don't want any fuss."

"It's not a fuss," Poppy said with a smile. "The ambulance will be here soon and then the hospital will take a good look at you."

"But you'll be there, love, won't you?" asked Audrey again, looking small and frightened and fragile.

"Here you go," the driver said, coming back and handing Poppy her phone. "I used it to take a picture of my license and of the number plate of the cab, so you know where to find me and that I won't nick your stuff. You tell me where you're taking all these bags and I'll make sure they get delivered where they're supposed to be while you look after this lady here."

Poppy sighed with relief and rattled off Midge's address before reaching into her pocket for the money Mel had given her.

"No, no, don't you worry about that. One good turn deserves another," the cabbie said, refusing the money. "You just concentrate on the patient here. Don't you worry none about your stuff, I'm in charge of that now."

Poppy could hear the sirens of the ambulance as it turned into the street. "Thank you," she said.

But the driver was already on his way back to his cab. She held tight onto Audrey's hand as the ambulance drew closer.

* * *

It was dark when Elizabeth got home. Dark and cold and there was no smell of cooking. There was no sense of anything, like the house was in suspended animation. It took her a long minute to realize that the house was completely empty and Poppy's belongings were all gone.

CHAPTER TWENTY EIGHT

El felt her heart beating in her mouth, felt her stomach turning over and over and was sure she was going to be sick.

"No, be sensible," she told herself out loud. "There's a logical explanation for all this."

Maybe, she thought with a spike of panic, Poppy was sick, or injured somewhere. But then, why would her stuff be gone too? That made no sense.

Maybe there'd been some kind of emergency? But what kind of emergency? A coffee shortage? A sudden desperate need for actors on *Eastenders*? What could possibly have called Poppy away?

She swallowed, trying to calm herself, trying to figure out what was going on.

She knew how today was supposed to go. She'd been expecting to walk into a house filled with the smells of food, into Poppy's arms, into the beginning of something that they were building together, however unstable and rocky it was right now.

Instead there was nothing and nobody, and try as she might to justify why the place was empty, she really could only come up with one decent explanation.

Poppy had gone. She'd moved out just as she'd said, but she'd decided not to come back. Elizabeth considered punching the wall, she'd heard that was the thing to do when you were angry. But when she looked down at her puny fist she really didn't think she could accomplish anything, which made her even more upset.

Of course Poppy had gone. After all, she'd practically pushed her out, hadn't she? One evening together and she'd been so anxious to tell Poppy that she should move that she hadn't even said it nicely, it had just spilled out.

She'd tried to control the situation, tried to force things into being the way she thought they should be, and now look. She was alone. Again.

Maybe this was just the way it was supposed to be.

She couldn't blame Poppy, she supposed. Why would someone so bright, so bubbly and fun and kind, want to be with a woman more than a decade older than her? A woman who didn't know how to feel properly, who was inflexible and stiff and... and English.

She'd never thought of her nationality as an insult before.

Tears were rising in her throat and she gulped them down, trying desperately to maintain her control.

So Poppy had gone. So what? Was she really any worse off?

She was alone, her life fallen down around her ears, but was that so different to how she'd been yesterday or last week?

Eli had left, her marriage was over, her house would be sold. All those things that had seemed so... inconsequential yesterday, were suddenly overwhelming all over again. Poppy had lit up her future and now that light had gone out again and she was stumbling in the dark.

For just an instant she considered giving in.

What would it be like just to go to bed and go to sleep and worry about none of this ever again? Not that she wanted to die. She just wanted peace. Calm.

Her phone rang in her coat pocket and hurriedly she dug it out.

Then she stopped.

It was Poppy, of course it was. Because Poppy was too polite, too considerate and kind, just to walk out without a word.

Her hands were shaking.

The first time she'd seen Poppy all she'd seen was her hands.

Delicate fingers putting a cup of tea in front of her on a cracked linoleum table.

She'd been so busy concentrating on Eli's words, on his face, on trying to reel him back in, that she'd noticed nothing else about the waitress.

And it was those words now that made her hesitate.

She just couldn't do it again, not so soon. The sting of Eli's explanations, of his justifications, was still there, buried just below her skin, and she just couldn't let Poppy do the same, couldn't let her strip away that healing skin by giving her more explanations and justifications.

Elizabeth buried the phone back into her pocket.

Eli, she'd figured a long time ago, had only told the truth to make himself feel better. She'd known that the first time he'd come to her and told her about an affair, rather than letting her discover it by herself.

After that, he'd told her every time he'd strayed.

There'd been no reason for her to know, and it had hurt her beyond imagining. But Eli had told her anyway because he'd wanted to pass along the heaviness of his guilt, he'd wanted to free himself a little. So he'd given her some of the weight and asked her to carry it instead.

She wouldn't carry Poppy's weight for her. Not today. She wasn't strong enough, that was the simple truth.

Oh, not that she was going to collapse. Not that she was going to draw the curtains and not leave the house. Not that she was going to stop living her life and making dinner and watching the news and everything else.

But it was going to hurt the whole time all those things were happening and she'd be doing them in spite of her feelings.

She took a long, shuddering breath.

If she could hold herself together for the next minute, then she'd be able to do it for another minute after. Which would add up to an hour eventually, then an evening, then a night and a day and a week and one day, she promised herself, she'd be able to stop focusing on keeping herself together and smile naturally again.

That was all she had to do.

She took another shaky breath.

It was after six. Which meant dinner.

She took herself into the kitchen and opened the fridge, selecting a few things and putting them on the counter.

See? She could do this. She could pretend to be normal until she actually was normal. And if that meant doing everything alone for the rest of her life then fine. At least the carpets would be clean and she'd always remember to take her shoes off, there'd be no hair in the shower that wasn't hers, no dents in the cushions.

Her life could be as perfect as she wanted it to be without anyone else there to interfere.

Which was probably for the best really, she thought as she calmly chopped a tomato.

She laughed a little to herself, the taste of it bitter in her mouth.

Poppy was right. Everything does turn out for the best.

The knife in her hand slipped and for a moment she kept on chopping, until the pain pushed through the coldness of her hands and then she gasped, seeing the red of her blood mixing with the red of the tomato juice.

Different kinds of red though, her brain told her, before she grabbed a tea towel and wrapped it around her cut hand.

She held her breath, trying to make the pain go away, holding the towel tighter and tighter against her hand as tears pricked and she blinked them angrily away.

Then something miraculous happened.

The doorbell rang.

In the space of that millisecond her heart beat again, her shoulders straightened, her hand stopped hurting and she practically flew to the hall.

It had to be Poppy.

There'd been some kind of horrible mistake.

Of course she wouldn't just leave.

She'd probably been calling to say that she was running late and, like a fool, Elizabeth had ignored her. She'd let past insecurities dictate how she responded and that wasn't healthy.

She was already breathing out in relief, sorry already on her lips, as she opened up the front door and…

"Darling, we heard," Amanda said, bustling into the hall. "Do forgive us for showing up unannounced."

"But you mustn't think that we're not here for you," put in Arabella, following close behind Amanda.

"And we completely understand why you'd want to ignore us," Alexandra said, coming in last and closing the front door behind her. "But you really, honestly can't. We want to be here for you."

"But not in a horrible pitying kind of way," Arabella said.

"Not at all, we're here to support you," said Amanda. "So please don't turn us away."

"We did try to call," said Alexandra.

"Stop," Elizabeth said, trying to catch up with what was happening. How could the three of them know? She hadn't even told them about Poppy, let alone that she'd gone, there'd been no time, it was impossible that they knew.

"It's absolutely none of our business," Arabella said softly. "And it wasn't all gossip, I promise. It was just that Hugh ran into Eli at some conference or another and Eli let things slip and then Hugh told me, and, well, I had to tell Amanda and Alexandra, you understand, don't you?"

Suddenly, Elizabeth did understand. They were here about Eli, not about Poppy.

"And then you wouldn't answer any of our calls or messages, not even when Amanda experimented with emojis," Alexandra put in.

"Sometimes those things are just too small to make any sense of," said Amanda. "It wasn't my fault."

"You sent a banana and a peach," Alexandra said.

"I was encouraging healthy habits and eating," said Amanda.

"That's not what that means," said Alexandra. "Not in the slightest."

"How was I supposed to know?" Amanda asked.

Elizabeth took a breath. It was hard to breathe in the narrow hallway with all four of them standing there. But she didn't want to invite them in further, didn't want anyone there right now. She wanted to be alone in her new normal. She might as well get used to it.

"Oh gosh," Amanda said. "You've hurt yourself."

"Oh dear, you have been in the wars," said Arabella. "Come on, let's have a look at that in the light. Alex, find the first aid kit, will you? There's a poppet."

Then Elizabeth was being hurried into the living room and the decision about whether to invite them in or not was fully taken out of her hands.

CHAPTER TWENTY NINE

It was after ten and the Tube was mostly empty. Poppy sat in a rattling carriage staring at her phone and wondering just what exactly had gone wrong and when.

She was so entranced by the blank, dark screen that she almost missed her stop, getting up at the last minute and running out of the doors that were closing so fast that she caught her foot on the edge of the platform and tripped.

"Mind the gap," she muttered, as she rubbed at her sore knees and picked up the pieces of her phone.

Mouth dry, she fit the jigsaw puzzle back together, but no matter how many times she tried, the phone wouldn't turn on.

"Great," she said. "Exactly what I need right now."

A late commuter in his pinstripe suit walked around her, carefully avoiding her eyes. She sighed. She must look insane.

Groaning, she stood up, feeling the fall in her legs, dropping her useless phone into her pocket, and then slowly limping to the escalator. And of course it was out of order.

"It was working just this morning," she said to anyone that cared to hear, which was nobody at all.

She was so entrenched in this run of bad luck that she expected the pavement to be empty when she came out into the dark, cold night. But it wasn't. She forced herself to smile when she saw Paul.

"Still here at this time?"

"Best time of night," he said. "Drunk commuters are a lot more generous than sober ones, trust me."

"I'll bet."

"You alright, Pops?" he said, his anorak hood up around his ears and his hands in his armpits.

She considered saying yes, but only for a second. Then she shook her head.

Paul shuffled over and patted the stack of cardboard next to him. "Come on then, sit down and tell your Uncle Paul all about it."

"Because that doesn't sound creepy at all."

He laughed. "Well at least you're over age, I suppose. Come on. I won't bite, and the cardboard'll keep you nice and warm, you won't freeze your bum off."

She walked around to his side then squatted down to sit, finding that the cardboard was indeed quite warm.

"Go on then, what's the trouble?"

"My next door neighbor, well, my ex-neighbor, well I suppose, no, ex-neighbor…" She took a deep breath. "It's complicated."

"Ain't everything?"

"Alright, so I've been seeing this woman. I mean, I like this woman. We just started. I was living with her."

"Moving fast," said Paul.

"Yeah, that's kind of the thing. So I'm moving out."

"Things gone that wrong already?"

"No, not like that. Well, yes, I suppose." She sighed again and swallowed. "Alright, maybe you should let me tell this, otherwise it's going to take all night."

"Righty-o."

"So we decided it would be healthier not to live together and I was moving out. I was supposed to get my stuff, move it, then go back and make dinner for us both. Except I didn't."

"Why not?"

She growled at him.

"Right, sorry, carry on."

"While I was moving stuff the lady next door had an angina attack and passed out in her front garden. She wanted me to go with her to the hospital so I did, and don't worry, Audrey, that's the neighbor, is fine and she'll go home tomorrow, but it meant I didn't make dinner, and now Elizabeth is angry with me and not even answering my calls. Not that I could call again if I wanted to, since I've knackered my phone."

"Oh dear," said Paul. He sniffed. "Doesn't sound that bad though. I mean, you can make up tomorrow, can't you? Just drop by her place or whatever with a bunch of flowers, it'll all be alright."

Poppy shrugged. "I don't know," she said. "Elizabeth is… She's got a way of seeing things, a way she wants things to be. And when things don't fit into that… Well, she doesn't do well. Plus, you know, it would be hypocritical."

"Hypocritical how?" A man appeared from the station and Paul picked up his paper cup. "Spare any change, mate?" The man ignored him and walked on.

"Well, if I truly believe that everything happens for the best, then I have to believe that this all happened for the best too," she said, thinking as she spoke. "And maybe it did. Maybe this isn't the greatest relationship in the world and I should let things go. She's not even divorced yet. If Elizabeth wants to talk to me, she'll call me, I guess."

"'Cept your phone's knackered."

"Yeah." She sighed and rubbed at her eyes. "It's not the only one. I'm beat."

"You know, when I was a kid, I had this boat. Big wooden thing it was, only a model, but long as my arm. I loved it, I did. And one day, I took it to the park and sailed it in the pond and the bloody thing floated off. Went right out in the middle of the pond."

Poppy frowned. "Okay," she said, not really sure what the relevance was here.

"So I sat down right at the edge and waited. Waited long past the time that I shoulduv been home. Until my dad came looking for me." He sniffed. "When he saw me, he asked what I thought I was doing, so I told him, I was waiting for my boat to come back. And it was still bobbing there in the middle of the pond."

Poppy shivered a little.

"He called me every name under the sun, he did," Paul went on. "Told me what a plonker I was. There's no bloody tide in the pond, my boat wasn't going anywhere. So I asked him what I was supposed to do. And he handed me a stick and told me to get my arse into the water and go get it if I wanted it so bad."

"Ah," said Poppy. "And did you?"

He nodded. "I think of that a lot, you know. Sometimes you've got to get your arse in the water and get it if you really want it."

"Sound advice," Poppy said, still a little unsure of its relevance.

"Think on it," Paul said. "I suppose you came for the thermos, did you?"

"I can't fill it up again in the morning if I don't have it now," said Poppy. "Besides, I'm staying with a friend and it's only a few blocks walk to her place from here."

"Here you go then," he said, passing it over. "And thank you kindly."

"I'll bring it back in the morning," she said, getting up. "You're gonna be okay for the night?"

"Got a pitch already scoped out, thanks for asking."

She nodded. "I, um, don't like leaving you here," she admitted.

"Go home, Pops. I got my life to live. I don't need no one feeling pity for me, not even you, and I like you a lot."

"Okay, okay. I'll see you in the morning then."

She started to walk and he called after her: "Don't sweat the small stuff, Pops. Isn't that what the Yanks say?"

She turned back and smiled at him. "Yeah, but I'm not a Yank, I'm a Canuck, remember?"

"Sleep easy, Pops. Things'll look better in the morning."

Except she wondered if they really would.

Elizabeth not answering her call had worried her.

Surely Elizabeth had realized that something had happened to detain her, that she hadn't deliberately not shown up?

But what if she hadn't? What if Elizabeth really thought, even after everything, that Poppy was the kind of person that would just disappear?

That hardly boded well, did it?

Maybe she should go back to Elizabeth's now. Except it was late and she was tired and if Elizabeth really was angry and didn't want to talk to her, well, giving her space was the respectful thing to do.

She hurried a little, the cold biting into her nose, wanting to get back to Midge's, wanting warmth and to sit down somewhere and rest her aching feet.

And would it be so bad if Elizabeth didn't want her?

She sighed. It wasn't like she wasn't used to situations like this. Mel had been right about Evelyn. She had run away to America, which given that Poppy had moved only two weeks before from Canada, had been a blow.

So maybe she needed to stay true to herself. Maybe she needed to stick to her mantra. Things would turn out for the best, whatever that best would be.

She turned a corner into a brightly lit street.

Okay, so she'd get her phone fixed or get a cheap burner and put her SIM card in it in the morning, and if Elizabeth called her back then it was fate. And if she didn't, then it was for the best. Right?

That seemed the simplest way to solve the problem.

Except this problem was so tiny, so small. So Elizabeth hadn't answered a phone call. So what? It was more than that though. It was why Elizabeth hadn't answered. She was angry, she'd assumed the worst instead of the best, all of which meant that she really wasn't ready to start something new, and Poppy should step back.

She sighed and a cloud of steam came from her mouth into the night air. She'd really liked Elizabeth.

Sure, she'd live without her if she had to. But for a second there, she'd been sure that they'd really connected, as different as they were, as unsuitably matched as they were.

The first time she'd seen her sitting in the cafe, Eli opposite her, she'd thought what an attractive couple they were. Her second thought had been how they must have walked into the wrong place because they were both dressed in outfits that cost more than the trailer she'd grown up in.

She hadn't even dared to imagine that someone as fine, as grand, as beautiful as Elizabeth could ever be interested in her.

And yet... And yet things had gone so differently from anything she could have imagined.

She turned into Midge's street. She hoped the cab driver had been honest and left her stuff as he'd promised.

Trusting in fate. That's how it should be. So just why did she feel like life was just a tad darker without the thought of Elizabeth in it? Why did she suddenly feel like the kind of person who carried a black umbrella, instead of the one that wore yellow rainboots?

She blinked away tears as the sweet shop came into view.

Things would turn out for the best. She had to let Elizabeth make her own decisions, whatever they were. Even if that meant she never saw Elizabeth again.

CHAPTER THIRTY

Wine was open on the table and glasses were all on coasters and Elizabeth was rather feeling like she'd been invaded.

And she was starting to get cross.

How dare they?

How dare they just walk into her house like this and assume they were welcome?

But Arabella had taken over the bandaging of her hand whilst Amanda had found the wine and Alexandra had ordered food and it seemed as though the three As were settling in for the evening.

Unless she could persuade them to go.

"Do you want to talk about it?" Amanda asked. "You don't have to, obviously, if you don't want to. But we're here to listen."

Here to find out the gossip, most likely, thought Elizabeth. But perhaps a little dose of the truth might send them running. Perhaps if she told them just how imperfect her life was then they'd go, they'd realize that she wasn't their kind of person at all.

"Eli left me for another woman," she said.

"How beastly," said Alexandra immediately.

Okay, ramp it up a little bit. "Oh, he cheated all through our marriage, I certainly knew about it. It's just this time it's different, he's found love, apparently."

"Men," said Arabella, rolling her eyes.

Elizabeth frowned. "So, of course, the house will have to be sold, I'll need a job. Actually, I have a job, waitressing at a bistro, but I'll need something more permanent."

"Of course," Alexandra said. "That only makes sense."

So far, so not good. Nobody looked even slightly shocked, let alone like they'd run away and desert her. Fine. Time to lay it on a little thicker.

"And then there was Poppy," she said.

"Who's Poppy?" asked Arabella.

"Well, it's like this," Elizabeth said.

She leaned forward and picked up her glass of wine and started from the very beginning. She started with Eli's little speech in the coffee shop and step by step she went through everything that had happened, or nearly everything. She left out the personal bits, the bits with feelings, because surely those parts weren't important anymore. And she definitely left out the sex parts because, well, because.

"She sounds thrilling," Arabella said, as Elizabeth got to the end of her tale.

"What did she do with the karaoke thing?" asked Alexandra.

Elizabeth was confused. "Um, she had like a portable microphone? And then she did something with her phone and made videos come up on the TV."

"Ah, she cast the YouTube app to the TV," Alexandra said knowledgeably.

"That sounds awfully fun," Arabella said, playing with her phone. "They have those microphones on Amazon, you know."

"That does sound quite exciting, doesn't it?" Alexandra said, leaning over to look at Arabella's phone.

"More wine, dear?" asked Amanda, picking up the bottle.

Elizabeth held out her glass to be filled and felt the annoyance building up inside her. This wasn't working out at all as she'd planned. Not even close. Okay, time for the big guns then. She steeled herself.

"And then I started to fall in love with her," she said. "Poppy, that is," she added for good measure.

"They do make whole karaoke machines you can have in your house," said Arabella.

"That's nice, dear," said Amanda, putting the wine bottle down. Elizabeth wasn't sure whether she was responding to her revelation or to Arabella's discovery.

Anger bubbled up inside her. "So we fucked."

"I do think a whole machine would be cumbersome," Amanda said to Arabella. "The portable microphone sounds much more convenient."

"Agreed," said Alexandra. "What about this one?" She and Arabella poured over the phone again and Amanda turned back to Elizabeth.

"That's nice," she said again, smiling brightly. "She sounds quite lovely. And good for you too, by all accounts. Where is she now?"

Elizabeth could do nothing other than stare at Amanda with her mouth open as Amanda's face turned from politely interested to very confused. Then the penny dropped and she smiled again.

"Elizabeth Marks, was that an attempt to shock me with your worldliness and savoir faire? Because I'll have you know that despite outward appearances, I'm just as worldly as you are."

"Just as worldly?" Elizabeth managed.

Amanda shrugged. "I went to boarding school, I had my experimenting phase just like everyone else."

"Oh, me too," Arabella piped up.

"Well, now I feel quite left out," said Alexandra.

"And I'm beginning to get the feeling that you don't particularly want us here," Amanda continued.

"It's not that," Elizabeth said, flushing. "It's just…"

"Just what?"

Elizabeth sighed. "I just… I'm not a part of your world. I don't think I ever truly was, and now I'm definitely not. I don't understand why you're here or what interest you have in me." She practically glared at Amanda. "You know there'll be no more expensive lunches, no more donations to the museum or fundraisers for the library."

"And you think we're only here because you're the right sort of person, do you?" Amanda asked. "Because you're one of us and we run in the same circles, and maybe because we want to hear what happened from the horse's mouth so that we can gossip about you at the club?"

Both Arabella and Alexandra were looking at her now too.

Elizabeth swallowed. She couldn't bring herself to lie, but she couldn't tell the truth either. So she said nothing.

After a long, hard moment, Amanda looked down at her hands. "That is quite offensive," she said.

"Mmmhmm," said Arabella and Alexandra in agreement.

Elizabeth's heart beat hard in her chest. Then Amanda looked up again.

"But I suppose I can forgive you given your current circumstances. You're obviously heart-broken. Just for the record though, I, at least, am here because you are my friend, Elizabeth. I'm here because I care and because I'd like to help you in the same way that I know you'd help me if I needed it."

"Me too," said Alexandra.

"Me three," added Arabella.

"So you can be angry with us if you like, you can send us away if you need some time alone, but don't think that we won't be back. If you can't do lunch then we'll have Chinese take out instead. If you can't donate money to the museum then you can donate time. If you can't go to fundraisers then…"

"Then we'll sing karaoke at home," said Arabella waving her phone. "I just ordered two of those microphones, they'll come tomorrow."

And slowly, slowly, Elizabeth's already cracked heart began to break into tiny pieces. She blinked, hard, trying not to cry.

"Better out than in," Amanda said, kindly, producing a vast, white handkerchief, which made Elizabeth laugh, because of course Amanda carried a handkerchief.

"You're all more than I deserve," she said, blowing her nose noisily into the crisp white linen.

"Not at all," Arabella said stoutly. "You'd do the same for us."

And Elizabeth wondered if she really would. Poppy would, that was for certain. But would the old Elizabeth? Or would she have kept her distance, not wanting scandal to tarnish her own reputation, just as she'd expected the three As to do?

"Yes, I would," she said, because now she would. Because now she would be kinder, better, nicer. It would be part of her new life.

"That's settled then," said Amanda. "Shall we open another bottle of wine?"

"I'll get it," Arabella said, getting up.

"You're wrong about one thing though," said Elizabeth to Amanda. "I'm not at all heartbroken about Eli. It was for the best, I see that now. We weren't terribly well suited. And he's happy, I can't begrudge him that."

Amanda raised an eyebrow. "Oh, I wasn't talking about Eli, dear. You're probably better off without him. I was talking about Poppy."

"Poppy?"

"Oh yes, obviously you're hurting. You can see it when you talk about her. I don't pretend to know what happened, and you absolutely don't have to tell me. But it's clear that you felt strongly for her and now you're miserable."

"I am rather," Elizabeth said, feeling strange admitting something like that. She sniffed. "Um, she left. She took all her things and moved out, which I told her to do. I mean, it seemed healthier that way, and the house is being sold anyway. But she was supposed to come back, to make dinner tonight, and then she never showed up."

"Ah."

Elizabeth sighed. "I tried to control things again. Tried to make them the way I thought they should be. I mean, who starts a relationship with someone they're already living with? And of course it scared her off."

"Or perhaps it didn't," said Amanda.

"I think it did."

Amanda sighed. "You know what I love about George?"

Elizabeth thought of stocky George with his red nose and red suspenders and shook her head.

"He makes my life better. Not in any immense way usually. It's simply that every day with him in it is slightly nicer than any day without him in it." She picked up her wine glass. "And I often think that that's the most you can ask from anyone, isn't it?"

"Here's a new bottle," Arabella said, putting one on the coffee table. "You should phone her, you know. Poppy, that is."

Elizabeth and Amanda both looked at her.

"What? I don't have ears in my head? It's obvious that you're batty about her, so phone her, see what happened."

Made braver by the wine she'd drunk, but mostly by the three women lined up on the couch in front of her, Elizabeth pulled out her phone. Was she really going to do this? Amanda smiled at her encouragingly and without thinking, she pressed the button to make the call.

The phone rang. And rang. And rang. It would have rung into eternity if Alexandra had gently prized open her fingers and removed it, ending the call.

"Here," said Arabella, holding out Elizabeth's wine glass. "Have a drink."

And Elizabeth drank, if only to help wash down the tears that were threatening to explode out of her.

CHAPTER THIRTY ONE

Elizabeth's head hurt with a sharp pain that she couldn't remember feeling ever before. She blinked, trying to make the pain go away, but it didn't. So she was forced to wake up fully and look at her surroundings.

The coffee table was pushed off to one side. A collection of empty bottles stood next to it. On the sofa, Alexandra was snoring, actually snoring. Elizabeth swallowed, her mouth dry. She felt a lot like she'd been body surfing across the Sahara.

"Here we go, here we go," said a voice.

Elizabeth squinted to see Amanda coming from the kitchen carrying a tray. She looked fresh, unruffled, and unreasonably chirpy.

"Why?" was all Elizabeth could manage as Amanda held out a mug.

"Why what?"

Alexandra snorted, turned over, and began snoring again.

Elizabeth tried again. "Why do you look like you went to bed after *Songs of Praise* with your hot water bottle and a cup of cocoa?"

Amanda perched on the coffee table. "Oh, I don't do hangovers," she said. "Never have. Don't believe in them."

"How can you not believe in them?" Elizabeth sipped at the

tea. It was either going to make her throw up or make her feel better. It was a bit of a toss up which.

"I just choose not to," said Amanda cheerfully. "If you try hard enough anything's possible."

"Bullshit," mumbled Elizabeth into her cup so that Amanda couldn't hear her. "How much did we drink?"

"Oh, a fair amount, I'd say," said Amanda. "Enough to sink a battleship as my old pa would say."

Elizabeth grunted and Alexandra snorted again.

"Best leave her," said Amanda nodding at Alexandra. "She's a bear if you wake her up too early. Leave her until ten and she'll be a lamb. Arabella took a cab home late last night. Has to do the school run, poor thing. Their nanny quit again, did you know?"

Elizabeth winced preemptively before shaking her head, but found it hurt less than imagined.

"It's the aspirin," confided Amanda.

"What is?"

"The trick is, you make good, strong builder's tea, drop one of those dissolving aspirin and an Alka Seltzer into it, mix it up well, add two sugars and just a splash of milk. You'll be right as rain in no time."

And Elizabeth was starting to feel slightly better. Her memories of the night before were hazy though.

"Oh, don't worry," said Amanda, patting her knee. "You didn't do anything awful, though frankly, if I don't hear the name Poppy again it'll be too soon."

Elizabeth groaned. "Was I that bad?"

Amanda grinned. "Hopeless," she said. "Hopeless and very much in love or lust, it's hard to tell the difference at the beginning, I find. Though you were pretty determined to get hold of her last night and tell her that she needed to come back."

"Ah." Then she remembered that Poppy hadn't answered any of her calls. "Ah," she said again, more sadly.

Maybe this was for the best. She couldn't just order Poppy to come back, whether she wanted to or not. The more she tried to control the situation, the worse it was sure to turn out. The problem was, she wasn't quite sure what else she was supposed to do.

She'd driven Poppy away, that much was clear. She'd driven her away by immediately trying to change their relationship into what she thought it should be. Pushing for a reconciliation now would be a mistake, even if she could persuade Poppy to answer her phone.

Her eyes started to itch and tear up again. She sniffed. "Mascara," she explained to Amanda.

"Mmm. Sleeping in cosmetics isn't a wonderful idea," replied Amanda, just as the doorbell rang.

Alexandra snored and shifted again and Amanda stood up, but Elizabeth stopped her by leaping out of her armchair and practically bouncing down the hallway to the door. This time it had to be Poppy. How could it not be? Everyone else she knew was already in the house, hungover, or presumably, in Eli's case, buried in paperwork in his office.

So when she opened the door to find a slight, older woman, the disappointment was almost palpable.

"Yes?" she said, rather more sharply than she'd intended.

"I'm looking for Poppy?" the woman said.

Looking more closely, Elizabeth could see that the woman looked tired and a little gray. "She…" She was about to say 'she doesn't live here' but couldn't quite bring herself to do it. "She's not here."

"Oh," said the woman frowning. "I did want to thank her."

"For what?"

The woman looked up at her and Elizabeth thought she looked familiar. "You don't recognize me, do you?"

"I do!" Elizabeth lied.

The woman harrumphed and then patted at her hair. "Well, I suppose I'm not looking at my best. It's Audrey, Audrey Lynton, from next door?"

Elizabeth squinted in the bright sunlight and finally placed the face. "Ah," was all she said.

"Your Poppy saved me yesterday. Did CPR and everything,"

Audrey said. "Not that I needed it, but still, the thought was there. And then the little dear not only rode with me in the ambulance, but stayed and waited in Casualty with me until I was settled up in a room. You should be proud of her, you should."

'Your Poppy.' The phrase made Elizabeth's heart swell and then deflate again when she realized that Poppy was no longer hers. Not anymore. Then the rest of Audrey's words sank in. "Wait, yesterday?"

Audrey nodded. "Spent the whole evening with me, she did."

So Poppy hadn't run away, Poppy hadn't left her, Poppy had been busy and then… And then what had happened? Elizabeth spluttered some kind of platitude that had Audrey nodding and smiling and then walking back to her house. Then she closed the door, slowly turning around to see Amanda standing behind her.

"I heard everything," Amanda said. "Just leave it to us."

"Leave what?" asked Elizabeth.

"Everything," said Amanda, firmly.

Elizabeth opened her mouth to protest, but Amanda shook her head warningly.

"Do you want to give up control and stop being so bossy or not?"

Elizabeth swallowed and nodded, because she really did, she didn't want to risk ruining whatever she had with Poppy in the same way she'd ruined what she had with Eli.

"Then leave things to us," Amanda said. "Just go with the flow, isn't that what the Americans say?"

Which Elizabeth thought was probably easier said than done, but she nodded again anyway because she didn't think she had much choice in the matter.

✳ ✳ ✳

Poppy hurried through the cold evening air, her nose running and her cheeks burning until she burst through the doors to the church hall. She breathed out a sigh of relief. Only ten minutes late.

Given the day she'd had, that wasn't bad at all.

She'd woken up late in a strange bed and it had taken her a second to realize that she was at Midge's. Then the whole previous day had come back to her and she'd groaned and wanted to crawl back under the blankets.

But she had to work and she was already going to be late.

So she'd dragged herself up and out and to the coffee shop, where she'd seen Jeremy for all of three minutes before he'd skipped out to go and buy himself a new suit for some important meeting he had.

The rest of the day had been a blur of orders and customers and deliveries. She'd barely had time to pee, let alone get something to eat. And her broken phone still bumped guiltily in her pocket. She shed her jacket. She'd get a cheap burner on the way home, she promised herself.

Not that she'd changed her mind about waiting to see how things played out. But still, she needed to be reachable.

She pushed into the hall to find Tanya in full rant mode, stalking up and down on the stage, her head clutched in her hands.

"What's going on?" Poppy whispered, sliding into a seat next to Midge.

"Cheryl's got to have an operation," Midge whispered back.

"An operation!" cried Tanya from the stage. "And only three days until we're supposed to open. She couldn't even do me the courtesy of waiting. Just what am I supposed to do now?"

"You could hire a professional to fill the role," suggested someone from the front.

"It's nothing serious," Midge said to Poppy. "Just something with her knee. But it obviously needs to be done. And with the NHS the way it is at the moment, once you've got the date, you don't want to reschedule, do you?"

"I suppose not," Poppy said, heart starting to throb in her chest.

"I don't think even a professional could learn the role in that amount of time. Besides, we can't afford it," Tanya was wailing.

Poppy cleared her throat and shifted in her chair. Tanya scowled at her then brightened and Poppy's heart beat even harder.

"Of course, of course, I could play the role myself," Tanya beamed. But then her face fell again. "But how could I possibly direct and star? It's an impossible combination."

"Does it have to be a woman?" asked Mr. Naipaul from the wings.

Poppy closed her eyes. She was sitting two rows back. Surely Tanya would have to see her and realize at some point.

"Yes, it does, Mr. Naipaul. We're not putting on a panto. Not only that, but a woman with a convincing American accent." She whirled around and glared at Poppy. "Poppy!"

Her smile already growing, Poppy started to nod.

"Do you have any acting compatriots, my dear?" Tanya asked. "A friend from home perhaps, who has an excellent memory and could learn the part or at least take a jolly good stab at it?"

"No," Poppy said, slowly.

Tanya growled in frustration. "Then what use are you to me!" she cried, throwing her hands up.

And Poppy snapped. Something inside her just gave way in the face of Tanya's incredible stupidity and ignorance and blindness and she couldn't help herself, couldn't stop herself. She was tired and cranky and it had been a long day and… And she'd had enough.

"What use am I?" she said, standing up. "Me? The North American who knows the entire part backwards and forwards and who's been sitting here in front of you for the last hundred rehearsals and who looks perfect for the part? What use am I?"

Tanya's eyebrows shot up so far they disappeared into her hair. "Of course," she said. "Of course."

Poppy waited for her to say something else asinine, like Poppy reminded her of her neighbor's dalmatian who'd be perfect for the role. But she didn't. In fact, she didn't say anything. So Poppy cleared her throat.

"I'd like the part," she said, loudly and clearly.

Tanya grinned, smiling so hard that her face looked ready to break in half. "Yes, of course, Poppy dear. You'll be wonderful, perfect in fact."

Poppy couldn't breathe properly and had to sit down.

Midge patted her arm. "See?" she said. "Asking for what you want is no bad thing. The worst that can happen is she says no. And the best, well, you've seen that for yourself."

Poppy turned to her and opened her mouth, but no words would come out because she finally realized that she might have been wrong this whole time.

Maybe sometimes things didn't just happen for the best.

Maybe sometimes you had to *push* things to happen for the best.

CHAPTER THIRTY TWO

Her feet were killing her in shoes that were too high, but Elizabeth gave her reflection a nod of approval in the glass door of the restaurant before she went in. The shoes, the suit, the briefcase, she looked every bit the successful entrepreneur.

She'd debated whether or not she was going to do this. This whole new 'hands off' policy concerning Poppy was distressing and difficult enough. Putting her trust in Amanda to figure things out was hard and felt wrong.

On the other hand, she had no other ideas just at the moment.

But in the end, her sense of fair play had won out. She owed Poppy this. She owed Poppy more than this, to be honest. This was the smallest thing she could do and it was the right thing to do, of that she was convinced.

Besides, she thought, as the hostess showed her to a small table, it was fun. And God knows, she could use a little fun right now.

She had enough time to order a bottle of water and have it arrive before Jeremy showed up. Considering how avid he was to get his shop franchised, he hadn't bothered to show up on time, Elizabeth noted.

He approached with an outstretched hand that she ignored.

"Sit," she said, pouring him a glass of water without asking whether or not he wanted it.

This was something she could control. In fact, this was the perfect outlet for her controlling tendencies. Jeremy needed someone to take him in hand, and that was exactly what she intended to do. Whether she and Poppy ended up together or not, she could at least give her this.

"You've got a nice shop," she began, elbows on the table. "Great coffee, excellent service, solid food, a nice location."

"Exactly," began Jeremy. His face was pale and Elizabeth wondered how often he got outside. "The perfect franchise. I've already started putting together—"

"Let me finish."

He bowed his head like a naughty schoolboy.

"You've got a good little going concern." And as far as she could tell, that was true. He'd sent her the financial records of the company as well as his business plan, and whilst she wasn't a numbers kind of girl, Alexandra had looked at them and pronounced them satisfactory.

"Right," Jeremy said. "And—"

She glared at him and he closed his mouth. "What you don't have is a franchisable business."

He grinned and then the grin slowly melted off his face as he realized what she was saying.

"You're not unique enough. There's nothing separating you from any other high street coffee shop."

"But we're Canadian," he began, sweat beading on his forehead.

"So what? The problem here is you," she said, really starting to enjoy herself. She'd had a pang of pity a moment ago, but then she thought of him leaving Poppy to work every shift, giving her no time off, depending on her and firing all the other staff, and her heart hardened.

"Me?"

"You," she said. "You don't know what you've got. You have an amazing barista that you don't pay enough and that you depend on far too much. Once she realizes that you're taking advantage of her, what do you think is going to happen?"

She didn't give him a chance to answer.

"She'll leave, and then what? You barely know how to work your own business, because you're never there. If the owner can't be bothered to run his own business, can't drum up his own interest in his own product, then how do you expect to sell that business idea to someone else?"

"I…" he started to stutter.

"No, the answer is no. You need to focus on what you have, which could be a very profitable little business if you actually ran it, rather than spending all your time trying to con other people into giving you money."

"That's not…"

But she was already standing up, pushing her chair back. "Your business is solid. You, on the other hand, are not. I wouldn't hand you a check if the money belonged to my worst enemy. I suggest you think about paying your staff living wages, employing someone other than that poor lone girl, and concentrating on actually running your business."

With that, she turned and walked right out of the restaurant, not even bothering to pay for the water she'd ordered. Jeremy could do that, it was the least he could do.

She smiled to herself as she walked toward the Tube station. The plan might not work. But it might. Maybe Jeremy would go back to the shop and offer Poppy a raise. Maybe he'd treat her a little better now that his bubble had been burst. Perhaps.

She walked past a bundle of blankets and cardboard and was inside the station vestibule before she realized that what she'd seen was a person. She took a few more steps and then turned back. Fishing a two pound coin from her purse, she dropped it in the cup in front of the man.

This was the new, nicer Elizabeth. The one who considered others. The one who was kind. The one who maybe, perhaps, Poppy deserved.

THE FOR SALE sign took her breath away when she saw it.

Not that she hadn't known it was coming, of course she had. But still. It was real now. And standing in front of her beautiful house.

She gulped and let the curtain fall back to hide the sign.

"It's a big change," Arabella said. "But it's nothing you can't handle."

"Right," said Elizabeth. "Of course."

Amanda cleared her throat and sniffed. "I, um, had an idea? Only I'm not entirely sure how you'll take it. I mean no offense at all, I need you to understand that."

Elizabeth sighed. "I don't think I'm really in a position to be offended by any ideas at this point." She slumped down on the sofa. She spent two hours looking at houses and eventually flats online and had only now realized just how expensive London was.

Her job paid so little there was no way she could rely on her wages for rent. She'd have to dip into savings and then what?

"Well, George and I do have a nanny flat," Amanda said.

Elizabeth raised an eyebrow. "You do?"

"Of course," said Amanda. "The children are far too old for that sort of thing now. We don't need live-in help anymore. And George has been after me to rent the place out for a while now, thinks it would be good for me to have a project. Only..." She blushed.

"Only the idea of letting a stranger live in your house is disconcerting?" supplied Elizabeth dryly.

"I know, I know, you did it with Poppy, but I don't know, I was sort of uncomfortable with the idea." Then she grinned at Elizabeth. "And, of course, I wasn't in need of a lesbian lover at the time."

"And you are now?" Elizabeth said, sourly.

"My point is, you're not a stranger," said Amanda. "The flat's furnished but doesn't have to be, there is a connection through into the house, but we can just lock that door so no one bothers you. And we can discuss rent." She cleared her throat again. "It was only an idea though. Of course I understand if you're not interested."

Elizabeth took a breath, then another. She could do this. She could make a new life. And that was going to mean accepting help sometimes. "That would be lovely," she said, smiling. "I'd really appreciate it for at least a couple of months. Do you think we could make a short-term lease while I figure out what I'm doing?"

"Of course," Amanda beamed, seeming just as relieved as Elizabeth was starting to feel. "We'll discuss all the nuts and bolts of it and make sure everything's above board."

"And we can stop looking at depressing flats in Havering," said Arabella, pouting.

"You can always take the train to visit me," said Elizabeth.

"I'd have to. I'm not sure a cab driver would go that far," she said, sticking her tongue out at Elizabeth. "And besides, it'll be nicer to have you closer. Don't forget we're doing karaoke next weekend."

"How could I forget?" said Elizabeth, wondering what kind of monster she'd created and whether she could find an excuse good enough to get out of Arabella's little girls-only party.

The doorbell rang and Amanda jumped up. "That'll be Alexandra," she said, rushing off to answer it.

Elizabeth heard the door open and close and the rustle of conversation and then both women were coming back in.

"Did you get them?" Arabella asked immediately.

"Get what?" said Elizabeth.

"These," Alexandra said, holding up a white envelope.

"Well, it's not air tickets, the envelope's too small for that. Don't drugs come in envelopes?" Elizabeth said doubtfully.

Amanda rolled her eyes. "They come in small baggies. How do you not know these things?"

"How do you know these things?" countered Elizabeth.

"Not drugs," Alexandra said, opening up the envelope and

pulling out four tickets. "We're all going to the theater."

Elizabeth groaned. "Really? Please tell me this isn't your way of taking my mind off things. I can't stand another evening of dreary Chekov or Shakespeare done in the nude, or whatever is popular nowadays."

"Oh, we think you'll like this play," grinned Alexandra.

"Want to bet?" asked Elizabeth.

"Absolutely," Amanda said. "How much? A hundred pounds? Ten? A thousand? Name your price."

"Oh, put her out of her misery, you horrible, horrible women," Arabella said, coming around and perching on the arm of Elizabeth's chair. She put a hand on Elizabeth's shoulder and Elizabeth didn't shrug it off even though she still wasn't completely comfortable being touched by her friends.

"Fine," Alexandra sighed. "You're going to love this play—"

"—because it's Poppy's play," Amanda finished with a wide smile.

And Elizabeth could only close her eyes and wonder just what the three were planning for her to do.

CHAPTER THIRTY THREE

"It's not that I don't love you, Pops," Mel said as Poppy finished stacking the cups by the coffee machine.

"I know that."

"It's just that sometimes I think you're a bit dense."

"Nice," said Poppy, folding her arms.

Mel rolled her eyes. "Poppy, come on, it's right there. Right in front of you. You're obviously miserable without Elizabeth, you had something going on whatever happened, and frankly I'm still not entirely sure what that is—"

"Audrey has angina and—"

"And Elizabeth doesn't answer her phone. Though why you can't call her is beyond me."

"Because—"

"Because you're waiting for fate to intervene which is more than dense, Pops. That's just bullshit and you know it. And if you didn't know it then the universe just sent you a big flashing sign in the form of a very relevant lesson."

"It did?" Poppy asked, slightly confused.

"You wanted a part in the play. You asked for the part in the play. You got the part in the play."

"I didn't just ask, I demanded," Poppy said with a shiver. "I can't believe Tanya gave it to me after that outburst."

"Of course she did, because you deserve it. And because you vocalized your need and made her aware of the fact that you wanted the part. You walk around expecting everyone to read your mind all the time."

"That's not true," Poppy said.

"Fine, you walk around expecting the universe to provide all the time. And that sounds stupid to me. Which is why I think you're dense. All it would take is a phone call to Elizabeth. Or showing up at her front door. Or, I don't know, renting a billboard with her name on it or graffiti-ing your love on a bridge on her way to work, or anything."

Poppy leaned on the counter. "Anything?" she mused.

Mel was about to scold her further when the shop door opened.

"We're closed," Poppy said.

"Hopefully not to me," said Jeremy coming in. "I do still own the place, you know."

"Ah." Poppy blushed. Not just because she'd mistaken him for a customer, but mostly because she was in the middle of closing the place up three hours early.

"What's going on here then?" he asked, looking around the empty shop.

Poppy exhaled. "Well, it's um, it's kind of like this, I, uh…"

"She's got a part in a play and tonight's her first night and she needs some time off to get to the theater," Mel said, standing up. "And since you weren't here to ask, she made an executive decision. Got a problem with that?"

Poppy held her breath. She really didn't need Mel talking her out of a job right now. On the other hand, she did really need to leave early.

"No," Jeremy said, after a long silence. "No problem at all. In fact, take the day off tomorrow too, Pops. You deserve it. I'll keep the place open tonight and open up tomorrow."

"What, really?"

He shrugged. "Why not? It's my business, isn't it?"

"Yeah, it's just…" She didn't know how to finish that sentence without actually getting herself fired.

Jeremy sniffed and nodded. "Right, I'll just go get my apron on and then you can get out of here." He paused for just a second, then added: "Um, we can talk about that raise when you come in for your next shift." Then, not looking her in the eye, he scuttled off into the back.

Mel growled under her breath. "See? You're impossible, Pops."

"Me? What did that have to do with me?"

"Just when I'm starting to get through to you and persuading you that the universe doesn't just provide, that you can't just hope for the best, something like that happens. The universe does exactly what you've been telling me it will. It's very frustrating."

"No," Poppy said quietly, realizing what had happened. "No, that's not everything turning out for the best. That's Elizabeth fulfilling her part of our bargain. She's met with him, talked with him. And it worked."

She hadn't realized until just that second that she'd never really thought that Elizabeth was going to do what she said. She's assumed, just like with everyone else, that she, Poppy, would do her part and then there'd be excuses or justifications for why Elizabeth couldn't do hers.

She'd assumed that Elizabeth would take advantage of her, just like everyone else did.

"Sometimes," she said. "Sometimes you've got to get your arse in the water and get it if you really want it."

"What?" Mel said.

Poppy shook her head. "Nothing, just something Paul said once."

Mel sighed. "Poppy, you need to act. If you want something, you need to actually get it, ask for it, do it, grab it, whatever. You have to act."

And Poppy was nodding. Nodding and grinning and feeling lighter than she'd felt in days. "Yes, you're right. I do."

Mel looked confused for a second, then a little panicky. "No, you actually have to act, Pops. If you don't leave now you won't make it to the church hall on time."

And Poppy was still laughing as she pulled on her jacket and ran out the door.

"See you tonight, break a leg," Mel cried after her. But Poppy barely heard.

POPPY WAITED UNTIL everyone else was busy painting faces and pulling on costumes and making fun of each other before she pulled the packet out of her coat pocket.

She was ready, as ready as she'd ever be. Her make up was done and her lines were word perfect, but she wasn't worried about going on stage. No, the whirling in her stomach had nothing to do with stage fright and an awful lot more to do with the package she now held in her hands.

"God damn it," she swore as she tried to pull the plastic apart. She gripped the thing between her teeth and tried to tear it, but it was no good.

She looked around, seeing a pair of nail clippers on the desk next to her. They'd have to do. With careful cuts she slowly, slowly extracted the phone from its packaging. It took a solid five minutes before she could turn the thing on.

Five minutes during which half the rest of the cast had disappeared, ready to get warmed up.

Poppy took a deep breath, then another as the cheap phone booted up. She was rewarded with a welcome screen and then a list of her contacts popped up. Thank God the thing worked with her SIM card. She was scrolling down to Elizabeth's name when someone called out to her.

"Just a second," she shouted, still looking at the phone screen.

She was actually going to do this.

She hadn't decided whether to text or call. Both were actions, said her brain, reasonably. Yeah, but calling was the bigger action, right? Which meant she really should call. Call and say what though?

"Poppy!"

"Coming," she said, not moving.

Just tell the truth. Just say that she wanted to see her, wanted to touch her, wanted to love her. No, that was too much. Maybe start with apologizing for not being there. That could do it.

Her hand was hovering over the call icon when a shadow fell across the screen.

"You're not nervous, are you?"

Poppy looked up to see Tanya sitting herself down on the table in front of her, kaftan settling into folds around her voluminous body.

"Not really," she said, itching to get back to the phone.

"Good," said Tanya. "Because you really don't need to be. You're a very fine little actress indeed."

"Um, thank you?" If she was so fine then why hadn't Tanya offered her the part in the first place?

As if reading her mind, Tanya said: "I deliberately didn't give you the part, you know."

This got Poppy's full attention. She put the phone down in her lap. "Deliberately?" she said. That hurt, a stinging hurt that made her want to cry.

Tanya nodded. "Deliberately." She sighed. "Poppy, you've been a part of this group for a long time now. And I'm not doubting that you haven't been an integral part. You've supported us all, me in particular, through many a production. We certainly could have done without you, but the process would have been harder and more arduous without you behind us cheering us on."

"Oh," said Poppy, not sure where this was going and whether she was being insulted or complimented.

Tanya tapped her red-painted nails on the tabletop. "I could see that you wanted more, that you wanted to be up there on stage, and yet I couldn't put you up there."

"Why not?" Poppy asked, remembering now all the times she'd watched everyone else perform, heard the applause they all received.

Tanya looked at her with sharp brown eyes. "You didn't even

have the confidence to ask me for a part, Poppy. How could I trust that you had the confidence to reveal yourself on stage?"

"But, I..." She trailed off. Tanya had a point. "I did," she said.

"Yes, I see that now. But I didn't before. You snapping at me was what it took." Tanya reached out and put her hand on Poppy's knee. "And I'm glad you snapped, dear. Because this play wouldn't be happening without you." She sniffed. "And to tell you the truth, you're a much more convincing American than Cheryl ever was."

Poppy felt her shoulders dropping, her spine straightening, her confidence brimming. She smiled and Tanya patted her leg.

"For a Canadian, that is," said Tanya with a wink. She slid down off the table. "Come on then, the footlights are calling, it's warm up time, my girl."

Poppy took one last look at the phone on the table then nodded. The phone call could wait. She would act. But first she had to, well, act.

CHAPTER THIRTY FOUR

In a city of nine million people it shouldn't really happen, and yet it constantly did. The one morning you go without make up is the one morning you run into the beautiful girl from the bakery on the Tube. The day you're in a rush is the day you bump into your chatty neighbor on the other side of the city.

Although, Elizabeth supposed she shouldn't be too shocked, given that Eli did work close by. She still had to physically stop herself from bolting the second she saw his face on the street though.

"I'm a grown adult," she whispered to herself. "I can handle this maturely." She took a breath of freezing air. "I have places to be and can't stop to talk."

Which was just about when she noticed that Eli wasn't alone. She glanced behind her but it really was too late to run. Besides, she didn't know another way to get to the church hall and she was supposed to be meeting everyone there in a matter of minutes.

"Elizabeth!"

He called from half a block away and waved and Elizabeth felt blood rushing to her face and a wave of heat despite the freezing evening. She swallowed and forced herself to smile and continue walking.

"Eli," she said, when they finally met. "What a surprise."

"What are you doing around here?" he asked, bending to brush a kiss on her cheek.

Elizabeth, who hadn't known that they'd reached a stage where kisses were appropriate again, blushed even further. "Um, going to the theater," she said.

Eli looked around at the tall office buildings then nodded. "Some kind of avant garde thing, I suppose, being done in an empty office block?" he said. Then he grinned, wide and free. "Elizabeth, I'd like you to meet Sally, Sally, this is Elizabeth."

From out of his shadow stepped a short woman with bobbed blonde hair. She looked kind, was Elizabeth's first thought. Her cheeks were pink and her blue eyes were sparkling, and she wasn't too thin or too fat. She looked comfortable.

A mature, grown woman, Elizabeth reminded herself mentally before sticking out her hand and shaking Sally's. "It's lovely to meet you," she said.

"I've heard a lot about you," Sally grinned. "And I love your coat, it's beautiful. You must be freezing though."

Elizabeth was cold, but she neither agreed nor disagreed because they were interrupted by the ringing of Eli's phone.

"Just a second," he said, stepping away to take the call.

Which left Sally and Elizabeth face to face and Elizabeth had the sudden realization that this was her opportunity.

She had Sally all to herself, Eli was out of earshot. If she was going to have her revenge, what better time than now? Okay, she didn't have picture proof, but she had her words. All she needed to do was tell Sally, woman to woman, that Eli was a serial cheater, about all the women he'd had, about how untrustworthy he could be.

Revenge had been somewhat abstract before. But right now, she could taste it. It was right there in the air. Maybe she could take Sally for a drink somewhere, explain everything.

She looked down the street in the direction of the church hall.

"I think you and I should talk," she said.

Sally smiled politely. "Of course, that sounds like a wonderful idea. Why don't we swap numbers? It would be lovely if we could all navigate this awkwardness gracefully."

Eli was still on the phone, marching back and forth.

Poppy would be getting ready to go on stage.

Sally's blue eyes were wide and kind and full of something that could be sympathy or could be hope.

And Elizabeth couldn't do it.

Maybe Eli would be different this time. Maybe Sally already knew his past. Maybe they'd be happy together.

But there was one certainty: this was no longer Elizabeth's business. No longer her business and she had more important things to tend to.

She stood up straighter and felt lighter and brighter than she had for months. She watched Eli as he rolled his eyes at whoever was on the phone and smiled. She knew his every gesture. But he belonged to Sally now. Sally who seemed genuine and sweet and… and happy.

"That sounds perfect," she said to Sally. "Eli has my number. Just give me a call and we'll do lunch." She looked over to where her soon to be ex husband was now laughing into his phone. "And I do have to run, I'm so sorry, but I don't want to be late."

"Of course," Sally beamed. "Have a wonderful time."

And Elizabeth was flashing a wave at Eli and then walking away, leaving everything behind her, the old feelings of betrayal and sadness, the false perfection, the ideal marriage that was really just a sham.

She was walking and then jogging as she realized the time, hurrying until she could see the lights of the church hall vestibule.

"We didn't think you were going to make it," Arabella said as Elizabeth stepped into the warmth.

"I'm here, don't worry," said Elizabeth. She looked at the three of them, all grinning, all dressed up like they were going to the West End, not some tiny little buried church hall with a minuscule stage. And she felt a wave of love.

"Just in time as well," grumbled Amanda. "I don't want to be stuck sitting behind some woman with a large hat.”

“You *are* a woman with a large hat,” Alexandra said, eyeing the frilly affair perched on Amanda’s head.

“I’ll take it off,” protested Amanda.

Elizabeth shook her head and sighed at the sniping. “So, what’s the plan then?” she asked.

“What plan?” Arabella said.

“You know, the plan, here, me, Poppy, what’s the plan?”

“Why do we need a plan? There’s no plan, is there?” Arabella looked from Amanda to Alexandra then back at Elizabeth.

“Of course there is,” Amanda said, comfortingly. “The plan is that we go and watch the play and then afterwards, you go back stage and talk to Poppy. See? A plan. A simple, easy, mature plan.”

“Lacks a little pizzazz though,” said Alexandra.

Elizabeth couldn’t help but think that she might be right. “Aren’t we supposed to be, I don’t know, showering the hall with balloons, or coordinating some kind of song amongst the audience or something? You know, something with big effect?”

Amanda sighed. “Do you particularly want to do that?” she asked.

Elizabeth shook her head vehemently.

“Well then, why don’t we stick to doing things the realistic way?” Amanda asked. “Shall we take our seats?”

Elizabeth wasn’t exactly sure about the plan or lack of it. She’d given up trying to control things though. She was going to go along with what the three As told her to do. And she was here. Here and she was going to see Poppy.

Her stomach flipped over a little at the thought of it.

But what was she going to say to her? What words could convey what she wanted, what she needed to say?

Her stomach flipped over a lot at the thought of that.

“Don’t think about it,” Alexandra said, taking her arm as they went through into the hall. “Just pretend everything’s fine and worry about later later. Trust me.”

Elizabeth let herself be seated, Alexandra on one side, patting her knee to calm her down. Then she leaned in. “There is one thing that's been bothering me," she said.

"Mmm?" said Alexandra, distracted by the paper program that had been left on her seat.

"How did you do this?"

"What?"

"This," Elizabeth said, waving a hand at the hall, the audience, the stage.

"Ah," said Alexandra. "I knew that Poppy worked in a coffee shop, but there are thousands of those in the city, so that didn't help. But you did mention that Poppy was in a theater group. And whilst there are plenty of theater groups in London, I could narrow down the choices quite a bit by selecting only amateur troupes. After that it was quite simple. Do you have any idea how many Canadians named Poppy who act there are in London?"

"Not a clue," said Elizabeth.

"Probably just the one," Alexandra said with a grin. "My original plan was simply to track her down and find out why she wasn't answering her phone. But then it turned out that opening night was coming up, and that seemed just perfect, so here we are."

Elizabeth narrowed her eyes. "You don't happen to work for GCHQ, do you?"

Alexandra shot her a glance but said nothing.

Elizabeth's mouth dropped open. "You do travel an awful lot," she said.

Alexandra raised an eyebrow.

"But no, you can't possibly be a spy. I'd know."

"And I couldn't tell you even if I were," whispered Alexandra as the lights dimmed. "Because then I'd have to kill you and neither of us wants that, do we?"

"Hush," hissed Amanda from Elizabeth's other side.

"Is Alexandra a spy?" Elizabeth whispered to her.

"Of course not," Amanda said.

"Wait, Alexandra's a spy?" asked Arabella leaning over Amanda's lap to better hear the conversation.

"For God's sake, will the three of you be quiet. It's starting,"

Amanda said rather too loudly. The woman in front of her turned around and shushed her, making Amanda turn bright red and Elizabeth laugh.

Then the curtains slid open and Elizabeth's heart started to beat triple time as she saw Poppy standing in the middle of the stage, a book in her hand, her beautiful face lowered into shadow.

"Oh, you've got it bad," said Alexandra.

"What?"

"You love her, don't you?" Alexandra chuckled.

She was still chuckling as Poppy started to speak and the play began.

CHAPTER THIRTY FIVE

Poppy forgot about the audience, which was probably for the best, because in that first second that she'd felt every eye in the house on her center stage she'd thought she might throw up.

The only thought running through her head was that if she did barf on stage then she'd only prove Tanya right and that she'd never get another part ever again.

But then quiet had settled over the little hall and the book in her hands had weighed heavy and she'd remembered that she wasn't Poppy Robbins at all, she was Nancy Grey-Horton, a young American debutante with a thrilling secret and an unrequited love.

"I do wish England wasn't quite so dreary," Peter's voice had come from off stage.

"Dreary is as dreary does," she said, eyes still on the book.

And she'd fallen into the play all over again.

In fact, she barely noticed a thing until she was lying on stage, eyes half closed, at the end of the third act, dead as a dodo, shot by her lover who'd turned out to be her third cousin and the local vicar.

The police led the culprit away and Poppy could feel a stirring in the audience and then the lights were coming up and she was springing to her feet, hardly able to believe that it was all over.

She grinned so wide it hurt her face and held hands and took her bows and then politely turned and clapped for Tanya, who took to the stage like a be-kaftaned albatross.

"Thank you, thank you," Tanya called, quietening the applause. "A little company like this owes so much to so many. But tonight we have a special thank you to say."

Poppy looked around wondering who that thank you might be for.

"One of our actresses unfortunately fell ill," continued Tanya. "So we all owe the success of this performance to somebody who stepped in at the very last moment and gave the part her all. Ladies and gentlemen, Poppy Robbins."

And Poppy found herself being pushed forward, bowing in the very middle of the stage as everyone cheered and applauded.

It was just as she was lowering into her second bow that she noticed them.

A group of four ladies cheering and whooping, already up on their feet. One of them was clutching a dubious looking hat, another was yelling Poppy like it was the name of her lost dog, and the third... the third looked an awful lot like Elizabeth.

She straightened up, smiled automatically, then went down into her third bow and checked to make sure.

Yes. There was no doubt about it. It was Elizabeth standing there and clapping and everything inside Poppy suddenly switched to the same channel, every atom of her suddenly had the exact same mission.

She had seconds, perhaps less.

Seconds in which to act.

And she didn't give it a moment's thought.

She straightened up, raised her hands above her head and pushed deep from inside her diaphragm so that when she spoke the words echoed out over the cheers and were crisp and clear and wonderfully, thrillingly audible.

"Elizabeth Marks I love you."

Five words. Five, short, sharp, beautiful words and the whole room stopped, there was a millisecond of silence and Poppy finally, fiercely caught Elizabeth's gaze and held it.

Come what may, she had acted. Whether Elizabeth liked it or not, whether she believed it or not, wanted it or not, Poppy had spoken her truth and she was never, ever going to take it back.

Her heart stilled in her chest, her lungs burst with the need for a breath, and still she held Elizabeth's eyes until slowly Elizabeth began to raise her arms.

It took a moment for Poppy to realize what was happening, a moment to understand that Elizabeth was opening her arms for her, was willing them together.

And when she did realize she leapt off the stage, stumbling over the first row as the audience hollered and began applauding all over again.

She could feel Tanya's eyes boring into her, scowling at her for ruining the moment, could hear Midge cheering her on, but all she could see was Elizabeth standing there, as she struggled to the aisle and then flew up the space and into Elizabeth's arms.

The audience cheered louder and Poppy didn't hear them as she pressed her face into Elizabeth's chest, as she smelled her scent and finally, finally felt like she belonged somewhere.

Then Tanya was clearing her throat, coughing, making an announcement, and the clapping became polite and rhythmic and then slowly started to fade away.

Poppy didn't ever want to let go. As far as she was concerned she could stay right here for the rest of her life. It was Elizabeth that gently pushed her away.

"Poppy, I'd like you to meet my friends," she said quietly. Then she shook her head. "No, strike that. Poppy I'd like you to meet my best friends."

And Poppy found herself being engulfed in hugs and air kisses from the three posh looking blondes that had surrounded Elizabeth and she was laughing because she had no idea what was happening.

She just knew that it was all right.

She'd done what she'd had to do.

She'd gotten her arse into the water.

She laughed as she thought how proud Paul would be of her, and reached out for Elizabeth's hand, clutching it like she wouldn't ever let go.

* * *

It was dark and cold and Elizabeth couldn't remember ever feeling so happy. The beginnings of a light fog were starting to wisp through the streets and she could smell wet leaves and smoke, the smell of the city she'd lived in nearly her whole life.

And Poppy was by her side, her stage makeup washed off, her hand tight in Elizabeth's as they walked their way home through the night.

"I am sorry," Elizabeth said, after enjoying a long time of silence. "Sorry for not answering your call. Sorry for assuming you'd just upped and left like Eli did. Sorry for thinking that you'd run just because I pushed you."

"And I'm sorry," Poppy said quietly. "For assuming that you wouldn't fulfill your part of the deal. For assuming that you were like everyone else. For not calling back."

"I did talk to Jeremy."

"I know," grinned Poppy. "He gave me the day off."

"Hmm, well, great oaks grow from little acorns I suppose," Elizabeth said.

"What happens now?" Poppy asked after they'd walked a little further.

Elizabeth exhaled. "I think we go home, maybe, um, go to bed."

Poppy laughed. "That's a given. I meant more... more in the long term."

Elizabeth stopped in the middle of the pavement. "In the long term? You want to make plans? I rather thought that we were just going to start slowly and see if we have something here. See where the universe takes us."

"We are," said Poppy. "If you want to, that is?"

Elizabeth started walking again. "You know, the problem with big public declarations of love is that the public tends to be there for them. Which means the important things don't actually end up getting talked about."

It was Poppy's turn to stop this time. "Wait, this isn't what you want?"

Elizabeth stopped and turned to her. Then that smile was lighting up the night. "Poppy, my darling, I can't think of anything that I want more." She took a breath. "You know, Amanda told me that the most you can ever ask from a person is that they make every day a little bit better."

"That's beautiful."

"Which is why I'm not so sure I deserve you," Elizabeth went on. "Because you've made every day a lot better and… and I can't imagine being without you right now. But I also know that we barely know each other, that I'm not even divorced yet, that so many things in our lives are changing. And perhaps we shouldn't make any promises yet that we don't know how to keep. Does that make sense?"

Poppy nodded. "What about promises we know we can keep?"

Elizabeth grinned. "Those are okay, I suppose."

"In that case," said Poppy, unwinding her scarf and putting it around Elizabeth's neck. "I promise that I will keep you warm."

Elizabeth took her hands. "And I promise that I will try my hardest to be worthy of you, to be kind, and to be less controlling."

"Hey, no promises we might not be able to keep," teased Poppy.

"Fine, I promise that we'll give this an honest shot. That we'll date and get to know each other and speak our truth."

"That I can handle," Poppy said. She stood up on tiptoes and pressed a soft kiss onto Elizabeth's mouth before taking her arm and pushing her to keep walking.

"There was something that I was wondering about," Elizabeth said after a few minutes. "It's only an idea and you should absolutely tell me if it's a terrible one."

"Deal," Poppy said.

"It was something I said to Jeremy the other day. That the cafe is a good, going concern. Which made me think, well, maybe I should buy it."

Poppy stopped dead in the middle of the street. "What?"

Elizabeth sighed. "It would solve a lot of problems."

"Like what?"

"Like me being practically unemployable. I can't get fired if I'm the owner," pointed out Elizabeth. "The house is being sold, I could use my half of the money to buy the place. Which would leave Jeremy free to pursue his next great idea. We could both work there, if you wanted to. And, um, there's a flat upstairs, isn't there?"

"We use it for storage right now, but yes," said Poppy.

"Well then, you could live there."

"Not you?"

"Maybe, one day," allowed Elizabeth. "But for now it should be your place. You can get a roommate in if you like, get help with the rent."

"There are three rooms," said Poppy. "I can definitely think of a couple of people that need a place to stay."

"So it's not a terrible idea then?" asked Elizabeth, because the whole time she'd been thinking about it she'd been afraid that it was.

"It's a wonderful idea," said Poppy. She squeezed Elizabeth's hand. "I didn't know it was going to be like this."

"What was going to be like what?"

"That being in love with you was going to be like this... like a walk through the quiet streets, calming, comfortable," said Poppy.

"You were expecting passion and being thrown up against a wall?" asked Elizabeth. "Because that can be arranged."

Poppy laughed. "No. Well, yes, maybe later. But this, this is good, this is... perfect."

"You need to be careful throwing around words like perfect," Elizabeth said.

"No," said Poppy, laughing. "You need to be careful with how you define perfect, that's all."

Elizabeth stopped again. "Okay," she said. "In that case, this is perfect. The soggy leaves, the graffiti and broken glass over there, the fact that I can't feel my toes they're so cold and I don't know where we're going to be in ten days, let alone ten years. This is absolutely perfect."

Poppy raised an eyebrow. "Uh-huh, right."

"No," said Elizabeth softly, putting a finger under Poppy's chin. "I mean it. This, right here, is perfect."

She leaned in, brushing Poppy's lips with her own until Poppy relaxed and let her in and then they kissed for a long, long time in the cold moonlight as the fog started to drift around their ankles.

EPILOGUE

Poppy fished around in the skip, pulling cardboard boxes to one side and really, really hoping that there wasn't a dead body somewhere in there. Then she heard it again. She sucked air through her teeth.

"Come on," she said as gently as she could. "Come on, come out."

She moved a large plank of wood and saw a flash of movement.

"Aha, there you are."

A tiny, black and white kitten poked its nose out between a cement wrapper and a box of old bathroom tiles.

"Come on," Poppy said. "I'm not going to hurt you. Come to Poppy."

With a small chirp, the kitten hopped up onto a plank of wood and unsteadily made its way toward Poppy. When she scooped it up, it purred then curled up in her hand as she quickly checked to make sure there were no other animals lurking in the skip.

"Looks like you're all by yourself," she said to the sleeping cat. Then she grinned. "Not anymore though."

She cuddled him close to her chest and climbed down from the skip, hopping to get her balance and then walking back the way she'd come, beaming from ear to ear.

* * *

Elizabeth was up to her ears in numbers and was far from happy. The problem with numbers was that they never stayed the same. She'd add them all up for one total, then add them all up again to double check and come up with a different total.

"Maybe I should only add them up once," she was muttering to herself when she heard the post land on the mat.

Anxious for any kind of distraction from the coffee shop's accounts, she leapt up and went into the little hallway. She was sorting through junk mail and bills when Poppy's key sounded in the door.

"Back already?" Elizabeth said, leaning down so that Poppy could kiss her cheek.

"I didn't make it to the shop yet," said Poppy. "Come on, I've got something to show you." She went off into the living room and Elizabeth followed her, remembering that the last time Poppy had had something to show her it had turned out exceedingly well. Who'd known that edible underwear was a thing? And that it was so much fun?

She was just reconciling herself, without too much anxiety, to leaving the accounts for another day and spending a rather more fun morning with Poppy, when she heard a plaintive meowing. Poppy knelt to place something on the rug by the fireplace.

"What's that?" Elizabeth asked, cautiously.

"What do you think?" said Poppy, gazing adoringly down at the kitten that was unsteady on its feet but desperate to explore.

"A cat?"

"A kitten. And he's all on his own. I found him in that builder's skip down the road. But he's not alone anymore, right El? He's ours now and I think we should call him Oliver. And, oh look, he's trying to eat the carpet."

"He's weeing on my rug," Elizabeth shrieked, rushing out to the kitchen to get a cloth.

Only when the rug was scrubbed clean again did she sit back on her heels. "Pops, why don't you take him home?"

Poppy sighed. "It's too much fuss there for a kitten. Mel and Paul are both packing up already to move. Then the renovations are going to start. It's safer for Oliver to stay here."

Elizabeth looked down at the little thing that had somehow got a hold of a piece of paper from her desk.

Then she looked up at Poppy, whose eyes were soft and warm as she looked down at the kitten.

Then she sighed.

Poppy probably had a point.

After two long years, the decision had finally been made. They were moving in together at last. Mel was moving in with her boyfriend, and Paul, somewhat surprisingly, was about to move into Amanda's guest room until the renovations at the shop flat were finished. Then he'd be moving into the flat that Elizabeth was currently living in.

No one had been more surprised than Paul at the fact that Amanda's children had completely fallen for him. And no one had been more surprised than Paul when Amanda had offered him discount rent in return for helping the kids with their homework, picking them up from school, and ensuring that they didn't fall into trouble.

Elizabeth, on the other hand, hadn't been surprised at all. Amanda was a soft touch, and after Poppy probably the kindest person that she knew.

The kitten meowed again.

"Fine," she said. "But you look after him and you clean up after him."

"Deal," said Poppy with a grin. She picked up the mail that Elizabeth had dropped onto the couch. "What's this?"

Elizabeth shrugged. "I didn't have time to open anything, you were bringing wild beasts into my home and I needed to supervise."

"Oliver isn't a wild beast," said Poppy as she tore open the large, cream envelope. Then her eyebrows raised.

"What?" asked Elizabeth, heart thudding.

Poppy passed over the thick, creamy card. Elizabeth read it and swallowed, unsure of how she felt.

"They're finally doing it," said Poppy.

"Looks that way."

"So? Are we going to go?" Poppy put a warm hand on her arm. "We don't have to if you don't want to, I think everyone would understand."

They would understand. But Elizabeth couldn't just not go. The shock of the invitation was starting to wear off. "Of course we're going," she said stoutly. "Eli and Sally's wedding will be the wedding of the year if Sally has anything to do with it."

"El?" Poppy squeezed her arm.

"That was my old life. Eli was kind to invite me and, well, as much as I didn't want to, I like Sally." She took a breath, this was the part she was bad at. "I feel… I feel a little sad, I suppose, but I think that's normal."

Poppy smiled approvingly. "Look at you, talking about your feelings like a champ."

"Don't patronize me," said Elizabeth.

"Would I?" Poppy said, leaning in so that Elizabeth was hypnotized all over again by her smooth pink lips, her dark eyes and her long eyelashes.

"You do constantly," Elizabeth said. "And by the way, your cat is pooing on the floor."

Poppy yelped and got up. "Okay, okay. I'm cleaning it and then I'm off to the pet shop. I'll get a box, litter, food, a bed, some toys. Is there anything else you need?"

"From the pet shop?" Elizabeth asked dryly. "No, I don't think so." But she smiled anyway because she knew it was just a habit for Poppy to ask if she needed anything. She did it practically every time she left the house.

"Look after Oliver," Poppy called as she ran out of the flat.

❊ ❊ ❊

When Poppy got home she dumped all her stuff in the hallway and rushed into the living room, anxious to see Oliver. Oliver opened one eye and looked at her before falling back to sleep on

Elizabeth's chest. Elizabeth didn't even open one eye.

Poppy stood for a long, quiet moment watching them both. It was obvious from the wet patches on the rug and the sponge on the mantlepiece that Oliver had had more than one accident while she was gone.

And yet Elizabeth was cradling him with one arm while she slept, unconcerned by the fact that he'd messed up her pristine flat.

In much the same way, Poppy mused, that she seemed unconcerned by how Poppy herself brought disorder to her life. Try as she might, she didn't always remember to take her shoes off, or to use the regular silverware instead of the nice stuff, or to fold her towel in the bedroom.

Speaking of which, she'd better pick up all the bags she'd just dropped.

She had poured litter into the box and was opening up a can of kitten food when Oliver's eyes flashed open. He gave a tiny meow and jumped off Elizabeth's chest.

"Ow!"

Poppy laughed. "Sorry, he was a bit eager for food." The kitten was practically burying his head in the plate she'd given him.

"Is that my best china?" asked Elizabeth, narrowing her eyes.

Poppy looked down at it guiltily, she really hadn't thought. "Um, maybe?"

Elizabeth sighed but said nothing and Poppy bit back a smile. "He'll grow on you."

Oliver growled as Poppy moved his food bowl to one side and Elizabeth laughed. "I think he already has." She sat up and stretched. "I had a thought while you were gone."

"Should I be worried?" Poppy asked, keeping a close eye on Oliver.

"Why don't we go to Canada?"

Which definitely made Poppy look up. "What?" she asked. She hadn't expected that.

Elizabeth shrugged. "The shop's doing well, and between them Paul and Mel can easily run it. The flat needs to be renovated anyway. And I've got some money left over from the sale of the house. Why don't we have a holiday? I've never been there and I'd like to go."

Poppy hadn't known she was homesick until Elizabeth brought up the idea. Now she was grinning like a maniac. "You mean we're going to have real syrup and Tim Horton's and go to a hockey game and eat poutine and see moose and everything?"

"I only know what approximately half of those things are," Elizabeth said, carefully. "But sure, why not." She cocked her head to one side. "And actually, if we're going to go, why don't we do it properly?"

"What do you mean?"

"It's going to be a good six to eight months before the flat is completely done. Why don't we travel around the country, it's a big place, make a real trip of it?"

Poppy was already pulling the laptop from Elizabeth's desk, typing furiously. She clicked open a few links and then frowned. "I don't know," she said.

"What is there not to know about?" Elizabeth laughed.

"Well, I don't think you can stay for more than six months," said Poppy, reading at a rapid rate. "I'm not sure though, there's a bunch of different visas but I don't know if you qualify. It's really complicated. It'd be easier if we were married, but—"

"Okay then."

Poppy's fingers hovered over the next tab as she looked up unsure of exactly what she'd just heard. "What?"

"I said okay then," Elizabeth said.

Poppy carefully put the laptop down, got up and came to sit next to Elizabeth. "You're only saying that because Eli and Sally are getting married."

"I'm not," said Elizabeth.

Poppy raised an eyebrow and Elizabeth shook her head.

"Listen, Poppy, I love you. Every day I spend with you is so much immensely better simply because you're there. I don't need a piece of paper to show me or you or anyone else just how much I love you. You complete me in ways I didn't even know I needed completing."

"Then..."

"But I'm not foolish enough or idealistic enough to think that in some ways a marriage certificate might make sense. There's the questions of visas for the both of us. There are tax advantages."

"So romantic," Poppy said.

"And there are other things. Like..." Elizabeth felt her throat swelling with sadness and had to swallow. "Like if anything should happen I'd like to be there for you, however that may turn out. I want to be able to sit by your bedside, I want to know that you're taken care of if I'm not around. There are plenty of sensible reasons to do this."

Poppy took a deep breath and nodded. "I see that."

But Elizabeth was already sliding off the sofa and getting down on one knee. "And there's one very unsensible reason too," she said as Poppy started to laugh. "I'm absolutely crazy about you, Poppy Robbins and I want to tell the world that you're my wife."

Then Poppy was laughing too and falling into her arms until they were making enough noise wriggling around on the floor that Oliver came to see what they were doing. Which made them laugh all the more.

"AM I LATE, please tell me I'm not late," Amanda said, bustling in through the door, arms full of bottles.

"Yes, you're late," said Arabella. "Which is astonishing considering that you literally live next door. As in, I could bang a hole in the living room wall and watch you bathe."

"Quiet, quiet," Alexandra said. "There's no arguing tonight. Tonight is pure karaoke fun and I won't have it ruined by silly spats."

"You know, anyone would think that this was your house," said Elizabeth, putting a tray of drinks down on the coffee table.

"Your place is the only one without interfering men in it, so it's only fair that you take pity on us poor married women," said Amanda, sinking down onto the couch.

"Ah, speaking of which," Elizabeth said. She shot a look at Poppy who was grinning fit to bust. "We, um, have a little announcement to make."

"Hey," said Poppy, pouting. "We have two announcements actually. The first is very important." She stood up. "I'd like you to meet the newest member of our little family…" She trailed off as she pointed toward the cat bed that was conspicuously empty. Then her gaze went toward the front door that Amanda had left open and her face paled. "Oh no," she said. "Oh no."

"HE'LL COME HOME," Elizabeth said. "He will."

"How does he even know that this is home?" Poppy wailed. "He was only here for a day."

"Because… because things will turn out for the best," said Elizabeth, desperately hoping that was true. She put her arm around Poppy and held her tight.

"There's nothing in the garden," said Amanda coming in, boots muddy. "And I feel awful. I'm so sorry about the door, I had no idea."

"It wasn't your fault," Poppy said. "You didn't know."

"That's kind, but—" began Amanda. She was interrupted by Eli who rushed in through the front door carrying a large cardboard box.

"Found him," he huffed, putting the box that was now yowling onto the kitchen table.

Elizabeth looked at Amanda who shrugged and said: "I called everyone I could think of. I thought the more people to help the better."

Eli was untying string around the box and pulling back the flaps. As soon as he did, a giant ginger cat leapt out and started strutting across the table.

"That's… not our cat," Elizabeth said.

"Oliver's a kitten," added Poppy.

Eli looked from one to the other. "But you've had him for years. Since right when I moved out of the house. How is he still a kitten?"

Elizabeth opened her mouth and then crashed it closed again. She'd almost forgotten about the night that Poppy had pretended to be a cat to cover up her presence in the house. And she wasn't about to tell Eli the truth now.

Eli hadn't taken things well at first. It wasn't so much the gay thing, it was definitely more the 'you tried to trick me with your girlfriend' thing. It had been unavoidable that he discover what had nearly happened, since the first time he properly met Poppy he'd recognized her immediately. For the first six months after he'd found out about Elizabeth's aborted revenge plan he'd avoided her entirely.

It had taken a very patient Sally to bring things back together. Sometimes Elizabeth wondered why she bothered. But then that was the kind of person Sally was. She hated fighting, hated confrontation, and wanted everything out in the open.

This should have boded badly for a confirmed cheat like Eli. Except Eli, contrary to everyone's expectations, was not only still completely besotted with his soon-to-be-wife, but also a doting father to their three month old daughter.

"It's, um, a different cat," Elizabeth said, hoping Eli wouldn't pursue the issue.

"And this is a girl cat," observed Poppy.

"I rather think that's Mrs. Cattington from next door," Amanda said. "Perhaps you could put her back in her garden? The Fishers won't be happy if you catnap her."

Eli stared at the cat, then at the three women, then shook his head, grasped the surprised cat, and marched back out of the house.

Poppy bit her lip and Elizabeth could see that she was trying to hold back tears.

"There's nothing out on the streets around here," Paul said, coming in rapidly followed by Mel.

"Didn't see a single animal. Ow!" Mel bumped into Paul who'd stopped suddenly in the middle of the kitchen. "What the hell?"

"Did you hear that?" Paul said, holding up a finger.

Everyone was silent for so long that Elizabeth, who was holding her breath in order to be more quiet, started to feel light-headed.

Then there was a small meow.

Poppy jumped up. "It's coming from the living room," she said. She raced inside, followed by everyone else, then stopped and looked around. "But he's not here," she said, confused.

"Quiet," ordered Paul.

Again, they stood still as statues, until another meow sounded.

"Jesus," Paul said. "I think he's under the sofa." He picked up the edge of the couch, tilting it back toward the wall, but there was nothing there. Then came the sound of scrabbling and another meow.

"He's inside the couch," Elizabeth cried. She ran to the kitchen, grabbed the nearest pair of scissors and ran back, holding them out to Paul.

"Are you sure you want me to cut into your couch?" he said doubtfully.

"Just do it," said Elizabeth, clutching on to Poppy's arm.

Paul ripped through the material at the bottom of the sofa, shoving his arm in as soon as he was able. Elizabeth held her breath again until he withdrew his hand, holding a small, meowing Oliver.

"Oh, Ollie," Poppy said, reaching out for him and holding him close.

Elizabeth let out her breath. "You can call the search off," she told Amanda.

"He never even left the house," Paul laughed.

* * *

Oliver was curled up in Poppy's lap fast asleep. She could feel his little heart beating against her leg. "Paul's already offered to look after him while we're on holiday," she said drowsily. "He's going to tell the kids tomorrow and I'm sure they'll be over to visit."

"Just as well Ollie's getting his rest then," said Elizabeth, bringing over two mugs of hot chocolate. "Although I'm not sure I need much more excitement after tonight."

Poppy pulled her face. "Sorry about the karaoke."

"Are you kidding? Any excuse to avoid listening to Alexandra's rendition of *My Heart Will Go On* is a welcome one. How about a film?"

Poppy checked her watch. "The BBC2 film should be starting in a few minutes. I don't know what it is tonight."

Elizabeth put the TV on and muted it. "Then we'll wait and find out. It'll be a surprise."

Poppy groaned and Oliver stirred. "We didn't even tell them," she said.

"What?"

"The others. We didn't tell them that we're getting married. We should have had a proper announcement and everything."

Elizabeth laughed. "That's really not necessary. We can send out a group text if you like?"

"Seriously? I'd have thought that you wanted formal announcement cards of betrothal."

"No," Elizabeth said. "Not at all. In fact, well, I don't really want any fuss. What about you?"

Poppy shook her head. "No fuss, no muss. But you don't want to do this properly, you know, a big wedding, white dresses, lots of things for you to plan?"

"No," Elizabeth said, putting down her hot chocolate. "I'd rather it was just you and me, our closest friends, and an afternoon at the registry office actually."

"Sounds perfect to me," Poppy said, snuggling up against her. The graphics on the TV changed and then Poppy started to laugh.

"What?" Elizabeth asked, distracted by Oliver's rounded and

very soft little tummy.

"Um, I swear this isn't planned," said Poppy, pointing to the TV.

The opening shots of *Strangers on a Train*, a cab pulling up in front of a train station, were flowing across the screen. Elizabeth reached for the remote and turned the TV off again. "I don't think we need to watch that, do we? I think I've had quite enough revenge for one lifetime."

"Mmm," agreed Poppy, gently moving the kitten off her lap and into his own bed. "Besides, not every revenge story has a happy ending."

"Not like us," Elizabeth said, moving in closer so that Poppy could snuggle under her arm.

"But then, things do tend to turn out for the best, don't they?" said Poppy, her breath warm against Elizabeth's side.

Elizabeth smiled and leaned down so that she could kiss Poppy's upturned nose. "Yes, things really do turn out for the best," she said, before moving down to capture Poppy's lips. "Want to take this party to the bedroom?"

Poppy nodded.

"Good girl," said Elizabeth, and Poppy melted into her arms so fast that Elizabeth laughed and Oliver woke up meowing.

THANKS FOR READING!

If you liked this book, why not leave a review? Reviews are so important to independent authors, they help new readers discover us, and give us valuable feedback. Every review is very much appreciated.

And if you want to stay up to date with the latest Sienna Waters news and new releases, then check me out at:

www.siennawaters.com

Keep reading for a sneak peek of my next book!

BOOKS FROM SIENNA WATERS

The Oakview Series:

Coffee For Two
Saving the World
Rescue My Heart
Dance With Me
Learn to Love
Away from Home
Picture Me Perfect

The Monday's Child Series:

Fair of Face
Full of Grace
Full of Woe

The Hawkin Island Series:

More than Me

Standalone Books:

The Opposite of You
French Press
The Wrong Date
Everything We Never Wanted
Fair Trade
One For The Road
The Real Story
A Big Straight Wedding
A Perfect Mess
Love By Numbers
Ready, Set, Bake
Tea Leaves & Tourniquets
The Best Time
A Quiet Life
Watching Henry
Count On You
The Life Coach
Crossing the Pond
Not Only One Bed
The Revenge Plot
The Queens of Crime

OR TURN THE PAGE
TO GET A SNEAK
PREVIEW OF THE
QUEENS OF CRIME

THE QUEENS OF CRIME

Chapter One

Ant stomped up the stairs. Sarah, of course, glided up them like she was some kind of fairy, her steps barely audible. But then, that was Sarah all over.

"Where are you going then?"

Sarah sighed. "I don't really know, to be honest."

"Then stay here," Ant said. "At least until you figure things out." Which was stupid and hopeless, she could see that. The relationship, if that's what you called a two month affair, had been winding down for at least half that amount of time. Still, she wanted to cling on for as long as she could.

"No," said Sarah. "A clean break is best for everyone."

"But where are you going?"

Sarah sat on the edge of the bed and folded t-shirts. "Away. Out of here."

"Helpful."

Another sigh and Ant could definitely remember when sighing was a good thing, when Sarah's head tipped back and her eyes half-closed and a sigh was a sign that things were going well.

"I'm not even thirty years old, Ant. I can't sit around a dusty, small-town bookshop for the rest of my life. It's not what I want."

"I could dust."

"Really not the point."

Ant had to concede that. She got the picture. And what could she do? It wasn't like she could move the shop or fly all the books off the shelves and into the hands of customers. Or force Sarah to stay. Not that she was actually sure she wanted her to stay, but still, it'd be nice to have the option.

"It's not you," said Sarah, putting the three folded t-shirts into her bag.

"Right."

Sarah grinned. "You are a bit weird."

"Am not."

"Ant, anyone that knows as much about crime fiction, detectives, and true crime as you is bound to be a little shady."

"I'm not shady." She sat down on the edge of the bed too, the mattress flexing.

"You are a bit," said Sarah. She grinned again. "But in a lovable kind of way. The kind of way that knows that Agatha Christie wrote hundreds of books and the first crime book was some fourteenth century Welsh manuscript."

Ant snorted. "John Creasey was the most prolific crime author, Christie doesn't even touch him when it comes to numbers, she barely cracked into the seventies. And Welsh? Seriously? Try Danish. 1829, for your information."

"Which kind of proves my point," said Sarah, shuffling a little closer and patting Ant's leg which in no way set off any kind of physical reaction at all. Except Ant's mouth felt a little dry.

"That I'm weird and you don't want to be stuck here with me."

"That you're special and passionate about something that isn't really my cup of tea," Sarah said gently. "And that's perfectly fine. We're both perfectly fine people. Just not well-matched, that's all."

"That's not what you used to think."

"Well, if every relationship started off with one partner

thinking that there was no future there'd probably not be many relationships," pointed out Sarah.

Ant nodded and kept her mouth closed. She didn't have an argument to make here. Sarah was right. They'd tried, it hadn't worked out. But then, neither had any other relationship she'd been in over the last decade.

Okay, trying to persuade a young woman to move to a tiny town like Whitebridge was hard. But try then moving said young woman into a tiny bookshop crammed with crime novels and you did end up looking more than a bit weird.

Ant had had to protest that she really, seriously didn't have any bodies hidden under the floorboards at least three times to various girlfriends. Which was twice more than she thought anyone should be comfortable with.

Not that she would ever, ever hurt anyone. She couldn't even kill the spiders in the bathroom and she'd left one box of books in the cellar to the mice because she didn't want to see them homeless.

Still though, she could see how a shop full of books on killing and blood and murder and everything in between might not make the best first impression. She could also see why someone like Sarah would want more.

Why anyone would want more.

"I'm going to stay with my cousin in London for now," said Sarah, standing up and zipping up her bag.

"Oh," was all Ant could think of to say to that.

"I'll text to let you know I'm there safe."

"Mmm." Apparently she'd lost the power of coherent speech.

"And Ant?"

"Mmm?"

"Don't dwell on this, okay?" Sarah looked at her with kind eyes. "Sometimes things don't work out and that's okay. We had a good time, didn't we? So let's remember the good parts and learn our lessons from the not-so-good parts, and move on."

"Right."

Easier said than done, Ant thought as she followed Sarah back down the narrow, steep staircase. She was trying to be kind. Sarah that was, not Ant herself. Ant didn't quite know what she was trying to be, other than to appear reasonable and not to fall to the floor and wrap herself around Sarah's legs to try and make her stay.

Again, not that she necessarily wanted her to stay. In fact, she was quite looking forward to having her bed to herself. Well, her and Maigret. The shop's cat glared down from the highest shelf by the door, the one that contained new releases and staff recommendations.

Ant saw that Mila had added a battered copy of *Fifty Shades of Grey* to the shelf again and gritted her teeth.

"So, this is goodbye," Sarah said, looking remarkably cheerful thought Ant sourly.

"Mmm." Back to the lack of vocabulary. For someone that read as much as she did, she really should attempt to communicate slightly better.

"I'll text when I get there," said Sarah again.

"Right."

There was a long, uncomfortable moment when they both looked at each other and didn't quite know what to do. Then Sarah leaned in and pulled Ant into a perfunctory hug, drawing back quickly as though she'd burned herself.

"I'll be off then." She turned toward the back of the shop. "Bye, Mila."

There was no answer, so with a determinedly steady hand she opened the door, flashed one last smile at Ant, then left.

Ant watched her walk away, not stumbling even once on the unevenly cobbled pavement. She thought she should probably be pressing her face up against the glass of the window or something, but given the current state of the windows she might catch Ebola or something else lovely. So she contented herself with wistful staring.

Again, not that she was so sure she wanted Sarah to stay. But having someone had been nice. If only for a little while.

But she'd fallen short again. It was somehow difficult to focus on all those good parts when she was left feeling like she always was, like she wasn't quite good enough. Like she didn't measure up. Like she couldn't offer the kind of life that a nice woman would want.

"Well, that was awkward," Mila said, popping up from behind the counter.

"You can't keep hiding away any time someone comes into the shop," Ant said wearily. "It defies the point of being an assistant."

"I do other things," said Mila, sniffing and pushing back her blue hair. "I stock shelves and carry boxes and..." She reached under the counter and pulled out a plate. "I make crisp sandwiches. Want one?"

"What kind?" asked Ant even though she knew she was going to eat it. It was the cheapest lunch she could think of.

"Softly sliced quadrilaterals of our finest *fromage* with a dressing of crisply roasted *pommes de terre* instilled with a tart *vinaigrette* and just a hint of *sel de mer*."

"Sliced cheese and salt and vinegar crisps then?"

"It sounds better in French," Mila said, pushing the plate closer.

Ant picked up a sandwich and took a bite, the crisps scratching at the roof of her mouth.

"So?" asked Mila.

"So what?" she mumbled through her sandwich.

Mila cleared her throat and looked pointedly out of the window in the direction that Sarah had disappeared in.

"Yeah, I don't have anything to add to that. She's gone. Obviously. Off somewhere more exciting than here. A little dusty bookshop not good enough for her." She was surprised at how bitter the words sounded.

"Still," said Mila. "At least you'll get your bed back. Maigret's been out of sorts ever since you tossed him out in favor of Miss Mop."

"Don't call her that," Ant said automatically, though it really didn't matter any more. Honestly, Sarah had mopped the back kitchen one time and Mila had found the very idea of water so close to the books so distressing that she'd practically had a fit.

"Better off without her," Mila said, picking up the other half of the sandwich.

"Didn't have much choice in the matter."

"I'm just saying," said Mila. "Trying to cheer you up and all."

"I don't need cheering up." Which was true now that she said it out loud. Oh, she was sad about Sarah leaving, of course she was. But life would go on. Things would keep ticking. It wasn't like she was completely heart-broken.

She was, she decided with another bite of sandwich, going to steer clear of women though. They were too much trouble. Besides, what did she have to offer? She'd be better off depending on Mila and Maigret, neither of whom minded when she smelled of salt and vinegar crisps.

Which reminded her. "If I find that copy of *Fifty Shades of Grey* anywhere near my bookshelves again, somebody is going to find out what a good whipping feels like, whether she enjoys it or not."

Mila sniffed again. "Thought the place could use some spicing up?" she tried.

"Well it doesn't. We're a crime bookshop. Detectives, police procedurals, true crime, the odd thriller that I let slip by. But that's it. Our customers don't expect to be assaulted by Christopher Grey when they come in."

"Christian," said Mila.

"Or atheist, it matters not."

"No, his name is Christian Grey, not Christopher. And what customers exactly?" asked Mila looking around the empty shop as though a stray customer might be hiding behind a shelf ready to jump out at her.

Ant gave up. "Go and make the tea," she said.

Mila danced off and Ant settled down onto her normal stool behind the counter, picking up a battered paperback and turning to her page.

The little shop seemed very empty now that there was no promise of Sarah coming back.

CHAPTER TWO

The bar was hygienic. Not entirely the description that Adelaide thought the owner was aiming for, but there it was. With white tiles and stainless steel trappings the place looked like an abattoir with the lights out.

Not that that was what was bothering her.

No, she was rather more bothered by the fact that this was a bar. A bar rather than a restaurant.

"And, of course, there'll be the normal bells and whistles," Joss was saying. "Interviews, the papers of course, and we'll get on to morning television as well."

Adelaide looked around, hoping for a waiter to rescue her, or at the very least provide her with another, very strong drink.

"Adelaide? Ad?"

She snapped back to focus. "Yes?"

Joss was peering at her with concern. "Are you even listening to all of this?"

Joss had a right to be concerned. As her agent, Joss had every right to be concerned. As her, up until just last month, purely British agent, Joss might have been less concerned. But given the fact that a month ago Adelaide had parted ways with her US agent and fled the country, landing safely at Heathrow and breathing a sigh of relief, and then informed Joss that she was now her sole agent, Joss had even more right to be concerned.

"Of course I'm listening," Adelaide said, crossing her legs and smiling slightly.

Why the UK, she wasn't entirely sure. Because they spoke English, that was a good start. Her high school Spanish was from so long ago that there was a fair chance they'd decided on a whole new alphabet or something since the last time she'd spoken it.

Then there was the fact that it was small. Small and cozy and, perhaps, just a little less cut-throat than the States.

And her books had always sold well in the UK. Well, Lloyd Franklin's books to be exact. But since Adelaide was Lloyd Franklin, it amounted to the same thing.

Plus, she'd told herself at the time, a change of scenery would probably be good for her. And plenty of Americans made their home in England. It was becoming quite the thing to do. Not that she planned on going full Madonna and developing the accent, but perhaps she could find inspiration here.

"Ad?" Joss said again.

"Mmm?"

"I was asking about a tour? Are you willing to go on tour?"

Adelaide raised an eyebrow. "There's an implication in there that I'm too old to be jaunting around the world selling my own books."

"There's an implication in there that there's been a world-wide pandemic and many authors are deciding not to tour. And with the rise of social media, tours are becoming less and less necessary," said Joss primly tucking a lock of blonde hair behind a perfect ear.

Adelaide sighed. She rather liked touring. She liked the adoring fans. She liked signing books and hearing stories and being surrounded by people that actually liked her. "I'll tour," she said.

"Fine," said Joss. Then she smiled, big and wide and genuine. "I can't tell you how excited I am to read the new Lloyd Franklin," she said. And Adelaide even thought she might be telling the truth. "The world needs more Detective Dennis."

Which wasn't what her last reviews had said. In fact, she was pretty sure she'd been called a has-been hack by the *Post* and the *Times* had said the plot was stretched thinner than fishnet and had about as many holes.

She'd stopped reading the reviews after that.

"What'll this be?" asked Joss. "Nineteen, twenty?"

"Twenty two," Adelaide said. Which was easy to figure out because she'd written precisely one book per year since she'd turned twenty two. Making this year somewhat of an anniversary she supposed.

"Well, I'll pull out all the stops, don't worry," Joss said, smiling. "We're honored to be your sole agents and glad that you've decided to move to the UK."

"Really?" asked Adelaide, sharper now. "Which is why you've decided to entertain me in a bar?"

Joss frowned.

"No fancy restaurants, no attempts to impress me?" It was clear she was making the girl uncomfortable.

She was a girl. No more than twenty five. Adelaide could remember when her British agent had been a man three times her age who'd taken her to Claridge's for afternoon tea and put his hand up her skirt.

Joss flushed. "Budgeting," she said. "I'm afraid expense accounts are the first thing to be cut."

"I see," said Adelaide. So nothing to do with the fact that her last two novels had failed to make the bestseller lists then. She looked down at her empty glass. "And can your budget stretch to another drink?"

Joss flushed even deeper red. "Actually, I do rather have to go."

"Ah. Another appointment."

"No rest for the wicked," said Joss, the flush lessening.

She wasn't even deserving of an entire evening then. Well, that showed her her place, she guessed.

"We could, er, pencil in dinner for next week?" Joss said. And Adelaide could see that she thought she'd made a mistake and was looking for a way to correct it.

"No."

"Ah. Perhaps the week after?"

Adelaide let out a breath. She really shouldn't piss the girl off too much. She was her agent, after all. And given the current state of affairs she needed her on side. If only to have someone to plead her case to her publisher. She did not, however, want a pity dinner.

"Or lunch?" Joss asked, shifting in her chair and anxious to leave.

"I won't be in town," Adelaide said finally. It was as good an excuse as any. "I was thinking about taking a road trip."

"A road trip?"

She shrugged. "With significant parts of the book taking place in England it seems only right to travel around, really get a feel for the place, for the people, the speech patterns. Research, you know."

"Oh." Joss frowned again and Adelaide could see that she was trying to put pieces together.

"Just the final touches," she assured her.

Joss's face cleared. "Right. Of course. Well, do stay in touch please, won't you?"

Given that Adelaide knew precisely one person in the entire country and that person was currently squirming in front of her and looking for excuses to leave, she didn't have much choice when it came to staying in touch.

Alright, this had gone on long enough.

"I'll stay in touch. And you should be running along to your next appointment."

Joss relaxed and called over the waiter that Adelaide hadn't been able to find. Five minutes later they were out on the street, cool air blowing up from the river, saying their goodbyes.

Adelaide waited until Joss disappeared around a corner before hailing a cab and climbing in. She spoke the address crisply to the driver and sat back in her seat.

Her agent's budget might be lacking, but her own was not. She could afford to buy herself dinner at Claridge's these days. Or perhaps she'd just have it sent up to her suite. There were certain advantages to writing bestsellers. Or to having written bestsellers. She hated herself for pushing that back into the past tense but couldn't exactly help it.

As the cab navigated the traffic she had plenty of time to think.

The road trip idea had been a spur of the moment excuse. But now that she came to give it real thought, it might not be a bad idea.

Research was always valuable of course. And she could stand to see more of the country. There were other pluses in there too, but the cab was drawing up in front of the hotel now and she was paying and climbing out.

"Ms. Park," said the doorman, holding the door open for her.

She walked through without even a nod of acknowledgment.

"Ms. Park," said the receptionist, handing over her room key.

Adelaide gave her an icy smile and turned to the elevator bank.

"Ms. Park," said the elevator man, pressing the button for her.

She raised a single eyebrow and stepped into the cabin.

She didn't need the mirrored walls to know that she looked perfect. Looking perfect was what she did. Her hair was more of an ash blonde these days, graying slightly, twisted up in a knot behind her head. Her eyes were bright blue, but the little webbing of wrinkles around them was becoming more and more noticeable.

So she didn't look at herself.

She let the elevator ride up until it dinged, then let herself into her own suite and locked the door firmly behind her before kicking off her shoes.

Yes, a road trip might be just what she needed.

If nothing else, it would keep her far away from London, and she had a feeling that being far away from London might be in her own best interest.

Because at some point she was going to have to tell Joss that not only was the new Lloyd Franklin book not yet finished, it also didn't actually exist at all.

Get Your Copy of The Queens of Crime Now, Only from Amazon!